The Ex Chronicles

By

Penelope Christian - LaKesa Cox - Yvette Danielle - Christina Grant - Meredith E. Greenwood - Elle Jaye - Lamesha Junior Johnson - Princis Lewis - Sharon Lucas - Tamika Tolbert Lucas - J.P. Miller - Michelle Mitchell - Dwon D. Moss - Cheryl Cloyd Robbins - Venita Alderman Sadler - J.L. Sapphire - Jeida K. Storey - Adrienne Thompson - Brenda A. White - Karen E. Williams

BROWN GIRLS BOOKS

Houston, Texas * Washington, D.C. * Raleigh/Durham, NC

The Ex Chronicles © 2016
Brown Girls Books, LLC

www.BrownGirlsBooks.com

ISBN: (Digital) 9781944359287
(Print) 9781944359294

Table of Contents

For her sixtieth birthday, Rhonda wanted to celebrate with her tight-knit family. And what better time to break the news that she was divorcing her husband of forty years. The announcement sends her family into shock when indiscretions and secrets are revealed.

After twenty-five years of marriage, Marcus makes an announcement that no wife wants to hear, but his wife's response proves to be the real surprise. In the end, what will become of their marriage?

Kelly didn't know she needed love, until love walked out the door. But when the world crumbles around her, will it be too late to discover she was wrong?

When Veronica meets Randolph for the first time at a local sandwich shop, his shoes live up to her 'judge a man by his shoes' motto. In fact, he fits all the 'must haves' on her list. But she soon discovers that while shoes can make a man, they tell you nothing about who he really is.

The decision to remain friends instead of lovers is hard, but after two decades should these two 'friends' give 'love' a try?

A sixteen-year-old lie resurfaces when Michol is forced to face her ex. Relationships, both new and old, will be tested when what was done in the dark comes to light.

Paige has finally achieved everything she's ever wanted. But when a lost love returns, he forces her to revisit the darkest parts of her memory and now she must decide whether to give into hidden desire or follow the path she so carefully designed.

Tracee and Wallace were close colleagues until he learned she was being considered for a promotion over him. Seeing a side of Wallace that she deplores, Tracee keeps her distance and warns her friend Charis to do the same when she finds out the two have been dating. When Tracee and Charis discover that Wallace has plans for them both, they will have to come together to avoid being casualties of love and war.

Why would a strange woman be waiting for Diane's husband at the hospital after his minor surgery? She seeks her answer with a tire iron and power swing.

Letter from the Publishers

Dear Reader,

Brown Girls Books is excited to bring you *The Ex Chronicles*, a collection of short stories by twenty talented writers who share tales about relationships that falter…among spouses, lovers, family, and friends.

Thank you for your support of this amazing group of writers. We were overwhelmed with the volume of submissions to this collection, and narrowing it down was extremely difficult. But we're excited at the final twenty that were chosen. And we hope you will be, too!

What you don't see is that behind the scenes, the contributors have created a strong sisterhood and a support system to assist in their personal and professional aspirations. That makes us at BGB, extremely proud.

Brown Girls Books was established to give publishing opportunities to new and established writers. We are excited about the opportunity to introduce you to fresh voices and reintroduce you to fan favorites. Our titles include something for everyone. We work very hard to bring you quality reading material that not only satisfies your hunger for good books, but that also gives talented writers the opportunity to tell their stories and have their voices heard, which is at the very heart of Brown Girls Books' existence.

We know that we would not be a success without your support. So thank you! And enjoy this amazing collection!

The Brown Girls Books Team

Too Old to Marry

By LaKesa Cox

Here we go. Another birthday. I swear it seems like the older I get, the faster they come around. At least I can say this birthday will be one to remember.

'Happy birthday to you, happy birthday to you, happy birthday dear ma-ma, happy birthday to you!'

I'm staring at the cake covered with sixty individual candles while my immediate family members sing to me. First there's Mark, my firstborn – thirty-six years old, never married, recovering drug addict, still trying to find his way; Melanie, my middle child – thirty years old, successful nurse, single mother of a three-year-old, who's bitter because her baby daddy married someone else; Malik, my baby boy, my 'I didn't know I could still get pregnant' child – twenty-four years old, recently graduated college and a new father with a three-month-old daughter and a new fiancée; then there's my husband, Lewis. We've been married for forty years, high school sweethearts. I followed him around the world when he enlisted in the Army, became the perfect Army wife and mother. I remember how I used to feel about Lewis back then, my first and only love. Now the very sight of him gets on my nerves.

I'm sure it was my firstborn, Mark's idea to put all those candles on the cake. He probably thought it would be funny while I'm wondering if the smoke detector is going to go off from all the smoke when I blow them out. Melanie is struggling to keep her three-year-old from putting his hands on the cake and burning himself on the candles.

Malik has his three-month-old daughter in his arms and his fiancée, Tracey, is standing protectively beside him.

I look around at my children and grandchildren, thinking to myself how much they mean to me. Between the stress of Mark battling drug addiction, Melanie's baby daddy drama and Malik taking six years to graduate from college because he couldn't figure out what he wanted to do with his life, it's a wonder I made it to sixty. And that's just a fraction of my stress. Lewis has spent half of our marriage running around with younger women, having bastard babies. There was one I was pretty sure of and probably more that I don't even know about.

Well, today was going to be the day I make the announcement to the kids. I promised myself I would wait until Malik graduated college and since he finally graduated three weeks ago, it was time.

"Blow out the candles, Mama!" Melanie says.

"Move the babies back before the smoke gets in their eyes. Mark, all these candles, I swear. I know it was your idea."

They all laugh.

I wait for Melanie, Malik and Tracey to move their bundles of joy away from the dining room table, far enough so they won't have to breathe in any of the smoke after I blow out the candles. Everybody cheers, the room fills with smoke and luckily the smoke detector doesn't go off. Now they have started to sing Stevie Wonder's happy birthday song. This has gone on too long.

"Okay, okay, enough of the singing. Thank you, thank you, thank you. Since all of you are here, your father and I need to talk to you. Take a seat." My formal dining room table has seating for six, which was just enough for the adults. Melanie, Malik and Tracey, who were standing in the doorway of the dining room and kitchen waiting for the smoke to dissipate, sit down with Mark and Lewis. I'm standing at the head of the table and Lewis is seated at the opposite end, scowling at me. I know he doesn't want to have this conversation today since this is supposed to be a day of celebration, but I don't want to wait any longer. The way I see it, this announcement is a celebration for me, too.

For years we have been putting up a façade of a marriage for the sake of the kids - twenty years to be exact - acting as a united front, when in reality, our marriage had dwindled us down to roommate

—

9

status. Sure we loved each other, but we hadn't been in love for a long time.

It's been easy to cohabitate since our work schedules have always allowed us to live together without having to see each other much. He works the overnight shift for Nabisco cookie factory after retiring from the military years ago, while I work the day shift at the post office. Getting married a couple of years after we graduated high school, Lewis entered the Army and we had been stationed at different places all over the world before we decided to move our family close to Richmond, Virginia where we'd both been born and raised. When he was in the Army, Lewis seemed to be committed to me and our kids, but after his twenty year stint, he retired and we settled into our beautiful home in Goochland County (a suburb of Richmond). That's when things changed.

It all started with him reconnecting with this woman named Linda who he dated before me in high school. We hadn't been back in town a full month before he ran across her at a gas station. The next thing I know, I was hearing about Linda and Lewis sightings and started smelling perfume on his clothes that didn't smell like mine.

Throughout the years, Linda kept her claws in Lewis and from what I hear, her nineteen-year-old son is Lewis's. Of course Lewis swears up and down her son is not his, but if you threw that boy in a bag with Mark and Malik, you wouldn't be able to tell any of them apart. Then there were the countless other women, too many to name with rumored "love" children sprinkled amongst them. Here again, Lewis denies having any other children other than ours.

So I got tired of being sick and tired and told Lewis a few years ago it was over. We argued about it, fussed, and finally he gave up because he knew it was inevitable.

One would think he would be happy to get a divorce so he was free to do the things he's been doing behind my back. I know what people were saying about me and how foolish I must look based on what Lewis was doing. But my focus has always been to raise my children in a two parent home, make sure they grew into adults who had memories of it, and not be a struggling single parent. I watched my mother do it with three kids my entire life and if it meant I had to be miserable for a little while for the sake of my children, it was worth it to me.

How did I do it? I wonder the same thing. I guess it's sort of like working a job you absolutely hate, day in and day out, but the pay is so good and so are the benefits so you just stay. People do it every day. Heck, I know several people on my job who are going through the motions and have been for over twenty years, despising the job and counting down to retirement. I guess you could say that I am about to embark on a marriage retirement.

"What's wrong, Ma?" Malik asked, breaking my train of thought.

"Nothing's wrong. But I thought it was time we let you all know that your dad and I are getting a divorce."

They gasp in unison, and oddly enough, they are all surprised.

"Divorce? Why?" Melanie asked.

"Well, your dad…"

"Your mother doesn't love me anymore, that's why," Lewis interrupts. Typical, he would try to put it all on me.

"Really, Lewis? You want to paint that picture? Go down that road?"

"Tell them the truth, Rhonda. This is all your idea. You don't love me anymore." Before I have a chance to respond, Lewis does the unthinkable – he breaks down and cries. Well, in actuality he makes the sound and gestures of a person crying, but not a tear in sight. His "crying" causes me to burst into uncontrollable laughter, which angers my children.

"Ma, why are you laughing? It's not funny, you're hurting our daddy," Melanie says.

"Mom, really, how could you laugh at a time like this?" Mark chimes in. Malik has since handed his baby to Tracey and moved closer to Lewis to console him. Tracey is staring at me like I'm the Grinch who stole Christmas. I realize I'm looking more and more like the villain in all this just because Lewis decided to attempt to shed a few phony tears. I'd been crying for years, tears they never had the privilege of seeing.

"Hurting your daddy? Hurting your daddy? Does anybody in this room know about hurt like me? You know what? It's not important. We're divorcing and we thought you all should know. That's it."

"But why? Why, Ma?" Melanie is on the verge of tears. I swear that girl is too sensitive for her own good.

"Melanie, your daddy and I made this decision together, right Lewis?" I look to Lewis for affirmation, but instead, he cries harder. This must be a joke.

"Lewis, seriously? Is this how you want to do this?"

He continues to make wounded puppy sounds and everyone is surrounding him, consoling *him*. Not only is this completely out of character for their military father, I don't think any of them have ever seen him cry.

The more I think about it, I don't think I've ever seen him cry either. Even when his father passed away last year, he didn't make a sound or shed one tear. I keep focusing on his face, waiting for some water to well up in his eyes, but they're dry. It angers me a bit, because I'm the person who's been hurt for years, cheated on for years, crying for years. But instead, the children are at the other end of the dining room table, rallying around their father and treating me like a traitor.

"Lewis, should we tell them about Linda?" Yeah, it was an immature move, but the buffoonery going on at the other end of the table was getting on my nerves. As expected, Lewis perks up and forgets about his "crying."

"Rhonda, what, what, what are you doing? Linda? Why would you do that?"

"Do what, Lewis? I just asked if you wanted to tell your kids about your friend named Linda, that's all."

The kids look at me with confusion on their faces. Mark speaks up first.

"We know Ms. Linda, your co-worker right, Dad?"

The color from Lewis's face drains.

"Oh yeah, she's the one who had that big cookout one year when we were younger and me and Malik went with Daddy. I think Mark was sick or something so Ma you stayed at home with him, but remember I got a big gash on my knee and had to go the emergency room to get stitches? I was pushing Malik on the swing and tripped and fell on some glass. That was a long time ago, though."

My mind starts to rewind back to the time when Melanie had to get stitches in her knee. I shake my head. Lewis told me they were at a cookout of one of his buddies, not once did he mention this was Linda's cookout. I remember the incident clearly because he brought Melanie home first and she was so upset because of all the blood. Lewis didn't think the cut was deep, but I insisted he take my child to the ER while I stayed home with Mark who was coming off of one of his drug binges.

I realize how stupid Linda and all of her friends thought I had to be, the wife sitting out in Goochland County without a clue, while he spent most of his time in town, courting Linda. Not to mention taking my kids around her, something I didn't know he'd done. I wasn't going to address that in front of the kids. Then again, it wasn't worth addressing at all at this point. But Lewis could see the fury on my face. It's one thing to disrespect me, but to drag my kids into it reaches another level of low down.

"Yeah, that was a long time ago, Mel. You know what? The reasons why your father and I are divorcing don't matter anymore. I will just say we have grown apart over the years and decided this would be best for both of us."

"I can't believe this. You wait until you get old to decide to get a divorce. Who's going to look after you, Ma, when me and Mark are busy with our own families?" Malik says, not realizing the insult.

"First of all, I'm not old. Second of all, I will be just fine looking after myself. I plan to sell this big house and get me one of those lovely condos overlooking the James River when I retire in five years."

"SELL THE HOUSE?" they all yell at the same time, even Lewis.

"Yes, sell the house!"

"Wait a minute, Rhonda, we didn't talk about selling the house. This is our home, our kids deserve this house be handed down to them."

He's such an idiot. We have three kids and one house. How does he plan on handing one house down to three kids? Oh, I get it, they

13

wait until we both keel over and die so then they can sell the house and reap the benefits of the proceeds. I don't think so. Besides, this hasn't been a home for him in quite some time. He spent his time laying his hat around too many places.

"Lewis, my dear Lewis, this house will be sold in five years, period. Now if you want to buy me out, you know, give me my share of what I put into it, and you stay here, that's on you. But trust and believe, when I retire, I'm leaving. In the meantime, you need to find somewhere else to go."

"Ma, this is crazy, I mean are you going through menopause or something?" Melanie asks.

I roll my eyes at her.

"Lewis, stop acting like this is new to you. We had this conversation several times and you know it's been long overdue. Kids, we both love you very much, but we don't have the love we used to have for one another anymore. Your father, well, he has other interests now which don't include me. Life is too short for me to sit out here in the middle of nowhere in this big house by myself while you all are off living your life. I'm not saying that to make you feel bad, I just want you to know it's time for me to look out for Rhonda. I took care of all of you for so long, now it's time for me to take care of me. Don't you think I deserve to be happy for a change?"

Mark turns away from his father and stares at me. A light bulb seems to go off in his head. Keeping his eyes on me, he asks his father, "Dad, are you having an affair with Ms. Linda?"

"Boy, take your time now. Remember, I'm your father."

"Mark, how could you ask him that?" Malik yells.

Then all three of them are going at it with each other.

For probably a minute, Lewis and I let them go at it before Lewis yells, "Be quiet, all of you! I don't care how grown you all are, you are still our children. The bottom line here is your mother and I are going our separate ways. Period. That's it. I plan on moving out in a couple of weeks so we can file for a legal separation. I'm going to be the man right now and say it's all my fault our marriage fell apart and I take full responsibility for the pain I caused your mother. Everything else is between me and your mother."

All of the kids seemed to have a revelation at the same time. One by one, they leave his side and come to stand by me. I never wanted them to have to take sides in all this, but Lewis asked for it when he tried to put on the show for them. Bringing up Linda wasn't part of the original plan either, but his childish behavior brought that on.

"Dad, how could you? All these years you preached to us about honesty and integrity. What happened to yours?" Mark asks.

"Boy, I already told you to stay out of it."

"No, forget that. I remember once I came home from rehab and you made me feel like the biggest failure there was. 'Son your integrity is one of those things you have complete control of and without integrity no one will stand to be around you'. Remember telling me that? So how can you preach to me about my integrity when clearly you don't have any? See, I always knew there was something up with that Linda woman. She slipped up once and said something to you and she said *'our son'*. I remember. You tried to make me think I didn't hear what I heard. So don't preach to me about integrity."

"What are you saying, Mark? Her son is dad's son? He's our brother?" Malik says.

Well, now it feels like we're in the middle of a Lifetime movie. All that's missing is the sappy music playing in the background. Poor Tracey has taken her baby to the family room out of the middle of this mess and my other grandbaby has been grabbing handfuls of birthday cake, eating it.

Lewis has the look of defeat in his eyes. He wants to raise his white flag, but it's too late. Instead of staying the course with the divorce announcement, he wanted to make me out to be the bad guy. I had no intention of taking the rap for his foolishness. I just wonder if he will continue to deny fathering Linda's child.

"No way. Is it?" says Melanie.

Lewis struggles with the decision to tell the truth or lie. I would imagine telling the truth would make him feel better, lift the invisible burden he's carried all these years. It amazes me how he crept around for so long, but stood firm with his lying to me about being faithful

15

and having an outside child. Why was it so easy for Lewis to lie to me, but when it came to his children it wasn't so easy?

Everyone waits for Lewis to respond. Mark has since pulled his chair closer to mine and wrapped his arms around me. The silence seems to go on for an eternity but when Lewis hangs his head, we all knew then. My sensitive child is now in tears, I'm sure thinking about the same betrayal she felt from her son's father. There was no way her father would do something like this. Not the only man she put high on a pedestal. Malik is in denial, shaking his head at the mere thought of his father betraying his mother in this way.

"Yes. Linda's son is my son."

"Oh, Daddy, how could you!" Melanie shrieks.

"Kids, believe me when I say, I'm okay," I feel the need to say. "For years I've tried to shield you all from my unhappiness and insanity for the sake of keeping you all happy. But I had an epiphany this morning when I woke up as a sixty-year-old *young* woman. I still have a lot of time left and I don't want to spend it protecting your father, pretending to play married when the marriage died a long time ago. Don't cry for me, I've cried already. Don't be angry for me, I've done that, too. Be happy for me because today starts my journey of true happiness. Your father has to handle his own demons but at the end of the day, he's still your father so don't hold a grudge. Be thankful we were able to give you all a great life as children. I don't know what the future holds for me. I might be too old to marry but I'm too young to bury, that's for sure."

Feeling those three wrap their arms around me was my reassurance that things were going to be alright. Sure I was nervous about a future that didn't include Lewis, but I knew whatever my future was, I would finally be content.

LaKesa Cox is the author of three novels, After the Storm, Water in my Eyes *and* Fetish for a Blue Skyy. *She resides in Henrico, Virginia and is currently working on her next novel. For more information, check out her webpage at www.lakesacox.com.*

That's the Way Love Goes

By Adrienne Thompson

"I want a divorce."

As I sat at the foot of our king-sized bed, I wasn't sure what shocked me more, the fact that my husband of twenty-five years had just uttered those words, or the fact that they'd slid out of his mouth so smoothly.

"Things just ain't the same between us no more," he continued.

I was only half-listening, because my eyes were glued to his stomach. He'd gained weight over the years and now had the physique of a middle-aged pregnant man. And he had the nerve to be leaving me? *Really?* Shoot, I kept it tight. Hit the gym five days a week. I'd lost count of the number of men who would hit on me nearly every time I left the house, and *he* wanted a divorce? The hell?

"I still love you, but I'm not *in* love with you. I mean, I thank you for being there for me over the years…"

I knew this was coming, though, so I don't even know why I was shocked. If I really thought about it, I think the first clue was one Sunday when we went out to eat after church and this Negro was sitting there putting ketchup on his fries. In all the years I'd known him, he'd never liked ketchup.

I even asked him, "What heifer got you putting ketchup on your fries?"

And you know what he did? He just sat there looking like a doggone deer in headlights, talking about, "Woman, you need to stop

17

tripping."

Mm-hmm, I knew I was right.

"This is hard for me. It was. . . it was a hard decision for me to make, but I really think it's for the best."

Negro was standing up there like he was God's gift to the world, like he didn't snore so loud that sleeping with him was akin to sleeping with a grizzly bear. I mean, really, after I carried his kids, two of which weighed close to ten pounds (I don't have to tell you what that does to a woman's nether region), he had the nerve and audacity to leave me. Me! Mm-hmm, I knew when he bought the motorcycle something was up. *Probably got him a young little hood rat stashed away somewhere and she's got him thinking he's the bomb-dot-com. Poor girl probably has no idea about his little blue pill dependency.* I closed my eyes and slightly shook my head, scoffed under my breath.

"I know you're upset, Kell. I know this seems unfair after all these years…"

Unfair? *Unfair?* I'll tell you what's unfair, me giving up on my dream of being a caterer so I could follow him to Bumfuddle, Arkansas, so he could coach golf at the local college. And speaking of golf, how was he going to act like I didn't spend years upon years stifling yawns and shaking the numbness out of my feet as I watched the world's most boring sport all because I was trying to support *him?* Humph!

"I want you to know there's no one else…"

Yeah, there is.

I opened my eyes in time to see him sit beside me on the bed. He fixed his sympathetic eyes on my face and said, "Is there anything you want to say? I know you're upset, and I want to be here for you, to listen. I still love you, Kell. I always will."

I tilted my head to the side and responded with, "When are you leaving?"

He frowned and released a quick breath. "Uh… well, I thought we should tell the kids first — together, the both of us."

"Tell them what?"

"That-that we're separating."

—

18

"Marcus, the kids are all grown. It's not like they'll need to decide who they're going to live with or anything like that. You can tell them on your own and if they want to talk to me, they can call or come by and I'll confirm that you want a divorce."

"O. . .okay."

"So when did you say you're leaving?"

"I *didn't* say. I mean, there's no rush, Kell."

"Well, dear, yes there is. You see, there's no way I'ma reside in the same house with you after that little announcement you just made, so I think you should go ahead and pack a bag and get on to wherever it is you really want to be."

He just sat there, dumfounded. Not a word passed his lips for a full five minutes. So I said, "You need my help?" and stood from the bed. I crossed the room to the closet and pulled out the biggest and best suitcase we owned — my gorgeous Louis Vuitton Zephyr 70. Although I knew I'd be paying that credit card purchase off from now into eternity, I didn't mind letting him take it. On second thought, I'd bought it with one of his credit cards so it was rightfully his. I smiled a little as I pulled it from the closet.

"Here you go," I said as I set it on the bed next to him. Then I left the bedroom and was back in a matter of minutes with his favorite set of golf clubs. "I know you'll need these for work and everything," I said.

He just sat there, his eyes shifting from the suitcase to me and back.

"But this is your bag," he said softly. "Your *favorite* bag."

I nodded. "Yeah, but it's okay. I'll get another one eventually." *With the alimony your lowdown behind is gonna pay me.*

He reached over and unzipped the suitcase, then he let his hand drop and raised his eyes, fixing them on me. "You don't have anything you want to say or ask, Kell?"

He wants me to ask him who she is and where he's going. "No, I think you've made yourself perfectly clear."

He opened his mouth to speak, then closed it and cleared his throat. "Well, I mean… don't you think we should talk about this?"

19

I frowned slightly as I leaned against the door. "Talk about what, Marcus? You just told me that you love me, but you're not *in* love with me and that you want to leave. We've already agreed that you'll tell the kids and since I don't work, it stands to reason that I'll stay here and you'll be the one to leave. That about covers it?"

"Damn, Kell. Twenty-five years and you ain't gonna shed a tear or nothing?" He said it so softly, I almost couldn't make his words out.

"I don't see you crying, Marcus, and you were with me those same twenty-five years," I rebutted.

"You got somebody else or something? Is that why you're so eager for me to leave?"

"You got somebody else or something? That why you want a divorce?"

"I already told you that's not it."

"Mm-hmm."

"You gonna answer my question, Kell? You been cheating?"

I folded my arms over my chest and shook my head. "You tell me you want a divorce and then accuse me of cheating because I'm not pitching a fit? Have you lost your mind, Marcus?"

He leaned forward, his brown eyes glued to me. "I'm just saying, I expected more of a reaction. All these years we been together. We got kids and grandkids, and you act like you don't even care about me leaving!"

"Wow, okay." I crossed the room, opened one of his dresser drawers, and pulled out the stack of underwear I had washed and neatly folded earlier that day. Then I tossed them onto the bed. "Let me help you pack," I said.

"Who is he, Kell?"

I rolled my eyes. "Good grief." I reached into another drawer and grabbed a stack of crisp white t-shirts. You could still smell the combination of Clorox bleach and Downy fabric softener. "Here," I said, shoving them toward him.

He snatched the shirts from me and muttered, "I don't believe this..."

"That makes two of us."

I stood by the door and watched as he huffed and puffed and shoved his underwear into the suitcase. He looked up and stared at me for a moment, then said, "Do you still love me, Kell?"

I shrugged. "Does it matter?"

His mouth hung open for a second. "Yes, it matters!"

"So was that what was supposed to happen? You were supposed to inform me of your intention to leave me and I was supposed to tell you how much I love you, beg you to stay?"

"No—I mean, yes—I mean, just tell me if you love me."

"Why?"

"Because I need to know!"

"Why?"

"Just answer the question, Kell," he pleaded.

I stood there for a minute, took in my tall, honey brown-skinned, handsome, albeit a little overweight husband's appearance. Remembered how thrilled I was all those years ago in college when he asked me out on a date, how after we'd been together for a while I would mindlessly scribble "Marcus and Kelly" on my notebooks, and how my heart leaped when after a year of dating, he proposed.

I remembered how he wept when I told him I was pregnant with our first child and how small Little Marc looked in Marcus's arms shortly after he was born. I remembered the births of our other three kids, the late night feedings and early morning risings. I remembered twenty-five years of meals cooked, beds made, and dirty drawers washed. I remembered weekends alone at home with the kids while he accompanied the golf team to some tournament or while he went on some recruiting trip. I remembered the snide remarks I'd endured from his mother who I always knew never liked me. I remembered "till death do us part," "in sickness and in health," "for better or worse," and the one that made me want to throat-punch him, "forsaking all others." I thought about the last twenty-five years I'd spent loving him and making love to him, and the only answer I had for his question was to turn and leave the room.

I walked through the second floor, down the stairs, and into the one room where I'd spent most of our marriage—the kitchen. I sat at the table, my eyes fixed on the stove, on the food I'd spent all afternoon cooking. The food that my dear husband had bypassed after coming home late to make his grand announcement. I had waited for him so we could eat together because that had always been important to me and at that moment I realized I was hungry, famished.

So I walked over to the stove and fixed myself a plate of the food I had been keeping warm for him. I sat back down at the table and was halfway done with my dinner when Marcus appeared in the doorway, the handle of my beloved Zephyr 70 in one hand, his golf clubs in the other, and his duffle bag over his right shoulder. "Well…" he said.

"Well…" I replied.

He stood there with an awkward look on his face for several minutes, I suppose waiting for me to say something like, "Please, don't go."

Well, if that was the case, he'd be waiting until the end of time. Finally, he said, "I guess I'll talk to you later. I-uh-left some stuff. Couldn't take everything at one time."

I nodded as I shoveled more food onto my fork. "Okay, just let me know when you want to come back and get the rest of your stuff." I placed the food in my mouth and shifted my focus back to my plate.

"Is that lasagna?" he asked.

"Mm-hmm."

He stood there for another few moments and I could almost hear his mouth watering. Then he finally left. When I heard the front door close and lock behind him, I told myself that I should've taken his key. Oh, well, I would just have to have the locks changed.

I finished dinner and walked through the quiet, empty house to my bedroom. I sat on the side of the bed and stared at the young faces of me and my soon-to-be ex-husband on our wedding picture, which sat on the bedside table. My hair was relaxed back then; my thin brown face held the promises of years of happiness to come. Marcus's arm was clutched protectively around my waist as he beamed with pride and excitement. We were so happy.

I sighed as I lay back on the bed, figuring I needed to try to get to sleep because once word got out about our separation, I knew I'd be bombarded with an endless barrage of phone calls and visits from concerned and/or nosy family and friends. The kids would be upset, but what could I do? Hell, I was upset, too, but I couldn't make him stay and I definitely couldn't make him be *in* love with me again.

I rolled over and sighed again as my eyes fell on Marcus's empty side of the bed, felt a little tug on my heart, and willed it away. I closed my eyes and had almost drifted off to sleep when I heard a sound. I quickly realized that living alone wasn't going to be easy. I was going to have to get an alarm system or I was never going to get any sleep.

I lay in the bed, trying to figure out if the sound was just a figment of my imagination when I heard it again. I sat up, searched the room with my eyes for some type of weapon, and chided myself for not keeping one of Marcus's other sets of golf clubs near the bed. A driver would probably make for a good weapon.

When he appeared in the doorway, I nearly jumped out of my skin. But before I could ask the man who'd just requested a divorce what he was doing back in my house, he dropped the golf clubs on the floor, laid the suitcase and duffle bag on the bed and began to unpack them, silently opening drawers and neatly stacking his clothes inside them. Once he was done, he put my suitcase back in its place in the closet, along with his duffle bag. The he left our bedroom and when he returned, he had a plate of lasagna in one hand and a glass of wine in the other. He handed me the wine as he sat at the foot of the bed and ate his dinner.

"You wanna have a barbecue this weekend, Kell? We could invite the kids over and everything. Make it kind of a celebration."

"A celebration?" I asked as I took a sip of the wine.

He turned and looked at me, nodded, and said, "Yeah."

I shrugged.

"And then maybe we can take a vacation. We haven't traveled in a while. As a matter of fact, I think we need to start traveling more often, get away more since the kids are grown and gone. I got plenty of leave saved up, may as well use it."

I shrugged again. "If you want to."

"And we need to eat out more. You shouldn't have to cook every day."

"Mm-hmm. Well, I guess you're right about that."

He set his plate down, crawled toward me, and kissed me deeply. "I love you, Kell. I love you and I appreciate you. I don't tell you that enough," he said. "And… I'm sorry for—for almost making the worst mistake of my life."

"You should be."

"And I'm gonna make it up to you."

"You better."

"Thank you for letting me come back, baby."

"I really didn't have a choice, because I love you, have for more than twenty-five years, and that's just the way love goes."

Adrienne Thompson has worn many titles in her lifetime: teenage mother, teenage wife, divorcee, registered nurse, and author. This mother of three young adults currently resides in her newly empty nest in Arkansas where she writes her stories full time. Learn more about her and her books at: http://adriennethompsonwrites.webs.com.

Never Too Late

By Cheryl Cloyd Robbins

His kiss tasted like crisp peppermint and I felt the color red pour down over me in a wave of love. My smile invited him to pull me closer. Life pumped from his soul into mine. The saxophone sang in my ears and I rested my head on his chiseled chest. Each note melted into the rhythmic soundtrack of love.

He nuzzled my neck, grabbed me tightly and lifted me off my feet. I was literally walking on air and his embrace kept me afloat. The saxophone continued its song as the high notes on the piano drizzled a love letter into the backdrop of our first dance.

White lace, draped just so, cascaded off my shoulders and down to my waist. The sharp darkness of his tuxedo reminded me of the night sky, and I was his light.

We existed in a space that transcended gravity while time stood still. He was the honey that would seep into my pores and make my life sweet.

Suddenly, I was startled by the blare of the saxophone. The light notes from the piano began to sound more like thunder. There was a screech that jolted me into consciousness and my feet hit the floor. He was disappearing into darkness as I was crashing into the light. What was happening?

The screech was like a train rushing through my head. My eyes fluttered open upon the morning light. The alarm clock on my nightstand was obnoxiously loud and the sun was unforgiving. A dream. It was another cursed dream of Keith.

Before I could distract myself, Keith's scent filled my nostrils. I'd washed my bedding a thousand times, but I still smelled him.

"These are going in the trash," I uttered. "I'm getting new sheets and a new comforter. Maybe I'll paint this entire bedroom."

I gathered the pillow in my arms, pressed it against my nose, and inhaled. It was like he'd never left.

"The pillows have to go too," I declared and kicked back the cover.

I willed myself out of bed, grabbed my phone and shuffled to the bathroom. While I brushed my teeth I checked for urgent messages or emails and then looked at my calendar for the day. Meetings, phone calls and more meetings were jammed into the nine hours I planned on spending at the office. Yet the date reminded me that this was the 124th day that I'd awakened to thoughts of Keith.

I spit my mouthwash into the sink and found my inspirational quote for the day staring back at me on the mirror.

Pain is inevitable. Suffering is optional.

You took the words right out of my mouth, M. Kathleen Casey. I began my morning prayer.

"Dear Lord, I thank You for another day. I thank You for Your love, Your grace and Your mercy. Lord, I ask You to be with me today that I may be focused and successful. Amen. Oh and Lawd. . .please take the image of Keith out of my mind. I can't bear to remember his face. Amen."

I flipped through the closet and found my "skinny pants." The broken heart diet was in full effect and I was happy to find a silver lining to my cloud. I tucked in my V-neck blouse instead of covering my waist with a sweater or blazer. My day was looking up!

I fixed a cup of coffee to go and even though I knew better, I added a shot of Bailey's liquor. Then I added another shot to keep the first one company.

My driver was right on time. I climbed into the backseat and sipped on my special brew of "Girl, get your life together" coffee.

I took my last swig just as we were pulling up to my building. It was a cool morning in Northeast Washington, D.C. I inhaled the autumn air and stepped inside my office building. I was early and the first to arrive, so I popped on the lobby lights and headed to my office.

I unlocked my door and just as I reached for the light switch, I heard a boom that stabbed my eardrums. For a split second I thought my lights had exploded. Then there was a second boom, louder than the first, and the floor beneath my feet began to tremor.

Next, there was a pow and a boom! Pictures jumped off the walls, books crashed to the floor. The lights flickered off and on before shattering into snowflake-sized pieces of glass around me.

"This is D.C., not California. This can't be an earthquake," I reasoned as I made a mad dash to my desk and crawled underneath it for protection. The windows cracked and I heard car horns blowing, sirens blaring and people screaming.

An eternity passed as I trembled, covered my head and waited for the world to stop crumbling around me. My desk had moved - with me under it - approximately eight feet, against the inner wall of my office. I snapped back into the present moment and realized I was trapped.

I pushed my shoulders against the back of the desk and tried to use my legs to make enough space for me to get free. But the desk that moved freely across the floor moments ago was like concrete now and too heavy for me to move. I began to panic.

I'd dropped my handbag in the race to get under the desk and along with it, my cell phone. I had no idea what had happened and more importantly, no way to call for help. I began to scream, but the heavy dust and smoke in the air filled my lungs. My eyes watered, my lungs burned and I coughed uncontrollably for several minutes before I could regain normalcy.

I pushed against the desk again, but it still wouldn't budge. I tried shifting into a more comfortable position, but there was little relief. I reasoned with myself that I should concentrate on remaining calm and thinking clearly. I remembered my morning quote, "Pain is inevitable.

Suffering is optional."

That mantra worked right up to the time my spiked coffee reached my bladder. It was then that I could no longer ignore the crisis I was facing.

I had no way of knowing what catastrophe had occurred. My co-workers hadn't made it to the office and could possibly be dead. My parents had died when I was young and left me an only child. No one would be looking for me. I could literally remain in this rubble for weeks before anyone realized I was missing.

The only person in the world who loved me was Keith. He was my lover and best friend. I was Bonnie and he was Clyde. I was Beyoncé' and he was Jay Z. I was Michelle and he was Barack.

I wanted him. I needed him. But I had been too full of pride to admit it. When he tried to provide for me, I found ways to let him know there was nothing he could buy for me that I couldn't buy for myself. When he attempted to protect me, I told him I could take care of myself. My foolish pride had pushed him away.

I took care of myself for so long, I didn't know how to allow someone to take care of me. I struggled with trusting him to be my blanket of security. He finally got fed up with having his masculinity rejected.

"What is it that you need from me, Kelly?" he'd asked in our last heated argument.

"I don't *need* anything from you," I hissed back at him. I proved my point but my victory was short-lived.

"Then I have no reason to be here," he quietly stated as he grabbed his keys and left me sitting on my bed, refusing to stop him.

I should have called him and apologized. We could have worked it out. Now it may be too late. I couldn't hold back the tears that were stinging my eyes, as they flowed down my dirty cheeks. My quiet whimper became a full-fledged sob as I considered I may never get the chance to take back everything I'd said and done to push Keith away.

I could still hear sirens outside but the sound seemed so distant. I was squeezing as hard as I could to avoid urinating in my skinny pants and surrendering even more of my dignity.

I'd pretended to be so strong, yet here I was with my tear-stained face, quickly giving up hope. I closed my eyes tightly and tried to regain my composure.

Suddenly, I heard the sound of crumbling bricks. The floor started to move while the foundation of the building began to shift. I was on the bottom floor. If the upper levels tumbled, I'd be buried alive!

I began frantically pushing against the desk again. I tried to kick, but the space was so small that I couldn't gain enough force to help.

"God, please help me," I prayed.

The sound of falling debris made me feel like a tomb was being built around me. I heard voices and screamed with everything I had inside. I coughed and choked, but I kept screeching. I used my elbows to knock on the sides of the desk. I yelled as loudly as I could for as long as I could. Then I heard a call.

"Kelly!"

God was answering me!

"I'm here!"

"Kelly!" The voice got closer.

For a split second I felt the familiar comfort of a voice I knew. But then the terrifying crash came from above my head.

"Kelly, baby, it's me!"

"Keith, help me. I'm under this desk." My hero had arrived to save me. Keith yanked out the desk drawers and peeked at me between the slats.

When I saw his face, I vowed I'd never let him go again. I cried out with relief, but quickly realized we were far from being safe.

"Baby, we have to hurry. When I count to three, I need you to push as hard as you can toward me. Ok, baby? Can you do that for me?" I nodded, because at this point I couldn't speak.

More debris fell from the ceiling. But I concentrated on waiting for Keith to count so I could push.

"One!" he yelled just before a beam slammed down behind him.

"Two!" I planted my hands and got ready to push.

"Three!" he yelled as he pulled with all his might. I pushed as hard as I could. There was no more holding my urine and I didn't care. We moved the desk about six inches on the first try.

"Now use your legs and push." This time he didn't count. When he pulled, I pushed and we moved the desk another twelve inches. It was enough for me to squeeze out while Keith pulled.

My legs had been cramped so long, I couldn't stand, but we had to move. Keith threw my arms around his shoulders and pulled me to my feet. I looked down and saw my wet pants.

"I had an accident," I said with embarrassment.

"Baby, I spent three hours digging you out, afraid you were hurt; I don't care about an accident. Let's get outta here and I'll buy you fifty pairs of pants."

Another shift in the foundation and the entire wall collapsed and blocked the doorway. Keith had covered me with his body and protected me from the falling wood and plaster.

There was now one way out and that was the window. It was already partially cracked and he used a chair to break out the rest of the glass.

My legs were regaining their feeling but I still needed help getting up to the ledge. Even on the first floor, we were still about six feet off the ground. There was no easy landing below us because the sidewalk was filled with busted brick and concrete, glass and debris.

Just as I was about to jump, the floor under Keith crumpled. I hesitated and reached for his hand, but he pushed me out of the window to safety.

"Keith!" I called hysterically. I couldn't see him.

"Keith!" I cried, and then saw him pulling himself up into the window frame. He jumped and yelled for me to run. We ran toward the street and looked back just in time to watch the entire building collapse. As the adrenaline began to deplete and my tunnel vision widened to my surroundings, I saw the remains of two city blocks flattened to the ground by what I would later discover were suicide bombers. I could hardly process the enormity of the cataclysmic event around us.

I stopped in my tracks and tried to bring my mind into the present moment. I looked into Keith's eyes and processed the fact that he had saved my life.

"You came for me," I said as I fell into his arms and we slid onto the ground.

He pulled me close, kissed my dirty forehead and said, "I'll always come for you."

***

Eight months later I found myself swaying to the harmonious melody of a piano and saxophone. I could feel the notes weaving our souls together. I inhaled and attempted to digest his scent.

Our heartbeats swayed in cadence with each other. We were as perfectly in tune as the instruments that played in the background.

I looked into his eyes, falling more deeply in love with him with each passing second. Our love eclipsed the crowd and we were momentarily encompassed in just each other.

Then the clinking of silverware on crystal glasses filled the air. I wrapped my arms around Keith's neck as he leaned in and kissed my lips. When I opened my eyes, he was still right in front of me and I knew this was a dream, and yet it was very much real.

Cheryl Cloyd Robbins is a native and current resident of North Carolina. Her love for writing has enabled her to use words to transport some of her readers in exotic places and times while also providing some of her readers with therapeutic tools for emotional healing. Cheryl is a co-founder and partner of Reign Incorporated. It is "Never Too Late" to discover more of Cheryl's work at www.cherylcloydrobbins.com or www.reignincorporated.com.

Pursue.Conquer.Destroy

By Yvette Danielle

My mother, Rojean, warned me to never buy shoes for a man because they'd be the ones he'd have on when he walked out of my life. It sounded crazy, but incited my obsession with a guy's feet... well, more so their shoes. I don't have a fetish or anything like that, but for me to allow a man anywhere near me physically, he must have nice – no - *perfect* feet that are clean, smooth, crust-less, fungus/corn free, non-funky and well- maintained. *And* his shoes had to be the same way. That was my thing.

I never predicted meeting someone who would make me throw these preconceived notions out the window. But it happened. This man stole my breath at first sight and I'd been winded ever since. I remember every detail of our first meeting.

It was 'hump day' Wednesday, and I had stepped out of my windowless office for a required dose of Vitamin D. I'd had enough of closed-in cubicles and airheads smooching on upper management's behind in the name of team building. The sunrays on my face were like baby kisses. I shrouded myself in the natural beauty I encountered on my lap around Center City Philadelphia's business district. The fresh air and change of scenery cured my claustrophobic outbreak and I headed over to Devon & Blakely to address my hunger pains.

"Those are some really nice shoes you're wearing."

The words were spoken whisper-soft directly behind my ear from a silky smooth tenor voice. It initiated a tremor throughout my body that I somewhat recovered from before looking over my shoulder. The warmest brown eyes and most amazing smile I'd ever seen on a chocolate black man greeted me.

I gasped.

"Are they Michael Kors?"

"No, DVF."

His forehead wrinkled slightly; he looked inquisitive.

"DVF?"

I looked down at my 4 1/2 inch black, t-strap leather Uffie heels, wrapped in leopard print calf hair around the toe band. "Diane von Furstenberg."

"I've seen something like them in Neiman Marcus."

I wrinkled my nose. "You work in the shoe department?"

His laugh was joyous and playful. "You're funny."

"Yeah, seeing as how I only shop the window at that place. These are from Nordstrom Rack."

"Well you definitely have great taste. Those stilettos look good on you."

"These are booties, but-"

"Now you're speaking my language."

He had to blow it.

My eyes rolled around in a circle. "You take care." I sidestepped around him to leave.

"Wait. Hold up, please." His buttery velvet voice saved me from moving. I envisioned planting my mouth on his full, succulent lips for a kiss. . . They looked so. . . soft. . .

"Yes?"

It was safer to view the Exit sign hanging above the door than to look at him.

"I'm sorry, did I say something wrong?"

"Your booty reference was offensive."

"My apologies, truce. May I start over?" He extended his hand, palm facing upward for me to take.

After that offhanded remark, I questioned if it was even clean. As if hearing my thoughts, he turned it over so I could inspect the other side or pop him like a child. That made me smile. He had clean, manicured fingernails and clearly took pride in his appearance. I shook his hand. He shined his bright, hundred-watt smile. I gasped again.

"Thank you."

"For what?"

"For another chance to speak to you, and get it right this time. Can I buy your lunch?"

"Well, now you're speaking my language."

We laughed. As we waited in line to order, I overlooked my hand naturally intertwined with his, like it belonged. I allowed it a few minutes longer. He squeezed warmth into my hand.

"Do you have time to eat here?"

"That depends."

"On what?"

"With… who? I don't even know your name."

He licked his lips and grinned. "Right, sorry. We haven't done that yet."

He dropped my hand and I regretted opening my mouth.

Turning to face me, he said, "Hi, how you doing? It's so nice to meet you before we eat together. My name is Randolph and… you are?"

I smiled. "Hi, Randolph. My name is Veronica."

"O' Veronica, Veronica… O' Veronica girl," he sang.

It was the chorus to the 1985 rap song by Bad Boys that had been a pain in my ass during my adolescent days.

I gave Randolph Rojean's signature look. That was strike two.

"What? Oh, come on. How could I possibly resist? Your name is a set-up!"

He was too loud for my taste.

"I swear I meant nothing by the jawn. Honestly, I come in peace."

"Riiiight."

"Can I help you?" the woman behind the sandwich counter asked, ending our conversation.

Randolph grabbed my hand for the third time in ten minutes. "Yeah, we're ready."

I peeked down at his feet, gasped once more, and then looked up. Beaming.

"Nice shoes yourself."

The remainder of the day was a blur. I recalled exchanging numbers before we parted ways and returning from lunch late. Randolph captivated my thoughts. I couldn't concentrate.

That man was fo-ine. Milk chocolate skin, close-cropped fade, goatee, an athlete's body, toned and chiseled muscles covered in fitted navy pants, a crisp white button-up shirt. . . and bulges in all the right places.

Yaaaass, honey, yaaaass!

Weeks passed like running water. The closeness between Randolph and I progressed through changing seasons. Although he worked nearby, I didn't know which building. He told me he was a surveillance analyst whose job was important to Wall Street. Whatever he did paid him nicely. The tailored Italian suits, *Blue Sole Shoes* with matching sock combinations and designer clothes he often purchased at Boyd's declared his job was serious. His wealth status never intimidated me nor did I feel inferior around him because of it.

We called each other throughout the workday, often sneaking into conference rooms for additional time. Our discussions were enlightening. We talked about five year goals: where we would be, if we would marry, have kids, our dream vacations and possibly, traveling together. Randolph was well-rounded. We talked politics, African-American history and even tackled the subject of religion. Neither of us was turned off by the other's beliefs, morals, or values.

He worked crazy hours. It kept him pretty busy and unavailable for weeks sometimes. The scarce moments we found together nurtured my desire to be near him but, romantically, he was lacking. My mind wrestled over whether this resulted from his work ethic or me holding out. Our intellectual foreplay kept things alive, but also fanned my anticipation for more time together.

One thing I could credit him with was patience. The more I made him wait, the more Randolph kept after me. It brought such satisfaction knowing he would continue his pursuit until he earned the prize he desired: to consume me entirely. He was not giving up until he did. I was not giving in until he earned it.

Despite Randolph's constant attempts to entice me, I held firm in my resistance to physical intimacy with him. Sex simply complicated things and clouded judgment. Especially good sex. I wanted romantic expressions without lustful intentions and knew that was not asking too much.

"The only time women go out and buy flowers for a man is for his funeral."

The dialogue between us was loose and easy as we enjoyed dinner together at my house.

Randolph pointed his fork in my direction. "I'm serious. Y'all don't buy them for us any other time. But you want to receive them."

"And we should-"

"On what basis? Because you're a woman? A *female*?"

"Absolutely."

"Bullshit." He laughed.

He stuffed his face with more of the four-cheese lasagna I cooked with chicken, hamburger, and a sprinkling of pepperoni and spinach. The combination was melt-in-your-mouth delicious. Homemade Italian bread and garden salad completed our meal.

"You don't have entitlement to flowers just because you're female. Hell, if anything that should be why we get them more than you. Because you came from us!"

"Are you serious right now?"

"I am. You were taken from my rib."

"You were birthed from my womb."

"Had it not been for me, there would be no you."

I set my fork down on that one. "If God had not brought wisdom into the world when he did - in the form of woman — there is no telling if you would still exist. Y'all would be extinct, and why? Because man cannot live without us. True. Statement."

The gleam in Randolph's eyes told me he was as amused with my banter as I was by his rhetoric.

"Look woman, all I'm saying is from time to time it would be nice to get treated the way you expect treatment. Buy *me* some flowers for a change. Bring me a stem. Give me mine while I'm alive to enjoy their smell and appreciate the sender."

"Uh-huh."

"Now see, you ain't right." He took another forkful. "Mmmn."

"What do you mean?"

"If I came through that door tonight with your favorite flowers and gave them to you, what would you do?" He picked up his Heineken bottle and took a long swig.

My cheeks grew warm and I struggled to contain the smile bubbling inside my mouth.

"Well," he prodded.

I lifted my head. "First, I would thank you for how incredibly sweet and thoughtful you were in doing so."

"What else?" he probed further, bedroom eyes watching me intensely.

"I, uh… I don't know…"

"Yeah, you do."

Silence. His words shifted the air current. It now felt warmer and lighter.

"You would want me to continue doing it, wouldn't you? Because you like it… right?"

I diverted my eyes from his sexy features. Picking up my glass of *Castello del Poggio Moscato*, a hard-to-find favorite of mine he brought for our meal, I took a moment to let its exotic fruitiness dance across my tongue.

Damn! This man was wearing me down.

"You didn't answer me. You like it, right?"

The deep and sultry tone of his voice hung in the air like dense fog at daybreak, thick, and heavy. My insides were moist. I nodded like a bobble head. The flickering candlelight in the center of the table crackled with the electricity and passion kindling between us.

I tried a series of kegal crunches to quiet the pounding from down under. But my vajayjay danced to her own conga beat. Randolph got up and walked over to me. I froze. My legs were still shaking.

"Dance with me, Veronica."

He took my hand and gently pulled me to my feet. Slipping his left arm around my waist, he twirled me away from the dining room into my spacious living room. I was more than tipsy. The alcohol - mixed with his ridiculously sexy cologne - had my head whirling like those eighties spin top toys. How did I get this lucky? I nestled my head onto his chest and listened as Ronnie Jordan fingered his guitar through my Bose system. The colors, music, and magic of that moment overwhelmed me.

"I like you," he whispered.

I had cotton mouth.

"I want you to know that I'm ready to do whatever it takes to make you mine. So if that means giving up my flowers to you, then I'm ready to do it."

I giggled. "I think you missed your calling as a comedian."

Randolph's chuckle vibrated inside my ear. "I'll stick to my day job. It pays the bills and will allow me to take really good care of you."

Oh, how I loved the sound of that! My arms tightened around his neck and I pulled him as close to me as humanly possible with clothes on. His erection pressed against my inner thigh. I yearned for all of him inside of me.

"Tell me what you want me to do right now."

How precisely on point he was with my thoughts freaked me out. I trembled.

"I want to taste you." Randolph nuzzled my neck, and then covered my lips with his.

What did he just say?

God. . . who am. . . my name is. . .

Now it was on! My vajayjay turned into an engine firing all cylinders at full throttle. *No* amount of kegels was going to work now. She was overly vocal about wanting wood - lots of it. Her lips screamed, *Just give it to me, give it to me, give it to me. Give. It. To. Me!*

I shoved myself away from Randolph and raced to the bathroom, pushing the door behind me a little too hard. It banged shut and I jumped and screamed.

A sharp knock was followed by the turning door knob. "Veronica, let me in. Are you okay?"

"I'm fine. It's okay. Really. I scared myself when the door slammed." My embarrassed chuckle became drunken laughter.

"Are you sure?"

"Yes, I'm good. Just feeling silly right now. Give me a second, please."

The three second pause felt like an eternity.

"Okay."

I relaxed and exhaled once his footsteps departed from the door. *Girl, get a grip.* What was wrong with me?

I knew.

I wanted this man.

Randolph was different. Special. He was unlike previous guys I had dated or been involved with, and I wanted to share more than just my body with him. I wanted to share my heart and divulge my all without having to spread my legs. Tie up my feelings, wrap them in a nice neat bow, and offer it to him as a sign of my purpose and serious intentions. But I didn't want to scare him. And I wasn't into Netflix and Chill.

Sex was off the table.

Which is why little V was cutting a whole fool right now. She was hearing none of it. Opportunity had knocked against my leg and she wanted to open and let it come on in. I had to shut her down.

Randolph's coat was in his hand when I re-entered the living room. He walked over and swept me into his arms. We spoke at the same time.

"You're leaving?"

"Are you okay?"

Then together, "Yes."

I moved out of his embrace.

"I'm sorry. I have to leave now. I got to go handle something."

"Is everything all right?"

"If it's not, it will be."

The way his nostrils flared and eyes went cold made me shutter.

He squeezed me tight. "I don't want to leave you like this. Are we cool?"

He was slowly melting my heart.

"Yeah. Go handle your business, but give me a call later so I know you're good."

"I will."

I had not heard back from Randolph since that night. I distracted myself with busy work to keep my mind off him, but he was never too far from my thoughts. When he finally contacted me to spend time with him Sunday afternoon, I was both relieved and excited. He showed up at my door holding a huge, bouquet of Calla lilies. I grabbed them from him.

"These are amazing! Thank you so much!"

I headed into the kitchen for a vase, leaving him at the door. He closed it and trailed behind me.

"You're welcome." His tone was short and his eyes were vacant.

"What's the matter?"

"Nothing, I'm cool. You?"

"Great, I've been working and keeping busy with other projects. So, did everything turn out okay that night you had to leave?"

"What? Oh, that. Yeah, it was nothing. Don't worry about it."

Geez! What was eating him?

"What's up? What you want to talk about?" he asked.

"Whatever's bothering you for starters. You look like you lost your best friend or found out *you are the father.*" My *Maury* impersonation was pretty good.

A half-hearted smile crossed his face as he looked away, but stayed quiet.

"What's going on?"

"Family stuff. You know how it is."

I didn't know, but clearly he wasn't ready to talk so I wouldn't pry. "I have something for you," I told him.

Now he was cheesing.

"You do? Give it to me then."

"Right now?"

"Hell yeah!"

We laughed.

"Close your eyes," I whispered.

"Hold up. I'm not into that bondage shit."

"Shut up!"

"For real, you aren't about to tie me up or handcuff me are you?"

"No."

"Burn my beautiful skin with candle wax."

This was the Randolph I knew. "Stop!"

"Pull out a whip or something like that to beat my ass."

"If you keep talking, I might."

"Don't try to put nothing in my ass, V."

"Shut up, Randy."

"What I tell you about calling me that? That's not my name. You play too much."

"You talk too much."

"Then give me some and I'll shut up."

"Boy, you drawn! Close your eyes."

"I mean it, woman, don't stick nothing in my-"

"Okay!"

This was my happiness. He was Martin to my Gina. It was nonstop comedy all the time.

He finally shut his eyes. I ran and retrieved his surprise from the bedroom. Randolph's back was to me when I returned.

"Okay, you can open your eyes."

I was standing in front of him holding a ceramic sneaker vase. It was designed and sculpted after his favorite pair of high top, brown leather Tom Fords. A sprawling arrangement of tangerine chrysanthemums intermixed with heavenly scented mini gardenias were inside.

"You don't strike me as the roses type." I extended the vase to him. "These are for you."

His reaction was worth every hour I spent in that pottery class. Randolph is an alpha male with a Type A personality to boot. This gift had to be God's work through me for him to like it. His teeth glistened like diamonds.

"These are my flowers?"

"Mums the word."

He took the vase from me, inspecting and admiring the handiwork.

"Tom Ford." He chuckled. "Nice... is that your signature on the base?"

My chin jutted out with pride. "Yep, I made it for you."

"Word, when did you have time to do this?"

"When I told you I was at the gym working out."

"O-o-ohhhh," he chortled. "You like being sneaky."

"No. Just clever."

He held the vase in one hand and hugged me with the other. His lips kissed their way from my forehead to my mouth. I relished the taste of his tongue. We paused for air.

"Thank you. I love it."

"Really? You do?"

He nodded sincerely. "This is the first time I've ever been given flowers."

"Did I get it right?"

"You did."

"Good, 'cause it was a first for me, too."

"Giving flowers?"

"I gave you a shoe."

"Do I get anything else?" The longing in his voice was quietly insistent.

"Yes, you certainly do."

Randolph stayed late that night. His lovemaking nourished my soul and afterwards he held me like it was his last act on earth. I had somehow won the super bowl championship of love, and had achieved more than a winning touchdown. I had brought home the good man trophy.

And all it took was some flowers, and a shoe.

I finally felt comfortable in my position with him and rested peacefully in his arms with that knowledge...

It was nearly six a.m. when I awoke to sounds of Channel 6ABC Action News playing from the living room. Randolph had left hours ago, taking his gift with him, and had lovingly wrapped me in a blanket. I climbed out of bed and headed to the kitchen to make coffee in the Keurig.

A handwritten note lay on the dining room table. I recognized Randolph's chicken scratch and smirked, but didn't walk over to read it until my coffee started brewing.

You were right about the baby.

I'm sorry.

My legs buckled as the noise level of the television increased. It was a commercial advertising birth control. I made it to the living room, grabbed the TV remote to turn it off, then abruptly stopped.

Randolph's picture was stretched across the fifty-inch screen. The caption beneath it read *Lover's Quarrel Turned Homicide*. I stared blankly at the screen.

"In what is being called a couple's dispute with a bizarre twist, police storm a West Philadelphia home at three a.m., responding to calls from area residents of a domestic altercation. Randolph Williams, age 43, was taken into custody for beating his 36-year-old pregnant girlfriend to death with what police describe as a ceramic vase in the shape of a sneaker. According to neighbors, the pregnant victim was seven months along with her first child, and Williams was identified as her disgruntled ex."

The picture cut from the field reporter on location to a uniformed policeman being interviewed. "The suspect made a full confession before his arrest, stating he learned today he was not the expectant father from DNA test analysis done by himself and the deceased. These test results were retrieved near the victim's body."

The picture cut back to the field reporter. "Randolph Williams is currently being held without bail and faces a series of charges. An investigation is underway, and no additional news is available on the welfare of the child. Authorities are not releasing the woman's identity until the family has been notified. This is Kim Collins, Channel 6 Action News. We will bring you more details on this story as it develops."

Yvette Danielle is a New England native, originally from Springfield, Massachusetts. A singer, thespian, playwright and poet/spoken word artist, she now resides in the Greater Philadelphia area. She is currently completing her debut teen novel, A Piece of My Love. To stay in contact with Yvette Danielle on Social Media, check out her Facebook Author Page (Yvette Danielle), or follow her on Twitter (@ydanielle) and Instagram (@yvettedanl).

The Ex I Never Had

By Christina Grant

1995 – Love At First Sight

Getting ready for another fun night! I was so excited to be living on campus and finally making friends.

"I had this bad chick uptown, she was whoa…." Black Rob blared through the hallways of my dorm, and as the RA, I felt all powerful playing that. Who was going to call campus security on the RA?

But tonight, I wasn't an RA; I was going to a Hip Hop version of Hamlet at the Student Theatre. Sounded corny, but all the fraternities and sororities came together for this event and in my never-ending dream of being a Delta, I had to be in the house. What was amazing was that a member of Delta invited me.

I met Erica during my freshman year. She was smart, beautiful, and although she came from money, she was super down to earth.

At first, I thought it was weird that she would invite me; I was her RA, but we only saw each other at dorm meetings. I had to quiet the voice in my head that told me to question the invitation.

I guess I questioned it because I'd always struggled with making female friends. I was what others called pretty (key word others): light skinned, with long flowing hair (that only a few knew was a weave) and a killer body. This caused me to make more enemies than friends because most girls wanted nothing to do with me and over time, that became just fine. I hung with the guys who were more welcoming to a pretty girl with a brain.

But now that I was entering my junior year, I was ready to embrace all of me – beauty, body, and brains. I saw the women of DST mastering their complete selves with ease and confidence, and I hoped one day to be welcomed into their sisterhood.

Walking across campus was always a scene. You had to look cute whether the sun was shining or it was freezing cold. I had a little extra strut as I walked today, full of confidence.

A couple of minutes later, I heard, "Stacy, slow down!"

I turned and saw Erica running and waving. As she got closer, her smile told me that she was glad I came out. She looked amazing in her treasured DST line jacket, black leggings, and stiletto boots.

She caught on to my nerves. "Look, after tonight everyone's gonna peg you as one of us, but you look amazing, so let's have fun and worry about Greek life tomorrow."

We walked and talked about everything and nothing. Erica was excited to be graduating in May and eager to head straight to Harvard Business School. (Third generation!) "Brains matter over looks every day!" she told me.

When we got to the event, I watched Erica in awe. Everyone knew her and it took over fifteen minutes for us to get to our seats. We were in the third row…and I was happy to finally be sitting down. These Louboutins were nice, but they hurt like hell.

Just as an announcement was made that the show would be slightly delayed, a male voice asked me to move one seat down.

"I want to sit next to her," he said, pointing to Erica.

I gathered my stuff, looked up, and saw a man who was just my kind of fine. He was short and stocky and handsome. I thought to myself, *Who is he and why hadn't I met him yet?*

I had been off the dating scene. College had proven to be a tough place for me on the relationship side and I decided to make my parents happy by getting my B.A. even if my heart desired my MRS.

Erica interrupted my thoughts to introduce me to her boyfriend, Michael. I felt the air slip out the room as she said the words 'boooooy frieeeend'.

My outside actions didn't betray my inside thoughts...super quickly I said, "Hey, nice to meet you," and then, I averted my attention away from Michael. My insides were on fire, but on the outside, I was cool as a glacier.

As Michael sat down, he said, "Aren't you like an RA or something...I feel like one night you kicked me out last semester."

I responded, "Well if it was past curfew, then you had to leave." I hoped that would end the conversation.

"Yeah, that was you," he continued. "You had on this green face mask and like a muumuu, but it was after nine and you were kicking fellas out left and right. We were giving you shit and all the fellas couldn't stop talking about the crazy RA in Wharton Hall."

We laughed and in that quick exchange, I felt like I'd known Michael for years. He seemed excited to meet the face behind the mask. Michael kept talking, asking all kinds of questions: What's your major? Are you from New York? Who's your favorite rapper?

I kept up with the pace trying to be polite, though I felt a bit uncomfortable. This was Erica's man, and I didn't want her to think I was trying anything. But she was in the aisle, talking to friends, and aside from introducing me to Michael, she hadn't said anything else to him.

Watching her, I kept answering him. And after a few more questions, I asked, "How long have you and Erica been dating?" I figured bringing it back to Erica would stop the conversation. But the way he answered, Michael missed the memo totally!

"Erica and I went to high school together. She's amazing, and such a people person." His eyes stayed on me. "Most people don't believe that high school sweethearts can make it, but four years later, we're still together."

I heard his words, but he didn't sound convincing. It was his body language mostly -- he didn't even glance her way.

Then, he asked, "Are you single?" He didn't give me a chance to answer. "Because without your green mask, you're stunning."

"Thanks," I said, appreciating the joke and the compliment. "I'm single."

47

"Really?" he asked as if he were shocked. "Well, some guy is gonna be very happy one day."

That made me blush and wish the darn play would begin. Or that Erica would sit down and talk to her man so that I wouldn't.

Then he surprised me with, "It's good to meet the girl that Erica has been talking about."

"She's been talking about me?"

"Yeah, I know you sing in the choir, have straight A's, apparently you're a mini Erica in the making. I'm pretty sure she's considering sponsoring you for initiation."

That made me smile.

"That's a huge deal," he said. "But I hope you're ready for the mess."

Now, I frowned.

He said, "The real question is, why do you want to be a part of all this?" There was a sadness in the way he said 'all this' and for a second, I thought maybe Michael didn't want to be here.

Even though I needed to stop talking to him, I didn't want him to stop talking to me. It had been super hard for me to have a conversation with any guy on campus, and besides my concerns about Erica and Delta, my spirit was at ease with Michael.

This was all super-wrong, but just as I was settled in for more questions, the lights dimmed and the stage curtains opened.

Show time.

Thank goodness.

2000 – Unexpected Pairings

While I sat in hospice care with my father, I spent most of my time talking to Michael via text. As with so many times in our lives since we'd met five years ago, Michael was there for me. Not physically, since he was sitting in a different hospital, here in the city watching the life leave his beloved mother. But he was here for me in every other way. We were going through the same thing, so he understood my pain. We were being forced to become adults long before we were ready.

We didn't get to see each other often, but we texted every day, the way we were texting now.

Michael: Hey, how's your visit?

Me: Today, he knew I was here. I had about five good minutes of him being fully present. He told me to go home, but he enjoyed me being here. I'm tired, but there's no place I'd rather be. You?

Michael: We are living the same life! I'm with mom and she's bossing me around. She's in great spirits and she's eating. As usual, she wants to know why I haven't married Erica? I'm pretty sure she doesn't care about Erica, she just wants grandchildren. ☺

Me: You guys are the poster board for black love, so get crackin! Glad she's in good spirits and harassing you! Thanks for always checking on me…it means a lot.

Michael: OMG not you, too! You know darn well Erica and I aren't ready. She doesn't even take time to come sit here with me. I'm not sure I can get past it.

There was a pause, but before I could text anything, another came in from him.

Michael: And you know Heather is being a beast, right...she's here as much as I am and I'm glad for the support.

This time, I was the one who paused. Heather was at the hospital with Michael? I didn't know why I was surprised. Heather and Michael met while he was volunteering at a school near campus. She was a teacher with a big heart and a lot of time to devote to Michael, though I never questioned their friendship because Michael and I were purely platonic. So, I figured he was faithful to Erica and he and Heather were just friends.

Finally, I texted back:

Me: You know I don't want to hear nothing about another woman. So we can stop texting now. LOL!

Michael: Fine, then you marry me!

Me: And with that, I'll leave you to have a good day! Give your mom a hug.

Michael: Fine, deflect...talk to you tomorrow and call me if you need anything.

I laughed; that was my once-a-year proposal from Michael. The joke was that I'd never touched Michael, kissed Michael, even gave a hint that I was interested in more than a friendship. But these last five years helped me to believe that men and women could have great friendships. And his friendship was important because I needed him by my side as I faced this life challenge.

It was funny that I was so close to him since he was still with Erica. For a while, Erica and I had actually become besties after I was initiated into Delta Sigma Theta Sorority, Inc. We were inseparable as we both focused on our academics, excellence, and ruling the world.

Then, during the Fall of my senior year, Erica invited me to Cambridge to visit Harvard. Now, I have to say I never thought I'd consider attending an Ivy League university, but Erica convinced me that between my grades, community service, and LSAT scores, I would get in. But then, my first night in Cambridge marked the beginning of the end of our best friend status.

I found my way to the campus and Erica's dorm and was blown away by her luxurious lifestyle. She'd traded her Honda Civic for a black BMW and everything from her hair to her shoes had been upgraded. Looking at Erica and other students on campus, I realized quickly that I was out of my (Ivy) league.

And if I had any doubts about my thoughts, Erica made me sure that I knew I would never fit in at a place like Harvard. After she gave me a quick hug, she snarled, "What the hell do you have on?" She frowned at my sweats. "You're at Harvard, for God sakes!"

I couldn't remember another time when she cared about my clothes, but I stammered to explain that I just wanted to be comfortable on my ride up.

"This isn't undergrad," she snapped. "If you want to be taken seriously, you need to look the part."

She went to her closet and threw a couple of outfits at me. "Change!" she demanded. "Because I can't be seen with you like that. Ugh! You can't be my pet project for the rest of your life!"

Her words stung and hurt to my core, but I'd never been one to cause drama, so I changed into something that she felt was appropriate. We went through the rest of the weekend without another dispute -- at least not an outward one.

But I began to see Erica with new eyes. As we engaged with her friends, she made a point of saying some pretty petty things.

"Stacy and I went to school together, but she attended on a scholarship."

"Oh, yes, Stacy is very smart. She's the first one to attend college in her family."

"Can you believe this is the very first time that Stacy has stepped foot on the campus of an Ivy League school?"

I wanted to say, 'Who cares?' to every one of her statements. Yes, what she said was true, but her tone reminded me of her earlier words -- pet project.

Erica didn't see or hear from me much after that, not that she seemed to notice. But what was interesting was that as Erica and I grew apart, Michael and I became closer, especially since Michael remained in New York while Erica was in Massachusetts.

Michael stayed local for business school, even though he and Erica got to see each other often since she had the money to travel back and forth. But, I didn't care about what was going on between the two of them. I was just happy to have Michael around as I navigated through the stress of law school.

I glanced down at my phone and thought about sending Michael another text, but then, decided I'd reach out later.

Putting down my phone, I turned my attention to my dad. He was resting and when his eyes were closed like that, it didn't even look like he was a man whose days were numbered.

Tears came to my eyes as they always did when I had that thought and I brushed them away. I took a deep breath; I wouldn't be the same when my dad passed, but I would make it. I could make it through anything as long as Michael was by my side.

2005 – Can We Try?

"Stacy, are you able to watch Samantha tonight? Heather and I need to talk and I really don't want Samantha listening to us argue."

This had become my new normal. Shortly after Michael's mom passed, he had a break-from-Erica baby with Heather and life as we all knew it changed.

He wasn't certain Heather was 'the one', but even after a decade with Erica, he wasn't sure about her, either.

And then, there was me. Michael was sure about me. I was the babysitter. The negotiator. The holder of secrets. And the best friend.

When I hung up from Michael, I went into the room where I had a toddler bed for times such as these. As I prepared for Samantha, I thought how much had changed in the ten years that I'd known Michael. While he was torn between two women, I was deeply in love and planning my wedding. I had met an amazing man, William, in law school and the best thing about him was that he thought my sweats were just fine.

Seriously, William was everything a woman could dream of: a deeply-devoted-to-God attorney who was so in love with me. He knew me in the most intimate of ways -- he'd seen me without my weave for god's sake!

But Michael was still my best friend, so when he dropped Samantha off, I didn't tell him what I always did -- that I didn't think he was over his mother's death and it was making it hard to see what was so clear -- that he was with Erica because that's who everyone expected him to marry, and that he loved Heather because of who she was and all the support she'd given him when his mother was dying.

At midnight, I was startled out of my sleep by loud banging. Even though I was sure it was Michael, I was still shocked to see him when I opened the door.

"What are you doing here?" I asked. "I'm not waking Samantha, so come get her in the morning."

"I just needed to talk. I'm tired, Stacy," he said. "It's been a long, exhausting day." He stared at the ground and kicked the carpet, like a kid preparing for a scolding.

It was 12:31 and he had chosen this time to become a three-year-old. *Patience, Stacy!*

When he looked up with tears in his eyes, I got scared. Now, Michael's not a thug, but he wasn't soft. In our years of friendship, I had never seen him cry.

"Okay…calm down…what happened at Heather's?" I guided him to the couch.

We sat down and Michael stretched out, laying his head on my lap. This was different for us, but felt natural. I started massaging his head of tight soft curls, something I'd never done.

"I just can't get this shit right, it's been so hard since Mom died and no one's happy."

Then, he sobbed, and I stayed quiet, just stroking his hair. This was good, a breakthrough. Like I said, he was still affected by his mom's death, having never shed a tear -- at least not in public.

His tears made me think of his mother -- and the last conversation we'd had.

I'd gone to visit her and she'd sent Michael away so that she and I could talk. I was nervous about it, at first. But then, she had put me at ease before she shocked me with her words.

"Would you like some tea?" she asked when we were alone.

"No, Ma'am. I'm fine."

"Why're you calling me ma'am? You've been calling me mom for five years. Don't get brand new."

I chuckled.

She said, "I just needed some one on one time with the woman who should be my daughter-in-law."

My mouth opened wide.

"Shut your mouth, girl." Then, she went on to tell me how while she thought Erica had the best intentions, she would never be able to take care of Michael and that I could.

"I don't have much time left." She held up her hand when I began to protest. "It's fine; I've lived a good life and I'm tired. But I just had to talk to you about this. I had to tell you that my son doesn't know it, but he's in love with you." My shock was showing, but she continued,

"There are going to be some rough days ahead for Michael." She took my hand. "Take care of my son. What I would love is for the two of you to get married, but honestly baby, just be there for him. Be there when he needs to navigate this, when he needs to break down...."

I heard his mother as if she were in the room with us now, and I just let Michael cry. He cried until he had no tears left, and then turned over and stared up at me.

He remained silent for a few moments, then, "Seriously, will you be my wife?"

All the other times he'd asked me, I laughed. But this time, it was so crazy and profound and weird...watching him cry and thinking about the words of his mother.

He sat up and we hugged, until Michael began to kiss me. He kissed my neck first, then my cheek, my forehead, and my eyes. I shuddered when he held my face with both hands.

Looking into my eyes, he said, "Trust me."

Two simple words that weren't simple at all.

I didn't even know I was crying until he wiped away my tears with his gentle fingers. We shifted, and I was on Michael's lap and our faces were so close, our noses almost touched.

I tried to pull away, but he pulled me closer.

"I'm in love with you, Stacy," he whispered. "You're my best friend, the strongest woman I know, and I want to spend my life healing your pains and proving that you are making a great decision to trust me."

For the first time since my engagement, I wanted another man to touch me. I leaned forward and kissed him. And then, our bodies shared an intimate beautiful conversation that was timely, but long overdue....

2010 – I'm Married Now

It was crazy that Michael's daughter was almost seven. She was my favorite little person, and I was pretty sure I ranked higher than her mom. With the back and forth with her parents, I had been the most consistent person in her life.

"Yes, Samantha, we should be there around six."

I hung up and smiled. This was a good time in all of our lives. Michael and Erica had completely parted ways and he and Heather had gotten it together, though they hadn't married yet. But they'd created a great space for Samantha.

"Honey, who was on the phone?"

I looked at my husband of two years. And in those few seconds, I thought about the wonderful journey that our marriage was.

I bet you thought I'd be living happily ever after with Michael. Well, we tried, but it didn't work. The morning after our night of passion, we talked about a relationship, but the sheer number of people who would be hurt by our actions, outweighed our desire to take our relationship to another level.

That was for the best because though Michael and I loved each other, in the spirit of who he was, he had to build a life with the mother of his child.

So after we had our moment, which was a great moment, we decided to stay on the friendship track and love the people who deserved to have us be the best versions of ourselves.

The Present - Here and Now

And that's where we ended up....me, with William and Michael with Heather. Yes, they finally married.

Michael is truly the ex I never had. The stars just didn't align for us, but that never stopped me from keeping my promise to his mother -- I would protect him, from this space of friendship. It is far more challenging than you would think, but it's a journey I wouldn't trade for the world.

Christina Grant is a writer, hopeless romantic, and believer in fairy tales!

BEST EX EVER

By Meredith E. Greenwood

Tiffany knew her man was up to something the minute she whipped her Nissan Xterra into the extended circular driveway. Even from the inside of the vehicle, the smell of country fried ham, fresh-baked croissants, and cinnamon apples consumed her nostrils and *almost* made her mouth water. Keith had gotten up extra early to fix his famous "sunrise surprise" breakfast. She closed her eyes and imagined every six feet, five inches of his shirtless, chocolate body standing at the stove. She smirked and thought about how she loved sneaking up behind him while he cooked and grabbing his...

"Wait, is that caramel vanilla coffee I smell?" Tiffany mumbled to herself. She rushed up the stairs to the front door and gave an explosive knock.

She gripped her stomach and waited for the door to open. It was time for another pep talk.

"Tiff, get a hold of yourself."

There was no time for lusting over the meal that she'd awakened to many mornings. There was no time for memories either, because at that very moment while she was *still* on the exterior side of the large glass front door of Keith's four thousand square foot lake-front house that they'd found and decorated together, her boyfriend of six years was on the inside; and he clearly had no plans of letting her in.

Tiffany balled up her fist and banged on the door extremely hard, definitely harder than she had the first seven times; and once she reluctantly accepted the fact that her knuckles were starting to bruise, she finally allowed two heart-crushing realities to slap her in the face. One - she had not been invited to breakfast, and two - there was another woman on the other side of the door and inside with her man.

If I could just get the double-paned window to open, I could stop whatever was about to happen, and get my man back.

Deep down she knew it was time to give up, but something equally as deep wouldn't let her.

"Ouch!" She struck the window, forgetting about the condition of her hand. She was so delirious with rage that it never occurred that she really *was* trying to break the glass.

"I don't care about this stupid window!" she screamed. Tiffany had stopped thinking about consequences a long time ago; not even Keith's alarm system would stop her. She was willing to do whatever it took to get inside; and that's why she was pleased with herself when she had the brilliant idea of climbing over the back fence and peeking between the slats of the wooden window blinds. *If I can't get inside, maybe I could at least see inside.*

Thirty minutes had passed. Fifteen minutes of banging on windows and doors, five minutes of the neighbors pretending to water their already perfect lawns, five more minutes of Bruno - Keith's Dog - barking at her, and five whole minutes of accepting defeat. All of that carrying on had left Tiffany in the same place where she'd started, back in her car. The only difference was that she was headed to her own house. . . alone, wet, soggy, and cold. Yes, soggy. During her attempt to break in, Tiffany had received a text message. She started to ignore it, but checked it, hoping it was Keith texting to tell her he'd finally opened the front door.

It was Keith, but it wasn't the message she was hoping for. She let out a string of curse words when she read it:

GO HOME.STOP ACTING CRAZY.CALLING PO-PO'S. SMDH

Tiffany wasn't worried. She knew Keith would never call the police on her. She wasn't going anywhere, that was until he turned on his sprinkler system. Everything in her wanted to ignore the fact that the dripping wet hair hanging over her eyes and face had her standing there looking like a deranged, psychotic stalker. But, she couldn't ignore it. While the downpour of water soaked into her clothes and washed away all of her hopes, tears soaked her face and Tiffany realized that she had officially hit an all-time low.

With sulking shoulders, Tiffany stomped back to her SUV. She hadn't thought about any outcomes. As a matter of fact, she hadn't thought at all. She just loved. She loved hard. Tiffany had given Keith the best six years of her life.

●●●

"It's my fault," Tiffany whispered in defeat. She shifted her weight in her bed and adjusted the elevation of her remote-controlled mattress. She'd already been in bed all day Monday and Tuesday. She'd rejected and ignored every telephone call, email, and text. She'd only picked up the phone once and that was to call the office claiming to be sick. It wasn't a complete lie, because she did feel like she was dying. Tiffany hadn't had a single bite to eat; in fact the only time she'd moved was to use the restroom and to grab more tissue for her tears.

Maybe I shouldn't have worked as many hours last week, or maybe I should've cooked more often. Or maybe I should've given Keith half of the house deposit like he'd suggested, then maybe I'd be living there with him and none of this would've happened. Did I do enough?

These were the things that played over and over in Tiffany's mind. And even though she had not gotten any definite answers from repeatedly asking herself the same antagonizing questions, she knew one thing. It *was* her fault that Keith had cheated.

"I hate him. I hate my boyfriend," Tiffany fussed and rolled out of bed, dragging herself to the restroom. "He's not your man, he's your…" She stopped mid-sentence and plopped down on the commode. She was frustrated. She had called Keith everything from an excuse maker to an extremely unfaithful jerk, but even with their history and his constant infidelity proving that he had never been exclusively hers, she still couldn't bring herself to call him that two letter word, her EX. It just didn't make sense. And that's what had Tiffany still sitting there when she heard someone calling her name. Keith.

The knocking at the door was like a drum, and Tiffany was drawn to its rhythm. She hurried up, left the restroom, fixed her sloppy ponytail, and ran full speed toward the front door. Keith was screaming and knocking and Tiffany's nerves made her struggle to unlock the door. It never once occurred to her why he was there, all that mattered was that he was there.

Tiffany took one more hard suck on the peppermint she'd grabbed from the hallway table. She hadn't brushed her teeth in three days and just in case Keith greeted her with a kiss she wanted to be ready.

Tiffany, stop! He cheated on you! She reminded herself. *Attitude, girl, attitude!* She swung the door open.

"Keith, what are you doing here? I hope you don't think you can just come over here and... don't you know I am the best..."

"Best thing I've ever had. I know. I miss you. I love you," Keith interrupted.

And that's all it took. Tiffany couldn't speak. Her neck had stopped rolling and her finger had stopped pointing. With just those words, she had drowned in the sea of sexiness standing in front of her. She examined his face; his eyes looked as if he, too, hadn't slept much in the past few days. It looked like he'd grown a few more gray strands of hair in his perfectly lined goatee. The grays didn't age him one bit, but gave him a distinguished look that drove Tiffany crazy. And that's just what she was...crazy. She took three steps backward to keep from falling into his arms. But Keith moved in closer and towering over her five-foot stature, he leaned down, and with his lips, he literally took the life right out of her.

Tiffany didn't know what happened next. Somewhere between Keith giving his sad "I'm sorry. . . she is just a colleague . . you caught me off guard. . . I just didn't want things to escalate any further" apology, the past no longer mattered. Keith grabbed her hand and led her to the shower.

Thirty minutes later Tiffany was clean, refreshed, and satisfied. She rolled over and kissed Keith's forehead. No side chick or one-night stand could ever replace what they shared. Things were going to be better this time. Why? Because the two of them had history and a bond that couldn't be broken. Keith was genuinely sorry, and despite his slip ups, she was and would *always* be the best thing that ever happened to him. Point blank. Period.

●●●

Lord knows I should've filled out one of those blue prayer cards again, but I'm tired. Church service was almost over and Tiffany had sent up a few extra prayers this particular Sunday.

Tiffany shifted sideways in her seat and turned up her lips as her stomach summersaulted in disgust. It wasn't enough that the elderly usher standing at the end of the pew beside her smelled like a mixture of evergreen, Vicks salve, and mothballs, but Tiffany was also disgusted because over the past four months, not much had changed with her and Keith. They argued every day; they'd only gone out once. Things were just as bad, if not worse than before the incident at his house. Keith wasn't as affectionate as he'd been and he was away on business a lot.

"Lord, help," she whispered.

Tiffany tapped the hand of the usher and signaled for a prayer card. That was one of the traditions at the church where she regularly attended with Keith. Every Sunday morning, two baskets were passed up and down each pew. The first basket was for tithes and offerings, and the second was for prayer requests. Tiffany had probably placed over three hundred cards in that basket over the past six years, anonymously of course. She figured that whoever read hers either didn't have a direct communication line to God or maybe they just read her cards for sheer entertainment. Still, Tiffany filled out her card and thought about the numerous times she'd begged Keith to write down prayers for their relationship, to no avail. She'd just have to pray harder for them both, she told herself.

The basket stopped in front of her, Keith leaned into her ear, "Did you say a prayer for me, Baby?"

Tiffany dropped the card and as Keith wrapped his arm around her, she nestled in beneath him. Had her prayer been answered that quickly?

After the deacon prayed, Keith gently guided Tiffany down the center aisle to the altar. Tiffany smiled. Why did it have to feel so good having Keith's palm resting on the lower part of her back? She knew God himself couldn't be happy with the distracting thoughts in her mind. But, she couldn't help but count her blessings. Regardless of the uneasiness she'd been feeling lately, all that mattered was that she was with Keith, in the House of God, holding hands during family prayer. FAMILY. No matter what or who came and went, Keith was her family. Her soon-to-be husband.

Their pastor had just finished praying for newlyweds when he was led to say a special prayer for all couples considering marriage. And that's when Tiffany's confirmation from God came in an unexpected way. When the preacher quoted "He who finds a wife, finds a good thing," Keith not only said, "Amen," but he squeezed her hand. That was all the hope Tiffany needed.

Tiffany burst into tears. As the preacher finished praying, she prayed along with him. She prayed for forgiveness for not having enough faith in God and His promise to give her the desires of her heart. Despite the affairs and separations, the desire of her heart was standing beside her and gripping her hand. Tiffany's loud prayers blended with wedding colors, numbers of bridesmaids, November or maybe December wedding, and if she'd calculated correctly, she and Keith should be married in approximately five months, three days, four...

"Tiffany! Tiffany!" Keith called to her as he shook her arm.

"I do," Tiffany answered, then snapped back to the altar where she and Keith were the last two people left standing. "I do love you, Jesus," she quickly said, trying to recover from her gaffe.

Tiffany had drifted off to another place and didn't realize that altar call was over.

Keith's eyes shifted between the pastor and Tiffany. With force and embarrassment he pulled Tiffany back to their pew, and she gladly followed her man. None of the side-eyed stares mattered. As she sat down beside him, she thought of all the wedding planning she'd do while Keith was away on business for the next three weeks.

As the choir sang, rocked, and brought the congregation to their feet, Tiffany made sure she gave an extra praise for the miracle that was being performed in her love life. She clapped, bounced, and rejoiced at the thought of finally becoming Mrs. Keith Fredricks.

●●●

Tiffany had almost given up, again. She'd changed her wedding color scheme about six different times. She'd selected the cake, the dress, and the menu. But, there was still one thing missing…the groom.

Keith had gone on his business trip as planned. The only problem was that the trip was more than three months ago. Tiffany knew that his position as Marketing Director of Shwartz & Heard Consulting Firm was demanding, but she had become suspicious of the amount of time he was spending out of town. Sure, he'd called once or twice, he'd answered half of her calls, and he'd even flown in once for an overnight meeting. But, that still wasn't enough. It seemed Tiffany and Keith were on different schedules and clearly, different pages.

Tiffany had had enough of the non-existent communication and was about to call off the wedding she was planning until that morning when Keith's sister, Traci, had called inviting her to her and Keith's parent's house for Thanksgiving. With everything that had been going on, the holidays had crept up. Knowing that everyone would be disappointed if she declined the invitation, and seeing as though she'd always gone to their holiday dinners, Tiffany accepted and volunteered to bring a few bottles of wine. Secretly, she was excited because she knew Keith would be there.

●●●

Tiffany couldn't wait any longer. She was hungry. She knew that the only reason they hadn't prayed and started eating yet was because Keith was still M.I.A., but the smell of turkey, dressing, and sweet potato pie was calling her name. Keith's dad was waking up from his nap while the women in the family were arranging the last few casserole dishes on the table. Tiffany had volunteered to help, but Keith's mom insisted that she watch the children. And that's where she was, rocking Keith's three- month-old nephew to sleep when the doorbell rang and she stopped singing the lullaby.

Tiffany jumped up and startled the baby. She eased his little body into the blue pack'n play, reached into her pocket and swiped some red lip gloss on her lips. "Please get the door, Tiff," Keith's mother yelled.

Tiffany headed toward the front door. "Yes, ma'am."

Her heart raced ahead of her to unlock the door. She was ready to greet her man.

"I've missed you K..."

Tiffany couldn't finish her sentence. No one and nothing could've prepared her for what she saw. She couldn't move. Who was this couple standing there? It couldn't be Keith, her Keith? And why was this lady, this heifer smiling, and holding this Keith look-a-like's hand? And why was she wearing a diamond ring?

"Keith, who is this woman?"

Tiffany knew she should've said more. She had every right to scream, curse, or slap him and the smile off that woman's face. But everything within her told her to give up because she'd finally lost her man. She just wanted to know the name of her winning opponent.

Keith didn't even acknowledge Tiffany's question. He slid right past her, hand in hand with the lady who was following him submissively.

Did she just brush up against me? Tiffany asked rhetorically. *And did she just look back at me and smile?*

Tiffany saw bright flashing lights. She was about to snap and become another crime of passion statistic. Her hands went up and her fists were about to connect with someone. Luckily for Keith and that lady, the entire physical confrontation was all in Tiffany's imagination and in reality, she was doing nothing more than still standing in the doorway and crying.

Keith's dad walked around the huddle of people in the middle of the living room hugging the new couple. He wrapped his arms around Tiffany, and with no words, he led her to the kitchen.

Tiffany didn't know how many more times she could push the same green beans around her plate. She'd mixed them with potato salad and cranberry sauce until the concoction had become a disgusting color. She couldn't eat. She knew she should've left a long time ago, but she was too weak to drive. Besides, she was a little tipsy. While everyone was meeting Keith's fiancée, who closely resembled his "just a colleague" friend, Tiffany had slipped into the restroom with one of the half-finished bottles of wine she'd brought. That was the only way she could keep her calm without causing a scene.

Tiffany pushed her plate back and let out a long embarrassing burp. "Congratulations, Keith!" And with that, she got up from the table and slowly drove home.

● ● ●

Tiffany knew she had to be dreaming. But why was everything so vivid and vibrant? And why were they so beautiful together? She'd logged on to her favorite social media website using the fictitious name she'd created a couple of years ago, KillingEmSoftlyJohnson. She had stalked his and her page fifty times in the past two days hoping to see something different other than the two of them plastered on the Internet. There they were sitting in front of some fancy water fountain smiling. It's not the picture that bothered her as much as it was the caption: Surprise! We're Engaged! Keith had never been one to publicize his relationship, especially not on any social media site, so why now? What was so special about this woman? How long had they dated?

Lord, forgive me, but I wish that water fountain could just rise up and cover them like the Red Sea did to the Egyptians. Tiffany's thoughts made her laugh.

"Shoot. No, no, no!" Tiffany was so caught up in the sight of them drowning that she'd accidentally sent Lynn, Keith's soon-to-be wife, a friend request. Luckily she was able to cancel it.

Tiffany checked a few messages, and paused when she saw one from Keith's sister. She could only imagine what Traci had to say. Maybe she was going to apologize for inviting her to the Thanksgiving dinner, or maybe she was going to apologize for her brother.

Tiffany opened the message.

I guess it had to come to that for you to realize that you deserve more. I am sorry that I can't feel sorry for you. The signs were always there, but you continued to give my brother so much of you, and never left any for yourself. You had to have seen it coming. He's a jerk. Girl, just move on and heal. You can't be anyone's best anything until you give your best to yourself. Sometimes you have to lose to win.

Those words sliced right through Tiffany's heart and hopes. Traci was right. She had to move on and get her life back and that's what she did.

Tiffany had no clue it would take that long to pull herself out of mourning. She'd gone through every phase: denial, acceptance, shock, hurt, the burial, and even purging. It had been several hard months, but after joining a support group she'd found, and donating every gift Keith had ever given her, she was recovering from the breakup.

The hardest thing for her to get past was that for years she'd placed all her faith in marrying Keith and because that wasn't going to happen, she questioned her own faith. She had always relied on the scripture that said that God will give the desires of one's heart. Tiffany struggled with that until one day during her prayers, her revelation came. She had jumped up from her knees and dug out a journal she'd written in years ago. She searched for the page "Godly Characteristics of a Mate." After all the hurt and time, Tiffany could finally see that Keith didn't fit any of those traits and she'd only held on in hopes that he'd change. But, Keith was never meant to love her, and he couldn't even if he'd tried, because he was not the true desire of her heart.

● ● ●

It was a chilly Sunday. Tiffany had wanted to stay snuggled in bed and attend church that evening, but she'd decided to go to the morning service. She hadn't been in a while, and today, she was going back. Besides, there was something she had to do.

When she walked into the church, she saw Keith and she knew he saw her, but Keith deliberately didn't make eye contact. His fiancée was sitting next to him, in Tiffany's old seat. Tiffany stared, and noticed that Keith looked different. Or was it just that her view of him had changed? She'd accepted that she had loved him with everything in her. She'd already forgiven herself for letting Keith misuse her.

The young usher handed her a stack of white envelopes to pass down the pew. Tiffany took one, passed the others, bowed her head, and wrote quickly on the blue card. As the basket passed by her, Tiffany slipped the card back into the envelope, sealed it, and placed it on top of the others. She noticed Keith peeking in her direction, and just as quietly as she'd entered the sanctuary, Tiffany got up and walked toward the exit.

"Goodbye, Keith," she whispered.

The touch of a masculine hand on her back stopped her. "Ma'am, you forgot to fill out the outside of your envelope." The usher had followed her to the door. "We need your name so the pastor knows who he's praying for."

Tiffany took a deep breath, pulled out her ink pen, and finally after six years she said what her heart wouldn't let her say. With newfound hope she signed the outside of the envelope: *Keith's Best Ex Ever.*

Meredith E. Greenwood, author of the fiction novel Faith, Grace, and Hope: Three Women, Three Letters, Three Trials…One God, is also a motivational speaker, playwright, and encourager. Meredith uses her creativity to motivate, uplift and inspire. Visit her at www.MEgreenwood.com, follow her Facebook page: Meredith E. Greenwood, and connect with her on Twitter and Instagram: MEgreenwood1.

Shame

By Penelope Christian

"Ms. Brooks, your pregnancy test was negative."

"I know."

"Did you know you weren't pregnant when you arrived?"

Maven didn't respond, and Nurse Know-It-All looked down at her with disgust. Her beady eyes peeked over her long beak nose and taunted Maven. Wasn't it time for a shift change? Maven didn't remember the woman's real name, and didn't care. She had endured her obnoxious mumblings, and snooty stares all day, and she was tired.

Scribbling in a frenzy on Maven's chart, the nurse sighed. "How is your head?"

"Fine. I'd like to get some sleep now," Maven replied in a curt tone.

That was code for get out, and Maven hoped she'd gotten the message. Running her tongue slowly around in her mouth, Maven felt lumps of flesh and tasted rusty iron. Pulling herself up in a sitting position, her shoulder pinched. Sucking in a sharp breath, Maven squeezed her eyes shut until the pain subsided.

The slow drone of the beeping monitors cocooning her bed signaled she was alive. Despite her puffy eyes and bruised body, she was grateful. For the most part. The night before she'd been wheeled in screaming, clutching her stomach, declaring her fake pregnancy in panic. Her performance in the E.R. was her attempt to hold on to the last thing that kept Maven human in her once family's eyes.

But Nurse Cock-a-doodle snatched Maven's last play away with a tube of her blood, and a condescending attitude.

Maven sank back down under the covers and closed her eyes. She wanted the woman to go without another peep, and after the nurse shifted her feet once more she was gone. Reaching up her hand to her head, Maven felt a dread missing at the nape of her neck. Examining her bandaged hand, she saw her usual flawless sable skin was ashy and bruised. Maven's door creaked open again. Gingerly turning her back to the door, she blew out a breath. She thought she'd made herself clear.

"Did your mind, self-respect, and fake baby all disappear in one night?"

Maven's eyes popped open to a camera flash. Her breath hitched. "Sofia?"

"Yeah, it's me and Kent's not here to save you now."

Sofia's words pierced Maven deeper than any wound she endured at the shelter the previous night. She hadn't heard from Kent. Where was he?

Turning toward the door, Maven closed her eyes on another flash. Sofia Peterson, her best friend of seventeen years, stood in front of her snarling behind a retro Polaroid camera. She was also dressed as a teenage boy. Her onyx mid-back curls were stuffed under an old baseball cap, and her body hidden in holey jeans and a worn out t-shirt.

Maven blinked back spots. "How d-"

"Haven't you learned by now I have ways to get to everything? Although, you surprised me. I didn't see you for a snake."

Maven swallowed hard. "Sofi, let me ex-"

Sofia threw a hand up and stepped forward.

Shrinking back, Maven's eyes darted around the room. "Whe-Where is your security?"

Pitching her body forward on her toes, Sofia scowled. "*I'm* asking the questions. Why?"

Maven's heart thumped in her ears, and she kneaded the sheets between her hands.

"*Why* Maven?" Sofia snorted. "I suppose I should feel sympathy for you being attacked last night?"

Sofia's scathing tone, brought fresh tears to Maven's eyes. She said nothing.

Sofia crossed her arms over her chest, reeling herself in. "I haven't got all day, Maven. Is that even your real name? As you pointed out, I don't have my security and any minute they will find me. Why? Just tell me why!"

One Day earlier....

"White or Red?"

Maven tossed her minced onions into a mixing bowl, and glanced over at Sofia. "White...Riesling, of course. Where is your sea salt?"

Sofia rummaged through her kitchen drawers for her wine opener, and slid a bottle of salt down the counter. "Riesling is too sweet. I'll open a bottle for you, but I'm having red."

Maven jumped as her phone vibrated on the counter, but she didn't answer it. She threw a dash of salt in the bowl, and shook her head at Sofia. "Since when? Back in college you drank whatever we had."

Popping the cork on the Riesling, Sofia poured Maven a glass. "You mean whatever was at the dorm parties."

They both laughed.

Hitting the silent button on her phone, Maven flipped the phone over to conceal the screen. "Yeah, until we turned twenty-one and could get into the real clubs. Are your bougie neighbors up for homemade food? I'm sure they expected this to be catered."

Sofia chuckled. "We don't have catered events every weekend. At least not on this coast."

Taking her wine from Sofia, Maven clinked her glass against hers. "With all these movie stars, and singers in your neighborhood, I'm not sure if Jazzy's request for sweet potato fries and burgers will go over well here on the East Coast."

Maven winked, and peeked out the kitchen window to the backyard. Her fiancé, Kent had his niece, Jazzy, under one arm and was chasing after her brother, Justin. Maven's face split into a grin thinking of their future children.

"Our L.A. neighbors might have opted for veggie burgers…is baby brother out there annoying my children again?"

Maven laughed. "You know Kent is the only one who will play with them for hours without a water break."

Sofia leaned over the sink, and yelled out the window. "Jazzy and J, you're supposed to be decorating with Uncle Kent. Party starts in thirty minutes!"

Maven's phone lit up, and she dropped it in her purse on the kitchen table.

"Who are you hiding from?" Sofia asked.

Maven's stomach dropped, and she darted her eyes around the kitchen. "No one, girl. It's just…job alerts."

Sofia set her glass down, and wrapped her arms around Maven's shoulders. "So you decided to start working again? What's up with Kent's side business? Why won't he let me help?"

Maven shrugged. "Sofia, you know how Kent feels about asking for help from you."

Sofia folded her arms. "No, I don't actually."

Maven shifted her weight, and leaned over the counter, sighing. "He doesn't want everyone to think his Oscar-winning-movie-star-actress-sister takes care of him. He said he can barely get work done at the office because the guys are always cracking on him about you."

Rolling her eyes, Sofia snorted. "Men, and their hang-ups. You tell him I said that, too."

Maven faced the window again to hide her expression. She agreed with Sofia, and that caused many exhausting arguments with Kent in the past. Fixing her face into a smile, Maven faced her best friend. "We're okay now. His I.T. business looks to be taking off soon, and we just closed on the house."

Sofia swept Maven into a hug. "Mav! That's so exciting! Why am I just now hearing about this?" She paused, staring off into the distance. "If the pictures…"

Maven rubbed Sofia's arm. "Don't go there. It's okay. You'll be back in Cali before I start decorating. Got any new projects coming up I don't know about yet?"

Usually mentioning a new project would bring Sofia back, but her eyes remained clouded and distant. Jacob, Sofia's husband, walked into the kitchen, and Maven froze.

"Baby, where do you want the playhouse?"

Maven had been awkward around Jacob since he and Sofia married. He was fine. Tuscan-brown skin, warm brown eyes, and a head full of straight coal black hair. He was the kind of sexy that never went out of style and he knew it. Maven thought he could use a few more inches in height though, and a stern talk on his wandering eye, but neither reason was why they didn't get along.

Every time Maven was around Jacob she felt him watching her. And when she would catch his eye, she could feel him staring right through to her soul. He didn't trust her, so interactions with him were always stressful.

Jacob came up behind Sofia, and kissed her neck. "The playhouse, Mami. Where do you want it? Jazzy wants everyone to see what we've been working on." Peering at Maven, he spoke to Sofia. "How's it going in here?"

Sofia zoned in, and wrapped her arms around Jacob's neck. "Baby, we need to be back in California before school starts, Mav and Kent bought a house I can't see yet, and why did we let those people run us out of our home? I'm Sofia Pet-"

Maven looked away as Jacob cupped his wife's face in his hands.

"Shhh, baby calm down. Everything will be okay. I told you I would handle it, right?"

"But I'm tired of looking for those…criminals. I just want to get back to my life," Sofia exclaimed.

"Listen, it will be over soon. The leads I have are close to finding the culprits. This is about our privacy…our children."

Tension stacked the air, so Maven plotted a quick escape.

Moving stealthily out the kitchen, Kent barreled in laughing, and grabbed her around the waist. "Whoa, where you going, beautiful? I came in for samples. What's cooking?" He looked around the quiet kitchen, then back at Maven. "What did I miss?"

"That my life is on hold for some S.O.B. that snuck private moments of my kids to the press." Sofia sobbed, and stomped out the kitchen.

Kent reached for her, but Maven grabbed his arm. "I got it."

She ran after Sofia, and followed her outside on the back porch. Sitting on a bench, Sofia brushed away her tears. Maven sat next to her in silence.

Sofia sighed. "I'm sorry, Mav."

"Sofi, don't apologize."

Sofia shook her head. "No, I have to. You and Kent flew out here to celebrate with us and the kids, not counsel me on something I asked for."

Maven raised her brow. "Asked for?"

"Yeah. I wanted to be the movie star. I wanted to be famous. No privacy for me, I get it. But Jazzy and J? I want the twins to grow up as normal as possible."

"I know, but don't blame yourself, please?"

Sofia shrugged. "What else is there to do when I see their faces splashed all over the blogs? Private moments in my home, in my neighborhood. Did you know Jacob fired all our staff? How could someone do this?"

Maven rocked Sofia in her arms, as she sobbed.

Looking up with red-brimmed eyes, Sofia said, "Did you know some nasty blog troll is trying to link Jacob with a neighbor in one of the photos?"

Maven squeezed her hand, and they both jumped when they heard shouting. Kent and Jacob tumbled out the back door pushing and shoving each other. A man Maven had never seen before, stood behind them staring at her. He was an older Hispanic gentleman, wearing a tight black suit and telescope-lensed glasses.

Jacob lurched forward toward Maven; Kent pulled him back and punched him in the face.

"Kent!" Sofia screamed.

Maven backed away, shaking her head. She didn't know the man, but she knew she'd been made. Sofia jumped between Kent and Jacob and pushed Kent back. He wiped at the blood pouring from his nose, and his eyes met Maven's. Pain, sorrow, and shame were there, and it turned Maven's stomach. She bowled over, and wretched violently, her morning eggs spilling over her shoes.

"Would somebody tell me what's going on!" Sofia screamed.

Leaning over, gripping her knees, Maven heard the man speak to her. "Hello, Misty."

"Misty? Who is that?" Sofia said.

Jacob spit at Maven's shoes. "The wench that sold our photos to the press."

Sofia paced the floor with her fist balled up. Her eyes narrowed, as if she was trying to process everything.

"I-is, this true?" she spat in Maven's direction.

"I-I can explain," Maven said.

Sofia was seething. "You could have told me you needed money. You could have told me a lot of things…but you chose to *betray* me by selling photos of my kids?"

Maven was convinced her hospital room came with a revolving door. Behind Sofia two boulder-shoulder twins squeezed in with matching outfits and earpieces.

An elderly nurse followed them in, and looked between Sofia and Maven. Assessing the situation, she spoke in a calm tone. "Excuse me, visiting hours are over. Please leave the patient alone to rest. Feel free to come back in the morning."

Sofia snapped another photo, and waved the film around in the air. "Maybe, I'll sell these photos on the market and make some money. I won't be back tomorrow, but you'll hear from my lawyer." She sneered, and walked over to her security. "Oh, and by the way, Kent wants nothing to do with you or your invisible child, and Jacob requested you jump off a bridge. Good night."

Sofia stormed out; Maven collapsed against her bed, and sobbed.

The elderly nurse took Maven in her arms, and rocked her slow. "Shhh, it's okay, child."

Maven's chest burned, and she couldn't open her eyes to face anyone. The darkness seemed much more forgiving. She clutched the old lady's body and cried until she was spent. Suddenly embarrassed, she pulled back and wiped at her face averting her eyes from the old woman.

"I – I'm sorry…" Maven sniffed.

"Hush, now."

The woman handed Maven a few tissues, and checked Maven's monitors. Her face was a smooth sandy-brown and her hair fell in pearly-white waves around her face.

Maven was caught staring at her, and the nurse gave her a warm smile. "Hello, Ms. Brooks. My name is Eugena Little. I'm your nurse for the evening."

Maven pulled the covers up to her chest, and blew her nose.

"Don't be embarrassed, child. We don't need proper greetings to comfort each other."

Tears pooled in Maven's eyes once again. Could this woman see to her soul, too? She covered her face with her hands. "There is no comfort for the evil."

Nurse Little drew back. "Evil?"

Maven nodded. "Evil. Pathetic. Disgusting."

Holding a finger up, Nurse Little spoke. "Quiet…don't speak those things over yourself."

"Why? They are true," Maven whispered.

"Do you want to talk about what happened?"

Kneading the sheets through her fingers, Maven let the tears fall. "I sold a few intimate family photos to the press of my best friend, Sofia, and her family." Maven sniffed. "I didn't think they would be spread over all the blogs…I lied to my fiancé about being pregnant so he wouldn't leave me because of it…I betrayed them both. Over money…guess that's what I get for thinking I belonged in their world."

Nurse Little stopped in the middle of checking Maven's vitals. "Their world?"

"Yes, I grew up poor, they didn't. Sofi didn't know when she met me in college, but I practically begged and bartered my way in. Sofia was beautiful, smart, funny…everything I wanted to be. And her brother. He was a prime catch. Fine, ambitious. . .unattached. I had it made when I met them. I finally had somewhere to belong. . .and now they're gone."

Maven shifted to get comfortable, and winced from the pain in her side. Nurse Little handed her two pills and a glass of water.

"How did you end up here?"

Maven downed the medicine and set her cup down. A wave of anger swept over her and she sneered. "What did they expect me to do? I wanted the big house, too. And the pretty kids. And the perfect life. Kent wasn't moving fast enough!" Picking up the glass of water, she threw it across the room and sobbed again. "Kent told me he was ashamed of me. Ashamed he fell in love with me. Ashamed to have even met me. He kicked me out of our apartment, and I had nowhere else to go. A few tramps at the shelter jumped me for the clothes and shoes I had on, and I ended up here. Frankly, I can see why he doesn't want me. I don't want me either."

Nurse Little sighed, and sat on the end of the bed. "Do you believe in Jesus, sweet child?"

"Sweet?" Maven snorted. "I'm anything but that. I do believe in Him, but what would He do with me? I've lied, and cheated amongst other things…why would He care what's happening to me? My granny would have thrown the bible at me three times if she could see me now. I don't even call myself a Christian anymore, with all the sinning I've been doing."

"If you believe in Jesus, it's not about what you've done, but what He's done for you," Nurse Little said.

Maven scrunched up her nose. "Huh?"

"Jesus died on the cross for our sins, so we don't have to carry them. We are cleansed of all our sin from the past, present and future. Forever. Jesus took that burden on Himself. He is Grace. Our undeserved favor from God."

Cocking her head to the side, Maven said, "What does that mean?"

Nurse Little squeezed Maven's arms. "It means that no matter how man sees you, *or* how you see yourself, God sees the *real* you through Jesus."

"And...who is that? Who is the real me?"

"Righteous. Justified. Favored. Extravagantly Loved. Always right with God."

Maven stared at the nurse who grew four arms, and legs in her head. Was this lady serious? "But...Isn't God ashamed of me, too? I've done horrible things."

Nurse Little shook her head. "No. Jesus came so that we may have Life. His blood washes away all of ours sin. We have been forgiven!"

"Forgiven? But that's..."

Raising her hands high, Nurse Little exclaimed, "The Good news! Grace is Jesus!"

"Will my fiancé' and best friend ever forgive me?" Maven pondered.

The nurse grabbed a hold of Maven's shoulders, and looked her in the eyes. "The question is will you forgive yourself?"

Maven paused, then said, "I don't deserve to forgive myself."

"Honey, none of us do. That's why this is over-the-top good news! Jesus came to die for us, even though we didn't deserve it. Grace is underserved. It's our free gift, for believing in Him...and if our mighty God can forgive us, you should forgive yourself."

The dull ache in Maven's chest slowly lifted. "Wow..."

Nurse Little cupped Maven's face in her delicate hands. "You are in Jesus Christ, sweet child. You belong to *Him*. Old things have passed away. Break up with your ex-self. That old way of living is gone. That old you is gone. *Believe* you are righteous, and move forward. Totally. Forgiven."

Maven stared at her in wonder. "No shame?"

A smile lifted Nurse Little's face. "No. Shame. You are forgiven and loved, Child of God. Run to Jesus."

Maven closed her eyes and let Jesus's light surround her and she spoke from her heart. "I. am. Forgiven."

Three days later, Maven hugged Nurse Little and walked out the hospital with her head held high. Opening the door to a cab, she smiled at the driver who was ready to take her anywhere she wanted to go. First thing on her agenda was an apartment. She hadn't heard from Kent or Sofia, but she was moving forward. Maven wanted their forgiveness but she wasn't going to live in misery. She'd been there and done that. The new Maven wanted to start over. To be guilt-free.

Her thoughts traveled back to Kent's face, then to Sofia's laugh, and she shook her head.

Maven spoke out loud, "I am forgiven. God Loves me. No more Shame."

Glancing at the hospital one more time, she slipped in the cab and shut the door.

Penelope Christian, is a freelance writer who often credits nature, random happenings at the airport, and quirky personalities as her creative muses. Her debut novel, Coffee & Cream will release in 2016. For more updates connect with her on Facebook: Penelope Christian and Instagram @ p_christian_ and www.penelopechristian.com.

The Circle of Life

By Sharon Lucas

Chapter 1

How did I allow my mother to convince me to attend this funeral? There are some things you just don't have to experience twice. For me, this man died years ago, so why am I sitting in the back of this dingy little storefront church trying to appear as if I am deep in grief?

I can't believe it. Was it really almost 30 years ago? I was 24 years old, had just received my MBA and recently moved into my first *really nice* apartment 200 miles away from home and my parents. I had a *good* job with a prestigious university, I was cute and I dressed flyyy! In other words, I was smelling myself!

Mom and Pop were old school! No dating until I turned 16; they preferred group outings, and the curfew was midnight until I left for college. Now don't get the idea I was a Miss Goody Two Shoes! I did my share of going steady – though no one knew about it except my best friend, Tarsha, my steady of the moment, and me! I was scared to go too far, because I had witnessed the wrath of my family toward my cousin Gwen, when, in her junior year, she had to leave regular school and attend the high school for pregnant girls.

Gwen's parents didn't play. They were supportive and didn't disown her as they were counseled to do by the Bishop Gray of the Temple of Divine Grace. But they made it clear that Little Ron – named for his grandfather because no one was allowed to even utter his dad's name in their home – was her child!

I once spent the weekend at their house while, my parents were away, and I wasn't there more than a few hours before I knew changing diapers and fixing bottles in between homework and housework was simply not my style. After that experience, I vowed to keep my little legs closed until much later in life. Goodness that was a lifetime ago!

Gwen had long since reprieved herself in the eyes of the family, when she finished school and went on to become a registered nurse. She and Little Ron were a twosome until she married a local dentist, a widower with two young girls. Little Ron and the girls were all grown up now, married with children of their own. Gwen and her husband still acted like newlyweds.

I kept my vow about closed legs through high school, through college, and even through grad school. Okay! I can't lie, even to myself. During my last visit to the doctor before I left home for my freshman year at Howard, I requested birth control pills. I knew it was time for me to pull up my big girl panties and prepare myself for womanhood. After all, Mom would no longer be sitting up waiting to see if I came through the door before midnight.

Chapter 2

My walk down memory lane was interrupted by the sound of the organist as he began to softly play "Amazing Grace." For several minutes I tried to listen, but soon I was again adrift in memories.

I never went back home to live once I left for college. I attended summer school one year, found a job on campus another, and then accepted a summer internship in San Diego, where I lived with my roommate and her family that last summer before graduation.

My goal was to complete my four-year program in four years. I didn't want to extend my undergrad experience by even one semester. I didn't want to end up like several of my friends who allowed playing bid whist in the student union to turn a four-year program into five years.

Don't get it twisted, I loved college life - the camaraderie, pledging a sorority and even the partying, but most of all I loved being free to make my own decisions. I had set a goal! I intended to have my Masters before I turned 24. Yes, I was naïve! I forgot that all work and no play would make Jill a very dull girl.

Suddenly, I realized where I was and that someone had sat down beside me and was talking to me.

"Are you a friend of the deceased?" she said.

I looked up. "Yes," I responded. "I was, but I hadn't seen him in years."

"I worked with him," the woman said. "Isn't it a shame how quickly he went after being diagnosed? That's why I stay in the doctor's office. Early detection is so important," she added. I simply smiled and nodded my agreement, praying all the while that this would not become an involved conversation.

She sat for a few more seconds and then announced she saw some coworkers and thought she'd go sit with them. I waited until she left before I exhaled a sigh of relief.

Again, thoughts of the past reclaimed me.

Chapter 3

Mom and Dad flew from Pittsburgh to Los Angeles for my graduation from grad school. It was their first time on the west coast and we made it a vacation. I was so proud to show them around. Once they learned I had accepted a position with Georgetown University as the Assistant Director of Minority Recruiting, you could see the relief on their faces. They were ecstatic to learn that their only child would soon be only a short drive away in D.C.

Because I had already spent four years in the city, it wasn't hard to get back in the groove. I knew a lot about the area and many of my friends from Howard were still there. Some were working and still struggling to get their degree. Some were married with families. Only a few of us had stable jobs with good salaries and were happily still single.

Back then D.C. was called Chocolate City and there were good-looking black men on every corner. Friday meant leaving work and going directly to the nearest and most popular watering hole. In most offices around the city, you could tell it was Friday simply by looking at the fashion show at work that day. We hadn't quite perfected how to transition from office attire to hang out gear, so Friday outfits were often a cross between "just a little too dressy and revealing for work" and "you better not wear that mess to church on Sunday."

I could no longer recall the names of many of those places, but I do remember Hogates on the wharf was one of my favorites. We thought we were so liberated. We thought we worked hard and felt we deserved to play hard.

I found a very nice and affordable condo in the Southwest section of the city. I could walk out, jump on a bus and arrive at work in less than 15 minutes. On a nice evening, I could walk to Hogates. Hogates! Where I met Him!

"The Lord giveth and the Lord taketh away. Blessed be the name of the Lord," was the line I heard the minister say as he slowly preceded the family down the aisle of the church to their seats.

"Oh my goodness," I thought, as I realized that during my last mental break from reality, the undertaker had closed the casket. Well, that did eliminate people looking at me funny had I been put in the position of having to nod a polite "no thank you" as I refused the usher's urging to view the deceased one last time.

I looked down at the program to try to gauge how long I was going to be trapped here. I soon realized I was in a Pentecostal church and it looked like all 35 people there with me – 10 of them in the pulpit – were listed to speak, sing or read.

Lord, please help me!

Chapter 4

Tarsha, my best friend from home, newly divorced and "ready for Freddie" came to spend the weekend with me that summer to celebrate her newfound freedom in style. It hadn't yet dawned on her that the two children she left with her mother for the weekend was an indication that she was not free. She would be tied to that man for the rest of her life and it was not going to be easy to find a new man who would accept and do right by her and the kids. But that's another story for another day.

I took off work that Friday so that Tarsha and I could go to Bubbles to get our hair done, and then we took the bus uptown to shop at Garfinckles. I loved that store where all of the "clear sales girls" wore black dresses and spoke in soft voices. I would be appalled today to shop in a store that so obviously didn't have any blacks on staff other than the lady who cleaned the Women's Room. A sign of the times.

We made it back to my apartment early so that we could be dressed and adorning a seat in Hogates before the regular working crowd arrived. It was important to have just the right seat where you could see the door and size up everyone as they came in.

I saw Him come in with a group of men all of whom were worthy of my attention. They took tall, dark and handsome to a new level. That suit was hanging just right and in all the right places. He looked like he had stopped to get a trim from his favorite barber that day. The smile, the dimples and his stride completed a package whose wrapping could only be rated a 10!

Back then, approaching a man to dance or to buy him a drink were not accepted practices, so I spent the evening smiling a lot and hoping he would look my way. I danced a few times but Tarsha, hot off a bad divorce, was definitely sending out "I am available vibes" and she spent most of the evening on the dance floor. Once, on my way to the ladies room, I hesitated at his table and he glanced up, but did not maintain eye contact. By the time Tarsha and I were ready to call it a night, I concluded he must be on the down low because he had spent most of the evening sitting, deep in conversation with two or three of the men he had entered with. Flyyy as I was looking, how could he not have noticed me or that I'd spent most of my evening watching his every move?

I was extremely disappointed, but life does go on.

Chapter 5

I should have made Tarsha come with me today. What's a best friend for if not to hold you up when you are stressed? If she were sitting here beside me, we could have kept up some distracting banter like, "Where did she think she was going when she got dressed this morning?" But here I sat alone and though I was amused by Ms. Dressed for the Nightclub sitting two rows in front of me, it wasn't as entertaining as it would have been had Tarsha been by my side. Maybe I could pretend I was checking my messages and take a few pictures to amuse the two of us the next time she and I were together. Just because we were in our fifties, did not mean we didn't still get down!

About a month after Tarsha's weekend visit, I ventured back to Hogates with a group from my job. It was the first time I had gone there since my weekend out with Tarsha. The group had eaten dinner at Bea Smith's first, so by the time we arrived at the spot, the evening was in full swing.

We had only been there a few minutes when I saw Him staring at me from across the room. Why didn't I get my hair done today? Why did I have on last year's outfit? I knew I should have put on that cute little number I picked up yesterday at The Brownstone. At least I had a mani and pedi done that day.

I was sitting with the group. He appeared to be alone until I saw what my mother would have described as a long, tall drink of water slink up to him. She was wearing the perfect little black dress, pearls and a pair of sandals to die for. I had priced the gold bangles on her arm and the hoops in her ears last week at the Greenan & Sons Jewelry Store in Silver Spring and knew immediately, I couldn't compete. Each strand of hair was in place and her makeup was impeccable.

My heart dropped.

Several times during the evening, I pretended I didn't notice him looking at me. By the time I made my way to the ladies room, I had convinced myself I needed to stop swooning and begin to look around the room for more promising prospects.

When the long, tall drink of water entered the ladies room, she walked right up to me and said, "Hi, have we met? My name is Naomi and I love your nails. Where do you get them done?"

I had just finished washing my hands, so I took a couple seconds to throw away the paper towel and clear my throat to be sure I could still speak. I finally answered, "I go to Fanci Nails on Pennsylvania Avenue, Northeast, near Union Station. My name is Jill."

"I'm going to give them a call tomorrow. But look, the real reason I followed you in here was to ask if you'd like to meet my cousin, Jason? He's been drooling over you ever since you walked in. He's the fellow you probably saw me talking to most of the evening. I just moved here from L. A. and he's trying to keep his promise to my mom to show me around town."

Well, knock me over with a feather.

Chapter 6

Thus began the most exciting six months of my life. Jason and I became a couple overnight. The morning after Naomi introduced us at Hogates, we met for breakfast at the Florida Avenue Grill and that was the beginning our daily routine. We wined and dined. We went roller-skating at the Kalorama Rink, to plays at the National Theater, long walks along Haines Point, late nights at Blues Alley and Saturday lunches at Ben's Chili Bowl.

After two months, Jason moved into my condo and I felt like I was in heaven. Surely the next step would be a ring and a walk down the aisle.

About four months into our relationship, I began to notice small things. Jason often begged off going out in favor of sleeping in. Some days his mood could change from happy to angry in a matter of minutes. One evening I came home to find him sitting on the couch in the dark, and when I asked if something was wrong he answered, "I lost my job today." He had been employed as a lobbyist for several years at The National League of Cities. Eventually, he stopped bathing on a regular basis and was hostile and suspicious of everything around him. I didn't know what to do.

I spoke with my parents and they advised me to ask him to move out. They were concerned for my safety. But I never had to do that. One day I arrived home from work to find Jason and all of his belongings gone. While I was relieved, it was also quite devastating to know that the fairy tale life I had imagined I would have with Jason was never to be.

For a few weeks, I looked for Jason everywhere. I called Naomi, who told me his parents asked her to share with me that Jason appeared to be following in the footsteps of his older brother, who had been diagnosed as schizophrenic several years prior.

Had I opened my home and my heart too soon?

Chapter 7

I hadn't seen Jason since that day more than 30 years ago when I came home to an empty apartment. That was why today I had no desire to view the body he left behind. I wanted to remember him as the fun-loving, bright, and promising young man I knew.

Suddenly I realized that while I was taking my walk down memory lane, the funeral service had concluded. The minister, who had led the family in, had now come down from the pulpit and was leading the casket and the family out of the church. The organist was playing When We All Get to Heaven.

Naomi nodded as she approached the pew where I was sitting. The beautiful young woman in front of her stepped over, grabbed my hand and pulled me into line with her.

Tiffany! Jason's daughter! My daughter! The best of both of us!

I found out shortly after Jason disappeared that I was pregnant. I contemplated my next move for less than a millisecond. Yes, I wanted to be a mother and I knew if Gwen could do it at 16, I certainly could handle it at 25.

My pregnancy was uneventful. My co-workers and parents were extremely supportive. Mom stayed with us for the first month of Tiffany's life and Tiffany is still the apple of her grandparent's eye! Tarsha proved to be the best Godmother ever; Tiffany spent most of her summers with her and her boys.

Though Jason disappeared for a while, his family was nothing less than awesome. Not once did they question Tiffany's parentage and they were there for and with us every birthday, Christmas and all times in between. Naomi was our bridge. Until Tiffany was old enough to travel alone, it was Naomi who traveled with her to visit her "Texas Family." And it was Naomi who, through the years, made sure we knew where Jason was and how he was coping with his illness. Though he never returned to me or to D.C., when Tiffany visited Texas and he was mentally and physically able, Jason was a father to his daughter.

Eventually, I met and married Matt, a professor at Georgetown. He and I raised Tiffany along with his son from a former relationship, Christopher, and our twin daughters, Jazmin and Jamie.

As I walked with the family from the church, after the homegoing celebration for a son and father who struggled to remain normal in what must have felt to him like an abnormal world, I knew in my heart the circle of this part of my life was finally closed.

Sharon Lucas is a retired wife, mother and grandmother, book club founder and president, and event planner. Following the success of her first book, a non-fiction resource guide, she took a leap of faith to write fiction, when she wrote this intriguing short story. Read more about her at sharonrlucas.com.

Losing Lily

By Jeida K. Storey

Whoever said, "Time heals all wounds," was a liar. Sure, the initial shock of the devastation wanes, but that wasn't what killed you anyway. It was the hollow feeling that crept on you; the constant reminder of the person missing from your life and the person you would have been if they were still around. Once my heart had been trampled, mangled, and smashed, nothing could heal it, but a little bit of prayer and a whole lot of tequila.

***

I had not seen or heard from Hunter since I ended our engagement three years ago. In that time, I'd grown accustomed to being alone. I had managed to remain unseen and unsought. No calls. No texts. No dates. No flirting. No Twitter DMs. No Facebook chats. I couldn't even get a Facebook poke. And, definitely, no sex.

Let us all have a moment of silence for my forgotten, unused and abandoned vagina.

Lately I'd been keeping busy, welcoming any and every distraction. I pulled a couple of overnighters at work, taking a hoe-bath each day in the restroom on the tenth floor. My boss urged me to go home during lunch and rest. The truth was I felt safer at work among people; I didn't trust myself to face the day on my own, but I couldn't stay at work forever.

I stumbled up the stairs to my messy, studio apartment, and headed straight to the shower. My back tingled from the rhythmic massage of the warm water. I bathed myself and washed my hair, then bathed again for good measure. After thirty minutes, the water started to cool down, so I exited the shower and wiped the foggy mirror with my hand.

I stared at my naked reflection in disgust. Mom would kill me if she saw how I'd let myself go. My curly hair was wild and unkempt, and I never wore make-up anymore. Or earrings. Or my contacts. I'll be honest. I looked like a black Ugly Betty. I could be pretty cute when I tried, but I needed a reason to try. Hunter had been that reason.

I was looking forward to a lazy afternoon wrapped in my favorite Snuggie, watching *America's Next Top Model* on Hulu. I strolled to the kitchen for a drink, plotting how I'd put the moves on José Cuervo when I realized I was out of tequila. It was probably a good thing as José tended to take advantage of a girl, so I decided to venture out for some wine.

In my mind, I heard my mother's voice reprimand me for daring to go out looking like I'd been smacked by Miley Cyrus's wrecking ball, so I brushed my hair into a high ponytail, threw on some skinny jeans, my Ugg boots, and a tight sweater. I put on a smattering of lip balm and took a moment to insert my contacts.

When I arrived at Wal-Mart, I noticed red and pink displays of hearts, teddy bears, flowers and candy. Nausea punched me in the gut.

February 14th.

Damn.

I loathed Valentine's Day like I loathed pap smears, root canals, and Donald Trump. Not because I was single, but I had my reasons.

I thought that I would have been strong enough to handle the sight of hearts and roses, but I felt a wave of emotion as violent as a tsunami. I stood watching as a swarm of people fought over the last pickings of cards and gifts. I hurried to the wine section. Glancing over each shoulder, I grabbed a bottle of Barefoot wine from the shelf and twisted the cap off, taking a long swig. Then another.

Wine in hand, I sauntered over to the frozen food aisle, snatched a bag of crinkle fries, and rushed toward the front of the store. I made a pit stop at the $5 DVD bin and considered grabbing the first few seasons of *Degrassi: The Next Generation.* I figured watching my favorite childhood TV series might put me in a better mood, but I rescinded that decision on account of the kid in the wheelchair who had more sex than I did.

I took another gulp from the bottle.

The checkout lines were endless. I should have gone to Target. I was tempted to leave my items and make a break for the exit, but I'd already downed nearly half the bottle of wine.

In hopes of finding a shorter line, I made an abrupt left turn down an aisle where I crashed into an unsuspecting shopper. My frozen fries made a crunching noise when they hit the floor, followed by the shatter of glass and splash of red wine all over aisle six. The impact of our collision sent the other person's shopping cart flying into the shelves, knocking over several boxes of Rice-a-Roni and Uncle Ben's.

I stumbled forward, but a pair of strong hands helped me regain my footing, rescuing me from further embarrassment.

"Are you okay?"

"God, I'm such a klutz," I said.

Flustered and humiliated, I reached down to grab the bag of fries just as he stooped to do the same.

"No, no. I can get it," I protested. Our hands brushed against one another. I could feel the intensity of his eyes on me--it felt as though he was using telekinesis to compel me to look at him.

I lifted my eyes to meet his and my fingers went numb. Then I heard myself inhale as he licked his lips and whispered my name.

"Heather."

The cadence of my name floated from his lips and tickled my eardrums.

Damn, he's still fine.

"Hunter," I said. "Oh, my God."

He smiled. "Of all people to bump into, huh?"

We both slowly stood upright. His blue eyes sparkled as he held my gaze. They traveled lower--to my lips, my breasts, then my hips, and back up again. His eyes always said things his lips did not.

A few stray tendrils had fallen from my messy ponytail. I smoothed them away from my eyes, but my disobedient curls refused to submit. I tugged on the bottom of my sweater, tucking my finger into a newfound hole at the hem. I cursed myself for not applying make-up before leaving the house, but it didn't matter because Hunter had a way of making me feel pretty.

"You look sensational," he said in a breathy tone.

"Thank you," I said, barely above a whisper. "You do, too."

He ran his fingers through his short, chestnut brown hair. I remembered a time when my fingers would comb through those locks. He used to have the sweetest baby face, always clean-shaven. Now he'd grown a mustache and a trimmed beard. Even underneath his Seattle Seahawks sweatshirt, I could see his broad shoulders and muscular chest. I couldn't help but wonder if he looked the same underneath his jeans, too. I blushed at the thought.

"So, how have you been? It's been a long time."

"Three years," I said before I could stop myself. "Um, I'm okay. Working at a new firm across town. What about you? Anything new?"

He chuckled. "There's always something happening in my world. I work with kids now at the community center in the sports and recreation department. It's right by the little park where we met. You remember?"

Just being in his presence made my heart stop and pound at the same time. "Yes, I remember."

I pursed my lips, praying to the heavens that my teeth weren't stained red from the wine. I took two steps back for fear that he would smell it on my breath. That's when I noticed his cart laden with Valentine's Day goodies. Although my heart felt as heavy as an anvil, I couldn't resist asking, "Who's the lucky lady?" I gestured toward the cart.

"Still nosy, I see." He stepped in front of the cart. Out of sight, out of mind did not apply here. "Man, I can't believe it's you. I was just thinking about you this morning."

I glanced at the cart again and scowled. "Why are you thinking about me?"

Hunter scowled. "Because today is…"

"Just another day," I interjected.

His expression softened. "Hey, Heather…" His voice trailed off.

My chin quivered and I squeezed my eyes shut. I would not cry in front of my ex-fiancé and a spilled bottle of Barefoot wine in Wal-Mart.

"I should go," I told him. I started to leave, but I could hear him following me.

"Wait," he called to me. "Don't go. Please. Wait."

I whirled around. His handsome face was solemn. We stood facing each other in a long moment of silence.

He reached for my hand and before I could protest, he pulled me into an embrace. I dropped the bag of fries on the floor and melted into him like butter on cornbread. I buried my face in his chest as I felt overwhelming grief overtake me. In his arms, I didn't feel like we were standing in the middle of a supermarket; we had traveled back in time to three years prior. When he'd held me as we wept together in the middle of our living room. He had been my rock when I found out we were pregnant, but he'd crumbled when we lost the baby.

My thoughts were interrupted by the sound of his racing heartbeat.

He pulled away to look into my eyes. "We didn't run into each other on this day for no reason. Don't you see? She brought us together—"

"Let's not do this," I said, wiping tears from my cheeks. "I can't handle all of this right now. All I wanted were my fries and my wine--"

"You've been drinking?"

"--so I really don't want to do this with you today, okay?"

He said nothing and I took that as my cue to continue. "I honestly never thought I would see you again. And I didn't want to be seen by you. Not like this." I looked down at my dirty boots and made another attempt to swipe my curls out of my eyes.

"You're every bit as perfect as you've always been, Heather."

My name sounded like a symphonic melody emanating from his lips. He lifted my chin with his finger and for a moment I thought he might kiss me.

A part of me wanted to stroke his cheek and savor the taste of his lips one more time, but the rest of me wanted to Usain Bolt out of there.

"I'm sorry," were the only words I could muster.

I stepped back and then turned away from him; his voice trailed after me.

"It wasn't your fault." I heard the emotion in his voice.

I stopped. Tears stung my eyes and I regretted wearing my contacts.

He walked up behind me and grabbed my shoulders. "It wasn't your fault. You didn't do anything wrong. You couldn't have changed anything."

Every insecurity I'd ever had came rushing back. "Sweet Hunter," I muttered. "I'm so sorry. You invested so much, loved me so genuinely, and the only thing I had to do was carry and deliver our baby...and I couldn't even do that." Now I faced him. "One more month. One more month and Lily would have been born a healthy baby girl. We would be married. She would be three years old now, twirling around in pretty dresses and calling me mommy—" My voice broke.

Hunter blinked back tears of his own.

"This day haunts me every year. Everyone around me celebrates the one they love, but I am constantly reminded that this is the day we lost Lily. I lost everything that day."

"No." The strength in his voice seemed to make the ground tremble beneath us. "You didn't lose me. *You* walked away from us. You changed your number, you moved. You... you vanished from my life just as quickly as she did. You didn't give me a chance to fight for you."

"I need you to know that I wanted to stay, but I didn't know how. Maybe I was selfish, but Lily's death devastated my soul and yours. I couldn't help put you back together because the shards of my own broken heart were bound to wound yours." Even with Hunter mere inches from me, he had never felt so distant. "I wish we hadn't bumped into each other. You should be going to surprise someone with those stuffed animals instead of talking about things we can't change."

He looked at the shopping cart, reaching inside to pick up one of the stuffed animals. For a moment I thought I saw a sad smile. "They're for Lily," he said.

"What?"

"These flowers and gifts. I take them to her grave every year. She's still our daughter. She's my sweetheart, just like her mother will always be...the only love I'll ever need."

I couldn't move. I didn't even budge when the Wal-Mart associate mopped around our feet, noticeably eavesdropping.

Hunter's phone started to chirp. He eyed the screen. "It's work."

"You should probably take that."

He silenced the phone. "It would be great if you would come with me to see Lily—" The expression on my face must have stopped him. He nodded. I was sure he knew that was something I couldn't do.

His eyes misted. "It was so great seeing you, Heather." He leaned in for another hug. He touched the small of my back and pulled my body against his.

He inhaled deeply. "You still use lavender shampoo." His chest vibrated against my cheek as he spoke. "Do you think I could call you some time?" His voice quivered.

When I pulled away, I saw a sadness in his eyes that mirrored the tears in mine.

I placed my hand on his chest and nudged him backward, creating space. "No."

He dropped his head.

"Be good," I told him.

He nodded. Before he could say another word, I walked out of his life. Again.

***

We all experience loss at some point in time and it affects everyone differently. It's an inevitable part of life that we all dread but, for most people, hope eclipses that pain. I wonder if anyone ever took into account that there are some of us who keep losing the same love every year.

Jeida K. Storey is an Atlanta native where she received her Bachelor of Arts degree in English and Creative Writing from Georgia State University. She lives with her husband in Orlando, Florida and is currently writing her first novel. You can find out more about her at www.jeidakstorey.com.

Fool Me Once

By Lamesha Junior Johnson

JAYLA

Keona had said she would never do it again. Now, Jayla felt more betrayed than a celebrity whose father leaked her secrets to the blogs. She slammed her laptop shut and imagined that Keona was in her grasp being shaken like a rag doll.

"Get a hold of yourself," Granny Shirley said with bugged eyes. "What in the world has you so upset?"

Jayla threw her head back and exhaled a long breath because one more outburst would further distress Granny Shirley. She was grateful the only other person in the small Houston coffee shop where they sat was in the kitchen and couldn't witness the emotions she felt.

She exhaled again. "Keona, stole my idea."

Granny Shirley rolled her eyes. "She's shown you her true colors so many times. I don't know why you befriended that girl again." Granny Shirley shook her head and huffed. "Just last month she stole your face mask recipe."

Jayla nodded. "According to her, since she changed one ingredient it wasn't stealing." Jayla smirked. That one change had caused pimples and blemishes to break out on the faces of the few women who tried Keona's product. Jayla felt bad for those women, but also vindicated knowing Keona didn't get away with playing her.

"And what about that time when you were in elementary school?"

If she hadn't been sitting right in front of Granny Shirley, Jayla would have rolled her eyes. Her grandmother remembered everything and now she wondered why she'd told her so much. Granny Shirley would forgive, but her forgiveness didn't say that one could remain in her life.

Jayla didn't know why it was like this with Keona, though. When she saw Keona for the first time in eleven years at her natural hair event, she'd been so excited that she'd stopped her session to hug her old friend. Their bond became strong again, as if days and not years had passed since the two had made their entire middle school think they were first cousins since they shared the same smooth chocolate skin, similar sharp features and the same last name, Washington.

During one of their catch-up lunches together, Keona confessed she was a huge fan of Jayla's Lifestyle and Beauty blog and she'd told Jayla that she had launched her own makeup blog.

"I wanna be just like you," Keona had confessed. "I'm tired of working at Dillard's. I want to blog full-time, too."

Jayla had been flattered by her friend and she'd encouraged Keona to follow her dreams. She just didn't know Keona was going to do it at her expense.

"Don't stare off in space," Granny Shirley said. When she rubbed her hand, Jayla came back to the present. "Tell me, what did she do this time?"

Jayla finished chewing a bite from her banana nut muffin before she said, "I contacted Keona about the two of us discussing fashion and celebrity gossip for my YouTube channel. I came up with the topics, lined up guests, the décor, and styled us. All she had to do was show up and talk. She knew I planned to launch my show next week, but she one upped me, duplicated everything I did, and launched it with someone else yesterday." Jayla opened her laptop to show Granny Shirley Keona's video. They watched for five minutes before Jayla said, "Now, I have to scrap all my ideas and start over."

Granny Shirley shook her head and looked angrier than when a flat tire caused her to be late for church. "That snake in the grass. Well, cut her off."

"I want to." Jayla lowered her eyes. "But, I missed seeing her the last time we stopped speaking."

As an only child, raised by her strict religious grandparents, Jayla had never had the opportunity to make many friends. Keona had filled that void until they attended different high schools.

Jayla looked at her ringing cellphone and silenced it. It had been a month since she heard that special ringtone she'd reserved for her now ex-boyfriend. When his side chick alerted her of their affair on Facebook, Keona had been right there for Jayla. Keona had trashed him, trashed the other woman and called both of them every dirty word she knew. Then afterwards, she'd taken Jayla out and bought Jayla her favorite Oreo shake. There were other times like that; Keona really did know how to be a good friend.

"You missed seeing her?" her grandmother said as if she couldn't believe it.

Jayla nodded. "Maybe if I tell her off one good time and never share my plans with her again, maybe then we can still be friends."

Granny Shirley placed her chin on her fist. "So, what will you talk about when you get together?"

Jayla shrugged. "I don't know."

"You're grown, but I know I didn't raise no fool," she said shaking her head. "Fool me once —"

"Shame on you," Jayla finished one of her grandmother's favorite sayings.

Granny Shirley clapped her hands, though there was no smile on her face. "You know how it goes. You'll be just fine when you kick her to the curb." She sipped the last of her tea. "Come on, you can work at home and I can fix you some food to take your mind off of it. With a full belly, you can plan something bigger that Keona can't steal." She winked at her granddaughter.

Jayla gave a quick glance to her watch. They'd only been at the coffee shop for thirty-two minutes and Granny Shirley was ready to leave. When her grandmother had said that she wanted to come with Jayla to the place where she did much of her writing, Jayla knew then that she should've made up some excuse to tell her no. Her grandmother preferred being home, lounging around in her duster, cooking and watching her soap operas. So now, she was ready to go back home before Jayla had even written one word.

"But, this is where I'm most comfortable writing and I can use their free Wi-Fi," Jayla whined.

"We have that at home," Granny Shirley countered in a tone that said her word was final.

Jayla closed her computer and gathered her things. On the ride home her thoughts turned back to Keona and she wondered if the good in their friendship outweighed Keona's occasional betrayal. Granny Shirley was wise, but maybe this once she was wrong and their friendship was worth saving.

KEONA

Keona didn't understand why Jayla was so upset. It had been a week since her new YouTube channel had debuted and Jayla had been upset the whole time; though at least she had called. It wasn't like Jayla had an original idea. Many people uploaded videos discussing fashion and gossip.

She rolled over in her bed and retrieved her phone. She checked the stats on her YouTube video and groaned. Keona had hoped to get some of Jayla's shine, but she had seen as much shine as a pair of dirty suede shoes. After a whole week, eighteen people had viewed her video.

Keona scratched her head aggravating her kinky strands. She should have done the show with Jayla instead of ticking off her friend.

Keona wanted to lie in bed longer, but she needed to clean up before Jayla came over. She got out of bed and tossed a week's worth of take-out into black trash bags, then loaded the dishwasher. She moved clothes from the couch and threw them on the bed. Then, she lit apple-cinnamon scented candles to mask the stench left from the moldy food.

She looked around at her messy studio that was much different from the four-bedroom, two-story house Jayla shared with Granny Shirley. Dust still lined her furniture and dirt covered the carpet, but by the time Jayla knocked on the door, she had managed to get a shower and fix her hair.

"It's open," Keona shouted from the couch.

Jayla entered with her purse swung over one shoulder and a large tote bag on the other. She turned her nose up. After they greeted each other, Keona motioned for her to take a seat next to her. Jayla looked around the room as if she wanted an alternative seat, but her choices were the couch, a bed full of clothes and dirty sheets, and a floor with red Kool-Aid stains.

She decided to sit on the couch and got right to the point, "Look, if we're gonna continue this friendship, I have to be able to trust you. You can't keep doing this mess." She folded her arms and pursed her lips.

Keona didn't like the shade thrown from Jayla, but she needed Jayla. "I'm so sorry. I couldn't get anything done thinking about what I did," Keona said. She was lying, of course. She wasn't sorry, and she had gotten plenty done filming another segment for her YouTube show, writing five articles for her blog, and working overtime at the department store.

"I couldn't get anything done either." Jayla bit her pinky finger that was void of the shellac polish and rhinestones that she usually wore.

Keona frowned. *Jayla never passed up a nail appointment. What else did she neglect?*

After a moment, Jayla unfolded her arms and relaxed. "I wasn't sure if we should end our friendship or try to make it work with new stipulations."

"What stipulations?" Keona asked with hesitation in her voice.

"You have to show me that I can trust you," Jayla said looking her in the eyes and displaying more force and confidence than Keona expected.

Keona put her hand on Jayla's shoulder. "I'm willing to do whatever you need me to do so that I can prove that you can trust me. Why don't we still do the show together?" Keona paused. "We could come up with – maybe a best friends discuss makeup show."

Keona hoped Jayla liked this idea. This would help her to be reintroduced to the huge audience that Jayla had. It had been thirty-seven weeks since Jayla had included photos of the two of them on her Instagram page.

Jayla shook her head. "No, I think we should separate business from personal from now on. That way we can work on our friendship."

Keona forced a smile. "Sure. That makes sense. Our friendship is more important."

Jayla nodded, then said, "What do you have to eat in here?" She pointed toward the kitchen.

"Nothing." Keona slouched on the couch. "Why don't we go to Pappadeaux?"

"No, I had that yesterday. How about we just order in Chinese?"

Keona frowned and shook her head. Jayla's fans were everywhere and they always wanted to take selfies with her. If she could squeeze into just one of those photos, that could make up for the mishap she had last week when she declined to take a picture and the woman dragged her on social media. That incident cost her several followers on Instagram and Twitter.

Jayla's phone chimed and she smiled after reading the notification.

"What's up?" Keona asked, leaning over trying to see what was making Jayla so happy.

"Nothing." She looked up at Keona. "I – well, I guess I can tell you since it's a done deal. I can't tell you all the details, but I've been asked to be the face of an online skincare line."

Keona wanted to roll her eyes, but she hugged Jayla to mask her envy. "That's awesome. I'm so proud of you."

"Thanks, sis," Jayla said ending their embrace.

"Yeah, it's something I've been working on for a while and there were a couple of other girls in the running, but I got it."

"Wow," she said, although a thought was already spinning in her head. Keona rubbed her stomach. "Why don't you run out and get something for us to eat? It'll be faster than ordering in. And while you're out, get an Oreo shake from me as a celebratory gift."

"That's a good idea." Jayla agreed and grabbed her purse, not even looking at her tote.

Keona stayed on the sofa until Jayla walked through the door, then she sprang up and ran to the window. Through the blinds, she watched Jayla drive away and when she couldn't see her car anymore, she went straight to her tote bag. Maybe there was something inside about that skin care line contract. She threw out the lip gloss, the iPad and at the bottom, found two notebooks. She scanned through the pages and stopped at what looked like Jayla's goal list. She smirked at all the check marks and the year wasn't even over. She had everything that she wanted, but a man.

"I'll find you a man, I promise," Keona whispered. Maybe that would be enough for what she was about to do. She flipped through more pages and found nothing. Tossing that book aside, she went to the next one. She searched through the pages until she found it -- the contact information for Antwan Rhodes of Antwan Rhodes Cosmetics.

Keona grabbed her phone off the coffee table, inserted his name into Google and learned that he was stationed in Atlanta and had started his business two years before.

Just as her fingers were poised to dial his number, she thought about the trip to New York that she'd taken with Jayla just last year. They'd gone to a Broadway play, and then hung out at a club and danced until the doors closed. Good times and Keona truly loved Jayla; but she needed this. Jayla had so much going for her including her degree. She didn't have all of that and needed this opportunity. She called the number and prayed -- prayed that she would make contact and prayed that Jayla would forgive her.

When Antwon didn't answer, Keona left a message, detailing that she was interested in becoming the face of his line. Then, she followed up with an email, pitching herself with pictures of her skin with and without makeup and she thanked God that the blemishes from her failed face mask had healed and her skin was now flawless.

Looking over at the sofa, she'd been so caught up that she'd forgotten put everything back inside Jayla's tote bag. She was filled with excited energy and she paced her living room. If she could just get this break....

Just as she had that thought, her cell rang. She blinked as she looked at the number, squealed, then took a deep breath before she answered.

"Hello," she answered trying to sound more professional than thrilled.

He verified it was her and then praised, "I didn't advertise this opportunity, but you are fabulous. I thought I'd found the face of my skin care line, but your pictures tell me that I may need to reconsider."

Keona leapt on the inside. "Thank you," she said in her normal voice.

"I have a photographer there in Houston," Antwan said. "Is tomorrow too soon?"

"No, no definitely not!"

"Great. If you can meet with him tomorrow, we might have a place for you with my company."

"I'll be there. Just tell me where."

Antwan relayed the information and ended the call. If she got this job, this would be her first paid modeling job. All she needed was a chance to get in front of his photographer; when that happened, she knew that she, and not Jayla, would be the face of his company.

She was still dancing around her studio when Jayla opened the door, catching Keona jumping in the air.

"What's got you so excited?" Jayla asked, placing the bags of Chinese food onto the table.

Keona said, "I'm just so happy that we're friends again, and I'm positive that things are turning around for both of us."

"Aww, I love you, too."

As they embraced, Keona squeezed Jayla tight, praying once again that this last betrayal wouldn't end their friendship. That somehow, her friend would understand.

JAYLA

A month had passed and Jayla hadn't heard anything from Antwan Rhodes, but she wasn't worried; he'd told her that the job was hers.

But then, this morning, she'd received a text from Keona: *Check my Instagram* was all that it said.

And now, Jayla was breathing heavy as she looked at the three photos of Keona: the new face for Antwan Rhodes Cosmetics. Even though her palms began to sweat, she still checked out the fifteen second commercial showcasing the products on Keona.

What happened? Wasn't this supposed to be her modeling gig? Why hadn't Antwan called her and told her that he'd changed his mind? Why hadn't Keona told her that she'd been contacted for this job? They'd been talking ever since they made up a month ago.

"I hope you can take a break," Granny Shirley said as she entered the study, carrying a lunch tray that filled the room with the sweet smoked flavor of barbecue. "Since I talked you into not going to that coffee house today, I hoped you'd have time to have lunch with me."

"Yeah." Jayla sighed as she looked up. "I can take a break."

"I know that face." Granny Shirley put the tray down and placed her hand on her hip. "What did Keona do?"

It was crazy that she didn't even have to tell her grandmother. "She's the new face of that line that I told you about. I want to be happy for her, but a part of me wonders why she didn't tell me sooner."

"I thought you two had decided not to discuss business."

"Yeah, but—"

"You think she stole the idea from you?" Granny Shirley narrowed her eyes. "Did you tell her about it?"

"No." Jayla scratched her head, then wrapped a curly red strand around her finger. Then, she thought back and remembered that day. She hit the desk with both hands. "I'm so stupid," she said and rolled backwards in her executive chair.

"What?" Granny Shirley walked over to her looking puzzled.

"I left my bag at her house with all of my information in there." She hit her forehead with the palm of her hand. "All this time I thought we were making progress and she betrayed me again."

Granny Shirley gave her the side eye. "Fool me twice."

"I know." Jayla looked down and fought back tears.

Standing over her, Granny Shirley said, "That girl is never going to do right by you." She took her index finger to lift Jayla's chin. "Let it go."

She wiped away a tear. "I'm gonna knock her out." Her voice trembled as she spoke.

Granny Shirley shook her head. "You're a lady. We don't fight. Plus, you don't know how," she teased.

Jayla laughed and Granny Shirley handed her a tissue. She stood and kissed her grandmother. She might not be able to slap Keona, but she wasn't going to let her get away with this betrayal.

She sat and ate lunch, but her mind was on all the things she was going to say to Keona. She tried her best not to rush through, but right after her grandmother cleared away their plates, Jayla told her that she had to run an errand. Jayla had just stepped outside the door on her way to Keona's, when her cell rang.

After she said hello, she heard, "This is Skylar Holmes."

That made Jayla stop walking. She'd taken photos for Skylar and his Olympia Natural Hair and Skin Care line several months before Antwan had called her.

He said, "I'm calling because we've finally made a decision. We didn't plan for it to take so long, but we've chosen you to be the face of our company."

"Oh, my goodness. Thank you."

"You're welcome. Check your email and get back with us as soon as possible."

"I will, and thank you again," she said rushing back into the house.

She spoke fast, explaining everything to Granny Shirley as she opened her computer and checked her email. Her eyes scanned the contract and she squealed when she saw the money she'd make; it was three times what she would have made with Antwan, plus more exposure. She'd have ads in two supermarkets, and would be making television appearances. She jumped from her chair and hopped around the room like a cheerleader.

"Didn't I tell you?" Granny Shirley said as Jayla danced. "God had something better for you. No attack from the enemy can stop the blessings God has in store for His children." She kissed her cheek before she left Jayla alone.

Sitting back in the chair, Jayla couldn't believe this blessing. She decided then that she wouldn't go to see Keona. They'd run into each other soon enough.

Jayla just didn't expect it to happen the next morning. She was at the gym, on the treadmill, running as fast as her size seven feet would allow. Keona got on the treadmill next to her and as competitive as she was, Jayla knew she'd try to keep up, even though she was not in the shape that Jayla was. Thirty minutes later, satisfied that she had worked her friend to almost throwing up, Jayla stopped her machine and told her to meet outside by their cars.

Within ten minutes, they were both outside.

"What's wrong?" Keona said, still breathing hard. "You haven't even congratulated me."

"You're expecting congratulations?" Jayla glared at Keona. "You're a thief."

"What are you talking about?" Keona said with a blank face.

"I know that you stole Antwan's information from me."

Keona paused and twitched her lips.

"Nothing?" Jayla placed her hands on her hips. "You don't care to respond?"

After a moment, "Yes, I did it," Keona snapped. "Because you're always acting like you're better than me."

Her words surprised Jayla; what was Keona talking about? This was not the way she expected this conversation to go.

"Well, Antwan chose me over you," Keona continued ranting, "and my face will be all over two pharmacies."

Jayla started to blast Keona with her new deal, but she made the mistake of telling her something too many times before.

"That's nice, but I'm sure I'll find something better than that. I always do. If you wonder why you're always at the bottom and I'm on top, it's because you can't win when you behave like a snake."

Keona shook her index finger at Jayla. "I love you, but this one time I deserved to win."

There was pity in her eyes when Jayla looked at Keona. "I would have done anything for you, but I can't have a friend who wants my life and is willing to do anything to get it."

Keona pressed her lips together.

When she didn't say anything, Jayla turned to leave. "There won't be another betrayal. I was a fool to try to bring someone seasonal back into my life."

Leaving Keona standing there, she got in her sports car and sped off. She had only one regret -- that she hadn't listened to Granny Shirley earlier. But there was no way that she would ever befriend Keona again.

It was months later when Jayla found out that Keona's ads never ran anywhere. It was all over the fashion news -- Antwan's company filed for bankruptcy and closed.

Just the opposite was happening for Jayla. Her deal with Olympia led to more magazine features and her big break was getting a regular Special Correspondent's spot with one of Houston's news channels.

All of her dreams were coming true and though she had felt a void with Keona being gone, that space was filled with new friends that God brought in her life. She wasn't sure how Keona faired, but Jayla was soaring and didn't have time to look back.

Lamesha Junior Johnson discovered her desire to write fiction after she obtained a MS degree in applied mathematics from Prairie View A&M University. She loves reading, sports, music, soap operas and volunteering. Lamesha is working on her debut novel and lives in the Houston area with her husband and son. Connect with her at www.LameshaJuniorJohnson.com or on social media on Facebook: Lamesha Junior Johnson, Twitter @LameshaJunior and Instagram @LameshaJunior.

NOT DADDY'S GIRL

By Brenda A. White

☐ MADISON

Color me dazed, antsy, and confused because two women approached me at Frenchy's Chicken and said I was their niece.

I was suddenly not hungry, so I closed my box, wrapped my lemon cake and rushed toward my car. My hands trembled so badly I dropped my phone. I fished it out from underneath the seat and called my sister, Shay. It went to voice mail. I slapped the steering wheel. "Shay, call me back, please. I have something to ask you."

I wanted to call my dad since I had just finished talking to him about moving my stuff back home after graduation. I pulled the hoodie over my head and rested against the headrest to calm my nerves. My chest moved up and down.

I had watched my family for years, wondering why I didn't look like any of them. I had always felt different, too. Though it had been awhile, I even questioned my parents on a number of occasions.

"Oh, girl, stop it, you do look like us," my mom said, then continued with what I know now were a bunch of lies.

I often wondered if I was adopted, but when I discussed it with Shay, she recalled my mother's pregnancy. She showed me pictures. My dark skin, high cheek bones, thick silky eyebrows, and full lips were totally opposite of her and the rest of the family.

Tears started to glide along my eyelids and my cheeks flushed a wave of heat. I wanted to believe it, but I thought *were those ladies telling the truth.*

My phone vibrated.

"Shay!"

"Hey girl. Why are you yelling?"

"You will not believe what just happened to me." I turned the radio off.

"Yes, I will. What?" Her tone excited. I loved her; she always showed interest in whatever was going on with me.

"I was sitting at Frenchy's eating by myself and these two ladies came up to me." I paused and looked around at the cars lining up in the drive thru. "They said that I was their niece."

"Girl, stop it. They are lying to you. How is that?"

"They said Momma messed around with their married brother and had me, while she was married to Daddy and that's why they divorced."

"Madison, how is that possible? Momma and Daddy divorced when you were almost eighteen." She paused. "Who would wait eighteen years after an affair to get a divorce?"

She didn't know it, but she was destroying my theory and desire of finally belonging. "I should call Daddy and ask; I just talked to him before I got here."

"Don't you dare," she continued, "If Daddy was mad at Momma about you; Aiden wouldn't be here, either."

"What if Aiden is not Daddy's either?" I twirled my finger around my hair.

"Madison, cut it out. Aiden looks just like Daddy," her voice elevated.

"I don't think so. He looks like mom to me. So, we really don't know who his dad is either." I mumbled and rested my elbow on the steering wheel.

"Madison! You are out of line?"

"What? No, I'm not! What if Momma is a hoe?"

She sighed, "I can't with you today."

Our conversation had gone differently than I had planned. I expected support.

"Okay, hear me out. Do you remember when they argued all the time, all of my high school years before they finally divorced? I thought Daddy had done something, because Momma did all the yelling. The arguments had to be about me, they've been telling lies all these years."

"Madison, that is not true," she yelled.

"You don't know." I wiped away a tear with the back of my hand. I didn't understand then, but it's all clear to me now... everybody started to treat me differently.

"That is complete nonsense," her voice filled with frustration.

"No, it's not," my voice trembled. She didn't respond, so I continued, "And Shay, I look just like the lady. So identical, I could be her daughter." I waited, still no response. "She gave me her number."

"Goodbye, Madison."

My jaw clinched and I took one long sniff as a sign to suck it up, because that was the last time I would cry about how my family treated me. Shay knew I was telling the truth. She had never hung up on me because she knew that pissed me off and everybody in the family knew what I did when I got pissed off.

JEAN

I always wanted a strong and noble man for a son-in-law. I watched Troy as he got out of the car, adjusted his ball cap, and rushed up the driveway toward the front door.

I swung the door open. "Hi Troy, come on in." I waved him into the house.

"I sure do appreciate you stopping by to look at my refrigerator."

"Come on, Mom. You know I'll do anything for you." His eyes beamed sincerity. Even after him and my trifling daughter, Ebony divorced three years ago, he'd always help with whatever I needed after Bill passed away.

They really needed a break, but I'd wanted them to fight for their marriage, because both of them cheated. Who hasn't? I wanted them back together. Happiness is really not that difficult.

"How are you and Ebony doing?" I followed him into the kitchen. "How long have you been back together?"

"Ms. Jean Hawthorn, what are you talking about?" He gasped.

"Troy, I've been around a long time and the streets talk."

"What are the streets saying?" his voice dripped sarcasm.

"That you two are back together."

"Oh." He busied himself pulling the refrigerator from the wall.

"Well, anyway, how is Madison?" She was my middle grandchild who always seemed so sad or mad. I always pray for her.

"She's fine. I talked to her earlier. She'll take her finals soon, then I'll help her move to my place," Troy said.

"Oh, that's good. She told me she would do it. Praise God, she pressed through." I clapped.

"Yeah, things were difficult for her, but she graduates in a few weeks so she'll be officially out of my pocket." He smiled. "Madison is my daughter. Don't get me wrong, I was mad at Ebony; I was wrong for shutting Madison out. It took me some time, but I eventually came around."

"Yes, you did. You're such a good man, Troy."

"I try, but it's not always appreciated."

I fiddled with the canisters on the cabinet. "You know Chester is causing trouble again."

He turned toward me, his eyebrows almost touching.

"Yeah, Ms. Essie called me earlier. His sisters told Madison—"

He dropped the wrench. "What? I talked to Madison and she didn't mention it." His shoulders visibly moved up and down.

MADISON

One week had passed since I found out about my biological father. I couldn't focus; I went from angry to happy to sad to wanting to seek revenge. I wanted to tell my parents, but I didn't know exactly how to approach them. I thought about the times I longed for my parents to just include me, talk to me, and support me. I wanted them to at least act like they cared. Grandma Jean with her poised and put together polyester was more supportive than them and I appreciated her for that.

I sat in the middle of my twin-sized bed taking deep breathes. The tiny dorm room, cold tiled floor, and beige walls made me feel like I was in a psych ward. I curled into a ball and closed my eyes. I dreamed of revenge and the confusion of how to seek it didn't escape me. I didn't know if I wanted to call them together, torch the house or hold them hostage and take them out one by one, execution style. I had no desire to go to jail so I resolved to continuous embarrassment to the Brown clan and unfortunately Grandma Jean, well, she's just guilty by association.

I had stared at that phone number scribbled on the back of a MD Anderson business card for hours. I needed to study, but I wanted to see what else "my aunt" had to say. I sat up, pulled my knees into my chest and dialed the number.

She answered on the first ring. "Hello, this is Joyce."

"Hi Ms. Joyce, this is Madison. The young lady you…"

"Oh, I know who it is. My niece. How you doing, baby?"

"Oh, I'm fine." I smiled. "Umm, can I meet my real dad, can I meet Chester?" I rocked back and forth.

"Sure, you can. I already told him I ran into you."

"Okay, I can meet him somewhere."

I met them the next day at the Starbuck's on Scott Street near campus. I got out of the car and my legs were wobbly, my heart was pounding as if it would beat visibly through my sweater. My biological dad, Chester and my Aunt Joyce were sitting at the table in the corner. He twirled his thumbs one around the other as I approached. He stood up, took a few steps, and embraced me. I looked a lot like him.

We spent four hours together. His stories were fascinating. He got divorced after the affair, had remarried, but his wife died in a car crash two years ago. And I have another brother.

I had spoken to him several times since our first meeting. His stories made me look at my mom and dad in a whole new light. He told me he wanted to acknowledge me a long time ago, but my mom continued to lie, so his sisters decided to track me down.

Another week had gone by and final exams were complete. I'm keeping my fingers crossed for passing grades. I didn't feel good about it because meeting my biological father had definitely distracted me. If I didn't pass, I couldn't start my job in January. I had so much to think about and so much to do, but was summoned to grandmother's house to celebrate a family tradition of trimming the Christmas tree. I didn't feel like hanging out at my grandma's trimming an ugly tree and listening to old people talk. I had packed my apartment and planned to move my things, but I didn't know where I was moving it to. I know I'm not moving to my mom's, my dad was already planning to move me to his place, and Chester had made an offer, too.

When I arrived late to Grandma's, I kissed her on the cheek, hugged my dad since he opened the door, waved at everyone else, and slid onto the couch.

"You need to learn how to be on time," Aunt Betty scolded.

I glared at her. I wanted to punch her in the face, but I'd think of a better way to punish her.

My grandmother stood in front of the crackling fire. She read a scripture and I totally tuned her out after the first sentence. "A good person leaves an inheritance for their children's children." My head was throbbing, my breathing heavy. I felt abandoned, betrayed, like nobody's child in that room. . Who cares that they took care of me. They would've gone to jail had they not done so. Food, clothes, shelter was it. Most of the love and affection came sporadically from my dad. Too bad there was no jail time for emotional neglect.

JEAN

I loved my family and I decided that I wanted to see them enjoy their inheritance while I'm still here. They behave badly at times, but they are still my family.

Madison strolled in late as usual, angry.

"Thank you all for coming..." I smiled and clasped my hands. "To our annual Christmas decorating party, but I wanted to add a bit of twist to it this year."

"And we thank you for having us every year," Pastor Jones chimed in and his wife smiled.

"I'm truly thankful for all of you." I paused smiled toward my grandson, Aiden. At twelve, he was the most innocent face in the room.

Ebony looked over and grabbed Troy's hand. I'm not sure why they want to sneak around; everybody knows they were dating again.

"I invited you all here to eat, help me to trim my trees, and..."

Madison sighed heavily. I felt sorry for her, but hated her attitude lately. Poor thing she's filled with so much angst and my sister, Betty didn't help by antagonizing her.

Ebony rubbed invisible lent from her jeans. "Madison, if you keep being disrespectful, I'm going to smack the taste out your mouth," she growled.

"I bet you won't," Madison mumbled.

I paused and took a few deep breaths and started praying silently. "Madison, sweetheart..." I placed my hand over my heart as a plea for her to cooperate. "As I was saying, I invited you all here to help me trim the tree and to share some things with you while I'm still here. Proverbs 13:22 says that a good person leaves an inheritance for their children's children, but a sinner's wealth is stored up for the righteous." I paused again to allow that scripture to settle in. "And no, I'm not dying."

"Well, praise God," Betty, chortled.

"Ebony, Troy, I see you two holding hands, I know you two are together again and so does everyone else in here."

"Oh Mother, we just..." Ebony tried to explain.

I held up my hand. "No need. You two have three kids together." It felt like a fur ball was stuck in my throat after that statement because we knew they had only two together. "If that's what you want, go for it." I took a sip of cider and my hands trembled as I set the cup on the saucer.

"Amen," my pastor called out.

"Hold up, Grandma." Madison held up one finger and stood next to me. My heart pounded heavily. "I have something I'd like to ask..."

MADISON

I had to interrupt Grandma. I could hear my heartbeat in my ears. I had to speak now. I flipped the light switch on so the extra lighting over the fireplace could shine down on me. I pressed my hands together to reduce the trembling. Then I pointed at my mother, "Mother, how old am I?"

She furrowed her brows. "Twenty-one."

"I've been in this family for twenty-one years. And for twenty-one years, you all have lied to me."

"Aiden, go upstairs." The man I thought was my dad instructed.

Aiden leaped from his seat.

"No, let him stay. He needs to hear this," I said.

Aiden stood frozen in place.

"Aiden, go upstairs, now." Troy narrowed his eyes at me.

Shay chimed in, "Madison, what are you doing?"

I waited until Aiden left the room.

"Anybody else want to leave? Okay, cool," I continued before anyone could answer. I knew they wanted to stay to hear what I had to say. There was something about the word *lie* that made people pause and listen.

"All of you have allowed me to live a lie. I knew I didn't look like anybody in this family because I look like my daddy, Chester Long. My last name is not Brown, it's Long." I stabbed my finger in the air. My face was getting warm.

The room was silent. No one in the room gasped, which means it was not a surprise, they all knew.

I continued, "How did that happen? Huh?"

Aunt Betty grunted and looked at my mother. Her grunt spoke volumes.

"When two people sleep around and get pregnant, they don't consider the child. All they think about is getting it in, then cover it up." My nostrils flared. "I knew I looked different, I knew I felt different."

"That's not true, we loved you and treated you just like we did Shay and Aiden," my mother combated.

"No, you didn't. You say you did, but you didn't." I was fighting back tears.

I looked over and saw Shay wipe her face. "Madison, don't do this," her voice edgy. I figured she was still mad at me from the moment I told her.

My mother lowered her eyes and fidgeted with her hands.

"Yes, we do love you, honey. We loved you and provided all of the same things we provided for Shay." Troy pointed at Shay. "And Aiden."

I shook my head, "No. Let me ask you, how many of my lacrosse games you came to? When I played volleyball, how many times did you come to see me play?"

No one responded.

"Just what I thought, Momma was too busy and you were too bitter. And that made me feel like I wasn't wanted. Shay and Aiden got everything they wanted and all of the support they needed. Now, either of y'all are at every game, coaching, cheering or whatever, supporting his whole team.

Troy shook his head. "I loved you just like you were mine because until you were twelve, I thought you were. I had to work through it, too. I couldn't abandon you."

His words softened me a bit, my heart even fluttered, but I had made up my mind to say mean things so I continued, "Dad, or should I call you Troy now? I know about your four-year old bastard son, Jayden, too."

He stood up. "You will not disrespect me."

"Oh, sir, you haven't seen disrespect yet and neither have you." I glared at my mom.

My mother started toward me, but Troy stopped her. "Girl, don't make me hurt you!"

The pastor starting coughing uncontrollably which was the reaction I wanted. He witnessed the heathens from his congregation first hand.

"You know what Dad, that's fair, you have indeed supported me financially and for that I appreciate you. Although…" I paced and pressed my fingertips against my lips. "You did all of that, but you're a weak man for not standing up for yourself and Momma," I paused. "You're a whore!"

My mother charged at me. I was pent against the fireplace as she struck me repeatedly until Troy pulled her off. "Ebony! Are you serious? That's our daughter."

I could taste the blood on my lip, my face throbbed. I straightened my sweater.

"Somebody has to pay the price for all the lies I've been told. It's not my fault I was thrown into this mess of a family, now I'm trying to make sense of it. And the first thing I'm gonna do is cut all of y'all off."

"What do you mean cut all of us off?" Grandma asked. "Wise people are careful and avoid trouble; fools are too confident and careless, that's Proverbs."

"I don't have a clue what you're talking about." I stomped toward the door. My mother raced after me and tried to block my path, but Troy pulled her away and called after me.

JEAN

"Baby, come back and sit down, let me explain it all to you as I should have done so long ago. Lord have mercy. I should let your momma tell you everything, but everybody's emotions are too high."

I shuffled back into the living room and ushered Madison through to my bedroom. I paused, "Everybody, I ask that you excuse yourselves as I tend to my granddaughter." I looked at Ebony. I was so disappointed in her and myself at the moment. I'm not sure where I went wrong. Maybe I allowed her to get too comfortable with me.

Ebony started toward me and Madison and I put my hand up. "No, you leave. You've done enough damage." She fell to her knees and sobbed. Troy and Shay came to her side.

I remember the day she told me how she ended up pregnant by Chester. She came in distraught and I ushered her back to my room just like I did Madison. The chaise in my bedroom was the spot where everybody told all. She stretched out and began to talk…

"I was at dinner with a friend and she said, *hmph, married almost nine years and never experienced an orgasm can send any woman over the edge. You need to find you a man who can turn your world upside down in bed.* Those two sentences kicked my imagination and my sexual desires into high gear and got me into trouble that would last a lifetime. Chester Long, you know him, Essie's son, married to Jocelyn, was a charmer and I allowed his charm and my inquisitive spirit to take control and send me from a simple conversation into a hotel room with my legs spread wide and had the biggest orgasm I had ever experienced."

I remember a hot flash came over me when she said that. She continued, "the affair didn't stop there, I mean, who could blame me, it felt good, but I hated myself for it so much so that I couldn't even love Madison the way I should have. I knew she was Chester's daughter, but I had to blame it on Troy and I hated him for not figuring it out. I wanted to stop, Momma, but I couldn't." She sat up. "I hated Jocelyn for figuring it out and setting out to destroy *my* marriage. Jocelyn left Chester the minute she found out, twelve years later. Of course, it took Troy several years longer to file for divorce."

I listened to her story and realized Ebony didn't know Chester as well as she thought she did.

Troy and Shay managed to get wailing Ebony to the car. I felt sorry for her, but they had to leave. My granddaughter needed me at the moment. I watched everyone drive away and I locked the door. I hurried back to my bedroom and Madison was curled into a fetal position on the chaise.

"Oh, sweetheart, I'm so sorry. Sometimes protecting someone does more harm than good. Your mother is …"

She rose from her position. "A hoe."

"No, no, no, we're not going to use that language." I moved over to sit next to her.

"Well, what is she then, getting knocked up by a married man?"

"…neglected."

"By who? You and Pawpaw didn't neglect her."

"Sweetheart, it's complicated. She and your dad had issues." I paused to determine if I should say it. "Sexually."

She jerked slightly and her eyes blinked.

"Yes and as an adult, she gave into peer pressure and encouragement to step out." I made a sweeping motion with my hand.

"Nobody can make me do anything that I don't want to do."

I smiled at her. "Yes, they can, which is why I hope you don't move in with a man you know nothing about. Your biological dad is a liar, a cheater… oh, help me, Jesus."

She narrowed her eyes.

"Yes, I know all about it. His mother Essie told me that he talked his sisters into hunting you down to tell you about him."

Her mouth opened.

"Baby, your daddy is mad because your mom wouldn't accept any more of his advances. When your dad has someone in his life he leaves your mother alone and when he doesn't, which is very rare, he stirs up trouble and he's a manipulator."

Her eyes turned glassy. "Grandma?" Her shoulders dropped.

"When you were twelve years old, your dad Troy, found out and now you're twenty-one when you found out. Why, because Chester plans things when it's convenient for him. His ex-wife Jocelyn didn't just find out, he told her."

Neither of us said anything until I broke the silence, "So, you're going to get your things and move in here with me."

She reached for a hug. "Thank you Grandma, I love you." Her beautiful skin was shiny from the tears; her right eye and lip were swollen. "So, he doesn't love me?"

"No." I pulled her into my arms and rocked her. "Troy raised you and provided for you even after he found out, not Chester. He was just a charming and charismatic man, but he is a master at manipulating people. How do you think he got your momma?"

She looked at me with an expression of disbelief. I had to tell her everything in hopes that it will help her to make better decisions.

"He was genuine, wasn't he?" I asked her.

"Yes."

"Hmph and plotting the whole time."

"Oh, grandma, I would've been better off not knowing. Why did this have to happen to me?" She fell into my arms.

"Sweetheart, why not you? You will be known by this testimony, somehow."

Her body stiffened as she pulled away. "I want to hurt them so bad. I don't want to ever see them again," she moaned.

"Aww, my baby, I love you. Don't say that." I hugged her again. "You worry about graduation this weekend, you have a wonderful life ahead of you with your new job; vengeance is mine said the Lord."

'No, Grandma." She shook her head. "Vengeance is mine."

MADISON
Graduation day…

I had planned for this day for a few weeks. I was excited my college years were finally over. I have a whole new life ahead of me. I had already made plans to work with a designer in New York. I was moving in less than thirty days and away from all of my family's nonsense to start afresh. I mailed over one-hundred invitations because I wanted everyone to be there for my big day.

I paid a technology intern to create a slideshow to play at the end of the graduation. I planned it, but I wanted to watch it unfold from a distance. Degree in hand, my breathing labored, I got up and slid out the side door of the arena just as the video started. The song "Holly Jolly Christmas" rang out in the arena for ten seconds, just long enough to get everyone's cheerful attention, then "Take a Bow" by Rihanna started to play and *Season Finale* appeared on the screen in swirly and capital letters. Underneath it was *The Lying Star-studded Cast*; it zoomed in large then switched to the next slide. There was a picture of Chester standing next to a fishing boat with the caption; *This is my biological dad… the liar, the cheater, the adulterer, the manipulator.* The next picture was selfies with me and my aunts at Frenchy's, Chester's sisters; *These are my two gullible aunties or lying aunties. I'm not sure which one.* There was a picture of Troy that I cut down the middle to separate my mom, *This is the guy who thought he was my dad, well, he is my dad. I love him, but I wish he'd man up and stop getting used.* The other portion of the torn photo transitioned onto the screen, *and this is a WHORE!* The picture zoomed in large, the music scratched to an abrupt stop and then *Merry Christmas and an Awful New Year, I'm done. ~MB* appeared. I should've put a picture with Grandma Jean and Ms. Essie, *Thank you for saving me.* But there was no need, Grandma knew I loved her.

The crowd gasped and chatter filled the room. Mission one, accomplished.

I guess I should've warned that I would embarrass them. Yes, I did, and that was just the beginning.

Brenda A. White decided to turn a childhood dream of becoming an accomplished writer into reality. Her novels are humorous and drama-filled stories of bringing your complete self into a relationship while being pruned through joy, pain, and adversity. Check out her website at www.brendaawhite.com/. You can also follow her on Facebook at Author Brenda A. White, and Instagram and Twitter @brendaawhite.

The EX Factor

By J.L. Sapphire

Taye walked out the front door of his home and slammed the door behind him. He hopped in his Ford Explorer, cranked the engine, and sped out of the driveway. He and his wife, Michelle, had just had another fight over money.

Taye and Michelle had been married for five years. When they met, it was in a nightclub. His only intent had been to find a cuddy buddy for the night. He'd spotted Michelle out on the dance floor, rocking a body-hugging red dress, and five-inch stilettos. He'd become physically attracted to her immediately, and knew he'd found the woman he would be going home with.

He'd walked over to her, and offered to buy her a drink…which turned into three drinks. From the way she kept rubbing his inner thigh underneath the table, it was clear that she was feeling him.

After the club closed, they headed to a nearby hotel, and made love in every way imaginable, until they heard birds chirping early the next morning. They'd exchanged numbers before they went their separate ways, although Taye had no intention of seeing her again. When she called him a little over a month later, he assumed she wanted to hook up. To his surprise, she was calling to tell him she'd missed her period, and that she was pregnant.

Taye immediately went on the defense, telling her they'd only slept together once, and the baby couldn't possibly be his. However, nine months later, after the twins were born, and a paternity test was done, in the famous words of Maury- he *was* the father. Wanting to do the right thing, he'd asked Michelle to marry him, and here they were.

They'd agreed that until the twins got a little older, Michelle would be a stay-at-home mom, because they didn't want to deal with trifling daycare workers who half paid attention to the children they were being paid to watch. Taye got two jobs - one at a paper mill plant, and the other as a shift manager at a fast food restaurant- while Michelle took care of home.

Only, she didn't take care of home. She'd told Taye that taking care of the twins left little time for her to cook and clean, and convinced him to hire a maid. Now that she had help with the kids, Taye told her it was a good time for her to find a part-time job, although she had several excuses as to why she shouldn't.

Michelle spent money like there was no tomorrow. When he'd tell her that she was spending too much, she'd accuse him of not caring about his wife having nice things, and that she'd sacrificed her life and body to have his babies. After she'd laid her guilt trip on pretty thick, Taye would usually buy her whatever she wanted, just to shut her up.

When her best friend, MiMi, got a brand new Dodge Charger, Michelle had begged and pleaded with Taye to buy her one, until he'd broken down and obliged her. Then, she told him she just had to have rims, tinted windows, and all the other accessories that made the car look more expensive than MiMi's.

When she told him that they needed new furniture in the living room, because what they had looked cheap, he'd tried to reason with her, telling her that it was fully paid for, and looked nice. Michelle threw a temper tantrum, until he relented and bought her brand new, top-of-the- line furniture for the living room and bedroom.

Shaking off his thoughts of Michelle, he drove around town aimlessly. He'd left the house because Michelle had started getting on his nerves, and he knew he needed to leave before he did something stupid, like slap her. Their latest fight had started because she'd had the audacity to come to him, telling him the Charger wasn't *'doing it for her anymore,'* and that she wanted a new car.

Taye had looked at her as if she'd been speaking Chinese. "Are you out of your mind, Michelle? I just bought you that car less than a year ago. What do you mean, it's not doing it for you anymore?"

"MiMi traded her car in and got another one and…"

"So, you think I'm going to keep buying you new cars every time your friend gets one? You must be crazy. Anyway, MiMi can do that, because she *works*."

"What are you trying to say, Taye?" Michelle had asked with an attitude while rolling her neck.

"I'm not *trying* to say anything. I'm *saying*, it's time for you to stop being lazy, and get a job. I was fine with you staying home when the kids were born, but we have a maid, who doubles as the nanny, whenever you leave the kids with her so you can go get your hair and nails done; if you can leave them with her to go do that, you can leave them with her while you find a job.

"You know what, Taye? You're a cheap bastard. I'm your wife. You're supposed to make sure that I have the best of the best…at all times. I knew I should have left your cheap butt in the club that night where I found you."

"Yeah, but since my cheap butt was buying you all those drinks you kept chugging down like you'd spent the last week in a desert, you didn't."

"You trying to call me a ho?"

"You said that, not me," Taye said as he kept eating his dinner at the dining table.

The next thing Taye knew, Michelle slapped him upside his head. "You didn't mind sleeping with me though, now did you?"

Taye closed his eyes, took a deep breath, and counted to ten in an attempt to calm himself down. "Look, Michelle; I'm really not in the mood for this. I'm not getting you another car. Hell, I'm still making payments on the one you have. If you're not happy with it, you can get a job, and pay for it yourself. End of discussion. But if you hit me like that again, so help me…"

Upset that she wasn't getting her way, Michelle dashed the glass of ice water she'd been sipping on at him. She wanted a reaction and she knew that if she pushed him, he'd get mad enough to want to hit her, which would lead to makeup sex, which would lead to pillow talk, which would lead to him giving her what she wanted.

Taye got up out of his chair, and she prepared herself for a fight. He looked angry enough to punch her. "What, you gonna hit me?" she taunted. "I wish you would."

Taye's nostrils flared and he rolled his neck from side to side, trying to calm himself down. "No, Michelle, I'm not going to hit you. That would be too easy." He walked out of the dining room and headed toward the living room to grab his keys off the key ring, with Michelle on his heels, still hitting him in the back of the head.

"Come back here, you're not going anywhere. You're always trying to run when you can't take the heat. You're going to stay here and..." her words were cut off as Taye slammed the front door behind him. She couldn't believe he left. Normally, he would have grabbed her when she swung at him, then he'd pick her up and carry her into the bedroom, and make love to her, until she got some act-right.

Taye noticed her looking out the front window as he backed out of the driveway. She probably was thinking that he'd be back. He was going to have to show her differently.

***

Taye found himself at the Galleria Mall. It was just after eight, and the mall didn't close until nine. He had driven around town for a while, trying to calm himself down, but gas wasn't cheap these days, and he was wasting what he had in his tank; so he came to the mall to walk around and clear his head.

He didn't want to leave Michelle, but she was giving him no choice. He'd tried being a good man...working two jobs to take care of her and their kids, but nothing was ever good enough. He'd grown up with both of his parents, and the last thing he wanted to do was have his twins grow up in separate households, but he wasn't sure how much more he could take. He was almost certain that if he left, she'd never let him see the kids and would drain his pockets of every penny he made in child support, so it was kind of cheaper to suck it up and deal with her.

He went into the GNC Nutrition store, looking for some protein powder. He didn't get much time off, but when he wasn't working, he liked spending time at the gym lifting weights and trying to bulk up a little more in his chest.

After he left there, he went to the food court and stood in line, waiting to buy a pretzel.

"Taye! Is that you?" he heard a voice say from over his shoulder.

He turned to look and immediately recognized the woman. "Brie! What's up, girl?" He gave her a hug and kiss on the cheek. He and Brie had grown up together…right next door to each other. Their families had been real close, and Taye and Brie were more like brother and sister, who just lived in different houses.

"I'm in town for our family reunion. I know you've heard it's this weekend."

"Yes, you already know your mom told me. She told me to come by, but I can't make any promises. I'm sure one of my jobs will be holding me hostage, even though I'm scheduled off this weekend."

"Well, you know mama; she'll make me bring you a plate if you don't come."

"How's she doing anyway?"

"Good…sassy as ever. Her and daddy are sneaking around again, even though they think we don't know."

Brie's parents had gotten married, divorced, and re-married again, more times than anyone could count. They couldn't live with each other, yet they couldn't live *without* each other, it seemed.

Taye got his pretzel and a lemonade, and waited for Brie to get one, then they walked and talked for a while.

"So, how's Michelle and those adorable babies?"

Taye rolled his eyes. "The kids are fine."

"Uh oh…I know that look. What's wrong, trouble on paradise island?"

They found a bench and sat down to rest for a minute.

"I'm trying, Brie; I really am. But, she just keeps pushing me. You know I just got her a new car not too long ago, right?"

"Yeah, you mentioned that the last time we talked."

"Well, she had the nerve to tell me tonight that she wants another car...just because her best friend got another one. I try not to call her the b-word, but that's exactly what she acts like- a spoiled, lazy, entitled... b-word."

Brie laughed. "That's what you get for picking up chicks in the club. You're having second thoughts about taking that big booty in the tight dress home now, huh?"

"Are you trying to make me feel better? Because it's not helping," Taye said with a pout.

"Aww...I'm sorry. Actually, I'm not; but I'll keep my thoughts and opinions about Michelle to myself." Brie had never liked Michelle, nor did she think she was the right woman for Taye, and she'd told him that...right up until the day he married her; but he'd told her he wanted to make an honest woman of Michelle since she had his babies, a decision he couldn't count the number of times he'd regretted.

"Hey, remember that pact we made back in high school?" Brie asked him as she stuffed the last of her pretzel in her mouth and washed it down with some ice cold lemonade.

Taye laughed. "Yep, I remember it. We said if we weren't married by the time we both turned thirty, we were marrying each other. I also remember that was the night you took my virginity."

"Hold up, I didn't *take* it...you gave it to me. You were a horny fifteen-year-old, and you couldn't wait to get some, because all your friends were already doing it. Anyway, you're married now, so..." She let her words linger.

"Yeah...but if things don't change, I won't be for long."

Because Taye and Brie had always been close, it was logical that they'd developed feelings that went beyond friendship when they were younger. One night, when their parents had gone out and left them home babysitting their younger siblings, they'd decided to experiment a little.

It was in the early 2000's- back when *BET UnCut* still came on late nights. As they looked at Nelly's *Tip Drill* video, Taye started getting really horny. He'd been trying to hold out and not have sex until after graduation, but he was losing the battle. All of his boys teased him, because he wasn't getting any yet. Brie had even lost her virginity - so he'd heard from one of the boys in the locker room.

They sat in bed giggling and watching videos, and, the topic of sex came up. "So, what's it feel like?" Taye had asked Brie when a commercial came on.

"Good," she said.

"I know *that*; but…what exactly does it feel like?"

"Don't you get yourself off…you know, with your hand?"

"Yeah!"

"Well, it feels like that…only better."

"Oh!" Taye said. His eyes scanned over her long legs up to her still budding chest. She'd definitely grown since they were little kids.

"Lie down," he heard Brie say after a while.

"What?"

"Lie down. I'm about to make a man out of you. It's time, Taye."

"Awkward as it was, you lost your virginity that night in my bedroom. At first, you were quick and clumsy; but before you went home, we gave it another shot, and you were significantly better," Brie said reminiscently.

"Yep, you laughed at me so much, I had to try and redeem myself," Taye said. After that night, there were a few more teenage sexual encounters between them. They dated for about three months, but they decided they were much better off as friends and their relationship remained platonic ever since.

"Okay, maybe I took it that first time," Brie said "but that second time was all on you."

"Okay, I'll give you that," Taye agreed.

"So, I assume you're no longer a minute man?"

"Still got jokes, I see," Taye said while playfully nudging her in the side.

Taye looked at his best friend. The years had been good to her. She'd always been slim when they were in school, but she'd picked up a little weight- not enough to where she was out of shape, but she was fuller in the chest and hip area, he noticed. The cutoff denim shorts she wore showed her long, shapely legs, and her tank top provided him with an eyeful of her cleavage. He licked his lips as he imagined tracing her womanly mounds with his tongue.

Although they had been kids when they messed around, Brie's curvy body caused him to have some very adult thoughts. Those thoughts slipped out of his mouth before he had a chance to stop himself. "Wanna find out?"

She looked over and arched a perfectly waxed brow. "Find out what?"

"If I've improved since we were teenagers?"

"You know I'm gonna clown you if you haven't."

"Wouldn't be you if you didn't."

Brie knew she should have declined Taye's invite to a sexual rendezvous since he was married, but the torch she'd always secretly carried for him trumped logic at the moment. "Cool. My hotel is just down the street from here. Come on, you can follow me there."

Taye and Brie left the mall, and he followed her a few blocks down, to the Holiday Inn Express. He'd never cheated on Michelle, even though word on the street was she was screwing around behind his back. He'd never caught her, but if he ever did, he was gone.

During the drive over, Taye had been more than ready to relive that night in Brie's room; however, now that they were alone in her hotel room, he started feeling guilty about cheating on his wife.

"Well, come on, why are you standing all the way over there?" Brie asked.

Taye walked over and sat down beside her. He'd had a complete change of heart and no longer wanted to sleep with her. "I'm sorry, I can't do this, Brie."

"What...why?" she asked. "If you're worried about Michelle finding out..."

"No, that's not the reason. Listen, Brie, I've liked you ever since we were kids. You're smart, beautiful, funny. I've always wondered what things would have been like if I'd married you instead of Michelle."

"So, why didn't you ever say something?"

Taye shrugged. "I don't know. I guess I thought since we'd already tried the dating thing and it didn't last long, it wasn't meant to be. We each moved on and started dating other people, so I just left it alone. Trust me, I've never stopped thinking about you. I can be myself around you without the fighting or petty drama. When you leave and go back home, I don't want my memory of our time together to be reduced down to a quick roll in the sack."

Brie was disappointed that she wouldn't get to make love to Taye, even if just for one night; but the respect her showed for her was admirable. "You're such a gentleman, Taye. That's one of the things I love about you. I really wish you had let me know you felt about me the way I've always felt about you."

Taye looked at her surprisingly. Brie had never admitted her feelings for him before. "Wait, did you say love?"

"I've always been in love with you…but, you've always known that."

Now she tells me, he thought. "Actually, I didn't. Had I known, I never would have married Michelle."

"I tried to tell you not to marry her; you always were hard-headed."

Taye thought back to when he'd told Brie he was marrying Michelle and how she kept saying he deserved better. He'd always assumed it was because he'd told her that he thought Michelle had trapped him by getting pregnant. Brie was always protective of him. Now he understood why she'd been against it. She was the better.

Rather than do what they'd come to Brie's room to do, they sat in the middle of her queen-sized bed, and cuddled, while watching re-runs of Martin, until Taye decided he'd better go.

"I really enjoyed spending time with you, Brie," Taye said as she walked him to the door.

"Me, too. I'll tell mama I saw you, and that you'll try to stop by the house."

Taye resisted the urge to kiss her luscious lips. Instead, he gave her a gentle kiss on the forehead before he turned and walked away. He'd wanted to make love to her, but had he cheated, he would have regretted it forever. He walked to the elevator and pushed the down arrow. Another lady walked up beside him, also waiting to get on.

Inside the elevator, she pushed the second floor button, and he pressed the one for the lobby.

The elevator stopped at the second floor, and the woman walked off. As the door was closing, Taye heard a loud, familiar laugh. Just before the door closed, he stuck his hand out, pushed the door back open, and looked into the hallway, just in time to see Michelle and another man, engaged in a very steamy liplock. The man's hands roamed all over her body while he kissed her neck, and she giggled like a schoolgirl.

Tears stung Taye's eyes, and he balled his fists. His heartbeat increased, and invisible steam flew from his nostrils. The angry side of him said to get off the elevator and beat his wife's lover to a pulp. Instead, he calmed himself and simply stepped back into the elevator. He was angry and hurt, but at least now he knew the rumors about Michelle's cheating were true, which would make it that much more easier to leave her.

He pushed the button to his desired floor, thinking that as soon as Michelle got home, he was going to tell her it was over.

The elevator stopped, and he stepped off. He walked to Brie's room, and knocked. His heart was beating fast, and he felt nervous butterflies in his belly.

Brie opened the door. "Taye, did you forget something?" she asked with a confused look on her face.

"Yeah, this." Taye pulled Brie closer to him, lifted her chin up to him, and kissed her. Brie wrapped her arms around his neck, and welcomed his tongue into her mouth, doing a sensual slow dance with her own.

"What changed your mind?" she asked once they'd separated.

"Let's just say, I had a sudden revelation that put a lot of things in perspective for me on the elevator ride down to the lobby."

"So…are you coming in, or did you just come back to kiss me?"

Taye stepped inside the room, and kicked the door closed behind him. He was sure Michelle would make the divorce process difficult and ask for spousal and child support. He would gladly pay any amount of money to take care of his children…no judge would ever have to force him to do that. As much as Michelle liked to hang out and party, he could get full custody of the kids before she could.

However, he wouldn't be that guy- the guy who tried to take the kids away from their mother, just to spite her. He knew the kids needed their mom. He would always be in their lives, regardless of whether he was living in the same house with them, or not.

Tonight, though, he was going to find comfort in the arms of Brie, the woman he knew he should have been with all along. And he was going to enjoy it.

J.L. Sapphire is the pen name and alter-ego of Joyce L. Blaclock-Thomas. She is a self-published author and blogger. As an introvert, she spends her free time reading and losing herself in the lives of the characters she creates. Follow her on Facebook on www.facebook.com/jlsapphire/ and check out her blog www.jlsapphire.blogspot.com.

Online Secrets

By Venita Alderman Sadler

I sat up in our bed, leaned against the headboard, and looked at my husband sleeping peacefully, oblivious to the fact that I wanted to knock him upside his head. I knew he was cheating, I just couldn't prove it. Especially since he kept accusing me of being paranoid.

Maybe I was a bit paranoid; I'd already checked our cell phone logs, and I would've checked his texts if I had his passcode. The thing was, though, what would I have done if I found a strange number?

We have been married twenty-five years. So, would I end our marriage? After three children? After all my sacrifices including giving up my own dreams?

All of those questions made me think I was being paranoid. After all, why would he cheat? I cooked, cleaned, raised our children, and had been a faithful wife.

But something was going on. He'd been distant, attributing his lack of attentiveness to being tired. But tired from what? He'd been a senior partner at Coles, Gentry and Williams Law Firm for the last ten years. All he did was bark orders, and give advice. Of course he litigated cases, but he had an arsenal of law clerks to do the hard research.

So, why was he suddenly so tired?

It had started about three months ago, right after our youngest daughter, Casmine went off to college. We were now empty nesters and I'd expected a life of fun and freedom with my man. But it had been just the opposite. I saw less of him now than when our children were home.

I was so stuck in my thoughts that I hadn't noticed that Wade was awake and staring at me.

"Hey, Beautiful," he said.

Those simple two words took me back...thirty years...to the day we met...

Going to the N.C. State Fair county fair was one of my favorite things to do. And now, my sister, Jasmine and I had taken our ten-year-old cousin, Kali to a day of fun. We'd been at the fair for a couple of hours when I played the basketball game, trying to win a teddy bear, but I couldn't score. After three tries, I wanted to give up.

Then, I heard, "Hey, Beautiful, I'll win a bear for you if you promise to go on date with me."

I turned around and laid eyes on four fine men, all around my and Jasmine's age -- twenty, twenty-one. But I didn't know which one had spoken.

So I said, "I'm Tiffany." Then looking at each of them, I added, "Who's volunteering to win my cousin that Mini Mouse?"

A tall brother who had the same complexion as my favorite caramel candy, stepped forward. He extended his hand. "Hi, Tiffany, I'm Wade." He smiled, showing his deep dimples. I just stood there taking in all his features...the same way I was staring at him now.

"What's wrong?" Wade asked.

"I was just thinking how handsome you are, even when you're asleep." I smiled, not giving him any indication of what I'd been thinking.

He sat up and played with one of the curls hanging over my shoulder. "Do you know how much I love you?"

I sighed.

He rubbed the side of my face and when he gave me a deep kiss, chills went through my body. I stroked his muscular arms, marveling as I always did at how he was still in great shape for a fifty-one year old man.

I leaned back, thinking that I had to be crazy to think my husband was cheating. And then, he stopped. He pulled away, rolled over, and swung his legs over the bed.

"Where are you going?" I wondered if he could hear my disappointment.

"To work; I have a long day ahead of me." He added, "Can you make me some breakfast?"

"Sure," I said as if his explanation was okay with me.

As he shuffled into the bathroom, I shook my head. I would've been happy with just five minutes, but I couldn't get that. Still, I wrapped myself in my bathrobe and took the long walk to the stairs, passing by each of my three children's bedrooms. This hall used to be filled with music, laughter and chatter. I missed my girls far more than I expected.

Inside the kitchen, I went to work, and by the time Wade came downstairs, I had a warm bacon, eggs and cheese bagel sandwich waiting for him. He grabbed his cup of coffee first, took a sip, and then reached for the bagel.

"Thank you," he said, as he bit into the sandwich. "You're the best."

"What would you like for dinner?" I asked him because I couldn't think of anything else to say.

He shrugged. "It doesn't matter. What are your plans for today?"

Now, I shrugged. "I'll clean up, go to the gym, then swing by the grocery store." I paused. "Why, do you need me to do something?"

"No, just making conversation."

It had come to this. We didn't have anything of substance to say to one another. After a few silent minutes, Wade wiped his mouth with a napkin, gulped the last of his coffee, kissed me on the forehead and left. I watched from the living room window as he got in the car and backed out the driveway.

Something was wrong.

But I pushed my paranoia away and cleaned up the kitchen. Instead of thinking the worst, I wondered what I could do to get us back in romance mode.

After just a few seconds, it hit me.

There was no surprise in our marriage. We used to be spontaneous and that gave me an idea.

I pulled chicken from the freezer and took out the Pinot Noir to chill. As I gathered the ingredients to make parmesan potatoes and a salad, I thought about what I would wear. It had to be something fitted to remind him of what he'd seemed to have forgotten. Yes, he was in great shape, but so was I. I didn't work my butt off four days a week at the gym for him not to notice that even at fifty, I could fit into size eight jeans.

It wasn't only my shape; I kept my whole body tight. I had few wrinkles, no bags, all my teeth were real and white and my eyes had become a lighter green- grayish color as I got older. I'd kept my hair shoulder-length and healthy. There were a few gray strands peeking out, but overall, I was still good to look at. Today, I was going to remind Wade of that.

Once I had all the food together, I turned my attention to my clothes. It was chilly outside, so I picked my white leather jumpsuit with the jacket. Yes, it was after Labor Day, but I cared nothing about those old-fashioned rules.

I added my red pumps, grabbed a red silk scarf, and was ready to go. With the lunch in the back of the car, I headed out. It was about twenty minutes before noon and I'd get to his office right before he ordered lunch.

I parked in the deck, and then took the elevators to his office. But before I could walk up to the receptionist, I looked to the left and saw Charlotte, Wade's secretary rushing toward me.

"Hello, Mrs. Howell," she said with enthusiasm.

That made me frown. Charlotte had been Wade's secretary for almost five years. She knew my last name was Gentry. She grabbed my elbow, swung me around and practically dragged me toward the elevators.

"Charlotte, what in the world are you doing?" I demanded to know.

With one press of the button, the elevator doors opened and she shoved me inside.

"Charlotte!" I yelled.

"Please Mrs. Gentry," she whispered. "I'll explain when we can get somewhere safe."

She pressed the button for the third floor, and I stayed silent as we rode down. What was going on?

When the elevator stopped and we stepped off, there were a couple of Korean ladies standing at the elevator banks.

Charlotte spoke to them -- in Korean!

One of the ladies nodded, then Charlotte led me down a hallway. I wanted to ask Charlotte all kinds of questions, like where did she learn Korean? But I only had one that I wanted the answer to right now. "What is going on?" I asked the moment we stepped inside the conference room.

"Mrs. Gentry, please have a seat," she said with more patience than I had.

I sat down and crossed my arms.

Charlotte took a deep breath. "Before I begin, I want to ask if you could keep me out of this. I really like my job and want to keep it."

"Okay," I said, slowly. "What is it? Where is Wade?"

"He's not here. He actually told everyone that he was leaving to spend the rest of the day with you...in the hospital."

"What?" I said. "What hospital?"

She held up her hands. "I'm just putting it together in my head. Let me ask you this -- were you in a car accident a couple of months back?"

"No." I shook my head. "Why would you think that?"

"Well," she began. "Mr. Gentry told us you were in a bad accident."

"What?"

"I know. We were all worried and I wanted to come and see you, but Mr. Gentry said that you couldn't have visitors just yet."

I could not get this information to compute in my head.

She continued, "We've been thinking that he was spending his time out of the office in the hospital with you."

"I haven't been in the hospital."

"I know that now. I knew that as soon as I saw you get off the elevator, looking like you were about to go shopping. That's why I had to act fast. To protect you and Mr. Gentry. I didn't want anyone who knew you to see you. I didn't want you to have to answer questions if anyone you knew saw you."

I let the information settle in and it didn't take long to realize that my paranoia was more like intuition. I'd been right.

The emotions that flooded me left me confused, hurt -- and angry.

I'd been sitting quietly for too long because Charlotte said, "Mrs. Gentry, I'm so sorry."

I guessed Charlotte had come up with the same conclusion that I had.

I shook my head. "There's no need for you to be sorry. I thank you," I said, now thinking about how horrible it would have been if one of the partners had seen me. "Can you do me a favor?"

She nodded.

"I know your allegiance is to my husband, but don't tell him that you saw me today." And if she had any doubt, I added, "And, I'll keep your name out of it." I stood, and turned toward the door.

"Mrs. Gentry?"

My hand was on the doorknob when I turned back.

"What about this?" She pointed to the basket that I'd prepared for our romantic lunch.

"You keep it," I said. "You can eat it, give it away, or throw it away, I don't care." Then, I had a second thought and I grabbed the wine.

I don't know how, but I made it to the car without breaking down. I didn't release my tears until I got behind the wheel. Even though this is what I'd been imagining, I couldn't believe it.

What was I going to do?

I called the only person I could trust, my sister, Jasmine.

My plan had been to tell her the story in a calm manner, but the moment she picked up, I started crying again.

"Tiffany! What's wrong?"

I wasn't going to have her playing twenty questions, so I told her what I'd been suspecting and what I'd just found out.

"I'm on my way," she said.

"No, you don't have to come. It's too far."

"Are you kidding me? I'll be there in three hours."

My sister lived two hours away, in Petersburg Virginia, so she was giving herself an hour to throw some things into a bag. I was so grateful; I really needed her.

For a while, I drove around, not wanting to go home and sit and think. So I stayed in my car -- and sat and thought.

When I was just too tired to drive anymore, I went home, changed into a pair of jeans and a T-shirt and went to baking. That's right -- I started baking cookies. All kinds of cookies -- chocolate chip, oatmeal. Baking was the thing that got me through whenever I was stressed.

By the time Jasmine arrived, I had about five dozen cookies ready to go.

"Are you hungry?" I asked her.

When she nodded, I was sure that my sister expected one of my home cooked meals, probably a steak, cabbage and macaroni and cheese. But all I had for her was some wine...and those cookies.

So we sat in the dining room and talked and drank and ate all the cookies. I cried and Jasmine listened.

"Okay," Jasmine said a couple of hours into what was becoming my drunken stupor. "You're going to stay in the hotel with me tonight."

"You got a hotel? I thought you were staying here."

"Not after what you told me. Before I got on the road, I made a reservation at the Marriott. We'll stay there tonight and figure this out."

I went with my sister because I didn't want to face Wade. Not when I had no idea what I was going to do. So, we packed an overnight bag and I left Wade a note, telling him I was with Jasmine.

I know, that was thoughtful of me. But even though he didn't deserve my consideration, I didn't know any other way to be.

But if I thought we were going to sleep at the hotel, I was so wrong.

"What are you going to do?" Jasmine kept asking me.

"I don't know," was my constant answer. But then, I added, "I can't do anything until I have proof."

"Don't you think you have enough?" Before I could answer, she continued, "Remember what Grandmom used to say -- beating or cheating, you need to leave him."

"But I don't have anything really, and I'm not willing to throw away my marriage without proof and an explanation."

Jasmine got that, so we came up with a plan. "You need to see it for yourself, so that's what we'll do."

It was almost dawn by the time Jasmine came up with the whole plan and then we drifted to sleep. I had dreams of seeing Wade doing all kinds of things, with all kinds of women. By the time I woke up, my thoughts had turned from Wade's cheating, to my revenge. But all that was on my sister's mind was food.

"I came all the way here -- I need you to cook for me since you didn't last night."

"Well where am I supposed to do that?" I asked her, looking around the hotel room.

"Doesn't this hotel have a kitchen?"

I laughed because I knew my sister was only half-kidding. Yeah, she was trying to lighten the mood, but she was serious.

"If these people knew who they had staying at their hotel, they'd be asking you to make breakfast, too."

I shook my head. My sister sure knew how to make me smile, taking me back to my dream of being a chef, the dream I'd put on hold to focus on my husband and our family.

"If these people knew what I knew about you..." She laughed.

I shook my head, but quickly, my smile went away. It was the look on my face, that made my sister become serious, too.

"Are you ready?" she asked in a soft voice.

I nodded and we dressed in silence before we drove to Wade's office in Raleigh. We drove into the parking lot to make sure that Wade was even at work; because of what I learned yesterday, I wasn't taking anything for granted.

"Suppose he doesn't come out today?" I'd asked Jasmine that question last night, too.

"Didn't his secretary say he left every day?" Like last night, Jasmine kept on before I could answer. "And if we don't catch him today, we'll catch him tomorrow or the next day."

Finally, around eleven, Wade strutted from the elevator to his car. It was a good thing that Jasmine was driving because I could hardly breathe as she cranked up her rental and followed him.

"Where do you think he's going?" I asked.

My sister didn't take her eyes off of the road. "We'll soon find out."

Just about a mile from his job, Wade stopped his car in front of Sullivan's Steakhouse, a restaurant that he'd taken me to many times. As he tossed his keys to the valet, I asked, "Do you think he's meeting someone?"

Jasmine didn't answer me as she pulled over to the curb a few feet behind the valet stand. I was just about to jump out of the car when my sister said, "Wait."

"Wait for what?" I asked. "I want to see who he's having lunch with."

"He didn't go in yet." She motioned with her chin.

I turned back; it was a good thing that Jasmine was with me because I would have confronted Wade when all he was doing was standing in front of the restaurant, glancing at his watch.

"Sit back," my sister said. "It shouldn't be too long."

Before I could become even more nervous, a small red sports car pulled up. Wade rushed in front of the attendant, opened the door, and a very tall, very slender woman with a short boob eased out of the car. She leaned into my husband and the two shared a lingering kiss.

My heart stopped beating.

It didn't start again until Wade and his mistress walked into the restaurant.

Putting her hand over mine, my sister asked, "Are you okay?"

I nodded; I couldn't speak.

So my sister did all of the talking as we waited. I hardly heard a word that Jasmine said because my mind was inside that restaurant with Wade and that woman. How could he do this? My mind was still trying to find an answer when Wade and that trick finally emerged. We sat low in the car as Wade gave two tickets to the valet, then just a few minutes later, both cars were brought around.

The red sports car pulled off first, then Wade followed her and as Jasmine pulled in behind Wade, she asked me, "Are you sure you want to do this?"

"Yeah, I already know where they're going." I swallowed the lump in my throat. "I just want to know for sure."

We were so close to the downtown Marriott that Wade and his woman could have walked. But again, he gave his car to an attendant, and holding hands, they walked inside.

That's when I lost my cool. I wanted to bust into that hotel, find their room, ram through the door and beat the man that I'd married to a pulp. The only reason I didn't was because my sister kept me restrained in the car.

"It's not going to do anybody any good if you go in there and go ghetto."

So, I sat and sobbed. And then when they came out almost two hours later, I really sobbed. Because they came through the doors laughing and holding hands. Another woman was making him laugh now. Our marriage was over.

When they got into their cars, Jasmine asked, "What do you want me to do?"

"Follow her," I said. My mind was filled with all kinds of thoughts and questions. I wanted to find out more about this woman -- at least wanted her name.

I was shocked when she pulled into the parking lot for WakeMed hospital.

"Oh, my God. He's been saying he was spending time in the hospital. I guess he wasn't lying."

We pulled right behind the woman, but she didn't notice us. Jasmine turned off the ignition as the woman grabbed a white doctor's jacket from the trunk. When she walked toward the hospital, my sister jumped out. I followed her, but she waved me back.

"Let me handle this," she said.

I only got inside the car because I wouldn't have known what to do anyway if I came face-to-face with her. But after about fifteen minutes, I wished that I'd gone with Jasmine and when twenty minutes passed, I was ready to go in and find my sister. That was when Jasmine trotted out of the hospital.

At first, Jasmine didn't say anything. Just clicked the camera icon on her phone and turned it toward me. I watched the video begin...

"My name is Jennifer Hodges and I didn't have anything to do with illegal gambling. I had no idea that Shon Spencer was the head of a gambling ring."

I frowned. "Who's Shon Spencer?"

"Just watch," my sister said.

The video continued, "I just met him two months ago on the Sweet Sensations dating website." Then, her voice raised a few octaves. "I promise, I didn't know he was involved in illegal activity and I will not be seeing him again."

Then, while the camera was still on Jennifer, I heard Jasmine's voice.

"Okay, I believe you. But you understand this is an active investigation."

"Yes."

"And so you won't say anything about talking to me?"

"No, of course not. I don't plan on ever speaking to him again."

"That's good. Because he's a dangerous man. And he's been having you followed."

"Oh, God," Jennifer said with tears in her eyes. "Do you think I'm safe?"

"You are. We'll make sure of it."

"Thank you," Jennifer said before the screen went black.

I waited a few seconds before I said, "So...."

Jasmine jumped in, "Wade posed as some guy named Shon. He's been hanging out on a dating website."

"But she talked to you...."

"Because I told her I was a federal investigator."

"Wow!" I said, in awe of my sister as well as in shock about my husband.

I didn't say another word, not even when we returned to the hotel. All I did was cry. I have no idea how much time had passed when my sister handed me a glass. I took a sip of the wine and cried. Took another sip and cried some more.

While I drank and cried, my sister called a friend, setting up an appointment for me to speak to a divorce attorney. When she got off the phone, Jasmine sat across from me. "I know you're hurting, I know you're upset, but you're going to have to get it together because there is one more thing you have to do."

"W-w-what?" I stammered.

"I want you to get on the website and meet Wade or Shon or whatever his name is."

"W-w-what?"

She repeated her request.

"W-w-why?"

She explained, "You need to have all the proof and I read this scenario once in a novel."

"A novel?"

"Yeah, you can get some good ideas from novels. Anyway, this woman hooked up with her husband on this website to trap him. Only when they met, they got back together. But don't you do that," she warned. "Wade doesn't deserve you."

Spoken like a loving sister.

I was too hurt and drunk to think about my sister's plan. So, I just laid my head down and was so grateful for sleep.

When morning came, I wanted to roll over and close my eyes, but Jasmine had to return home to her husband and no matter what, I was going to have to face Wade one day.

"Don't let him know what you're going to do," Jasmine said as she dropped me off. "You always want to have the upper hand in situations like this."

Solemnly, I agreed, then hugged my sister before she drove away, leaving me feeling lonelier than I'd ever felt in my life. I stepped into our home, glad that Wade wouldn't be home for hours since now I knew he was doing all kinds of things during work and after work. Inside the kitchen, there were flowers on the kitchen counter.

I missed you, I can't wait for a home cooked meal.

I imagined all the things I could do to his home cooked meal, since he thought of me as no more than his personal chef. I tossed the card back onto the counter, then took my bag into our bedroom. I didn't even unpack before I stripped and climbed into the bathtub that I'd filled with very warm water and vanilla bath salts.

I soaked away the tension as the situation settled in my mind. My husband was having an affair. Probably multiple affairs. By the time I got out of the tub, I felt better. Not better in the sense that I felt good about Wade. But I'd accepted it and now I agreed with Jasmine. I needed to have the upper hand so that I could get whatever I wanted out of this marriage.

Inside the kitchen, I relaxed some more as I poured myself a glass of wine, then prepared chicken stir-fry and rice.

After fixing a hefty plate, I sat in front of my laptop and logged onto SweetSensations.com. I let the homepage just sit there for a while. Did I really want to do this? Didn't I already have enough on Wade?

But my sister was older. And wiser. So after taking many more sips of wine, I created my profile:

Name: Angela Cole.

Age: Thirty-ish.

I answered all the other questions, said that I worked in the pharmaceutical industry, and then I found a photo online of some random woman to use as my profile. The picture was cute enough, not as cute as me, though.

That thought made me sad. What was it about me that made Wade want to do this? I pushed that thought away along with the wine. This was not my fault, this was all on Wade.

I completed my profile, uploaded everything, and before I could stand up, a bing came over my laptop.

I had a hit already. My heart beat faster as I sat down. Was it Wade? No. Some guy named Brandon:

You're cute, want to go to dinner tonight?

Wow! He worked fast. But all I did was smile. I had no plans of responding.

But Brandon gave me the confidence, so I stayed on the site and searched through the photos. There were so many -- black, white, Asian, Hispanic. How was I going to find him?

Then, another bing.

I sighed. Maybe I shouldn't have put such a cute picture up there.

I opened the message and my jaw almost hit the floor.

Shon: Hello Angela, I'd like to get to know you better. ☺

I had to steady my fingers.

Hi Shon, how are you?

Shon: I'm good. What about you?

I'm just getting in from work.

That wasn't a complete lie. I'd just prepared a nice lunch and if I were doing what I wanted to do with my life, making lunch would've been working.

Shon: You're in the pharmaceutical business, I'm a lawyer. Are you originally from NC?

I told him that I was from Virginia and he told me that he wanted to show me around the area.

Really? That was fast. No wonder he was always tired with me.

But I just had to ask him the one question I wanted to know. I took a deep breath and typed:

Are you married?

His answer came back right away.

Shon: Divorced.

It was like a kick in the gut.

I guess I took too long to answer because he came back with:

Shon: Don't let the divorce scare you. My wife wasn't career-driven, she was lazy, didn't work. I had goals and she didn't.

If someone had been telling me this, I wouldn't have believed it. There was no way that Wade was saying this. I was only home because of him. I'd always had my dreams, but I'd put him and our daughters first. That's what I was supposed to do. That's what he told me he wanted.

Shon: What about you? Are you married?

No. I never found anyone worthy of me.

Then, I added:

Maybe that will be you. Let's pick this up later.

Shon: I can't wait to spend time with you. I'll be waiting.

I didn't bother to say goodbye, just slammed my laptop shut. Then, I called Jasmine and told her.

"Perfect," she said. "Next time print out the conversation and email it to me." She gave me more instructions and told me I had to keep up the charade for at least a week. I wasn't sure how I was supposed to do that, but since I wanted to nail Wade, I was going to do the best that I could.

After hanging up from Jasmine, I went about doing what I would normally do, focusing first on dinner. I thawed frozen Salmon, then barbecued it, serving it with a side of "dirty" rice. I kept the plate in the warmer until I heard Wade pull into the garage. By the time he got out of the car and came into the house, his plate was on the kitchen table and I was curled up on the sofa in the living room.

"Hey, Beautiful."

I took my eyes away from the television and looked up at him. Those two words used to melt my heart; now they felt like a stab in my heart.

I didn't respond, but he didn't seem to notice. I guess his mind was on other things, other women. He gave me a kiss on the cheek. "I only saw one plate on the table; you're not eating with me?"

I shook my head. "I ate earlier, I'm not hungry, I don't like Salmon."

He frowned a little, then chuckled as if he thought I was telling a joke. "Okay."

That was the end of it. I didn't have to put on much of an act after that because when he finished eating, he didn't even bother to come into the living room. He went to our bedroom and I fell asleep on the couch.

It was eleven when I woke up and went into our bedroom. Wade was sound asleep, but when I slid into the bed, he rolled over and wrapped his arms around me. He held me and I cried myself to sleep in his arms.

For the next few days, I kept our normal routine, cooking, keeping a clean house. Then, while Wade was at work, I handled my business the way Jasmine advised me. I gathered all of our information: bank records, life insurance policies, our wills and everything I could find on Wade's financial interest in his law firm.

Then, I met with the attorney, Phylicia Lynnwood, who had been working with my sister. The two had hired an investigator and when the attorney showed me all that they'd found, I was even more stunned.

"It seems that your husband has been quite busy on this website," Phylicia told me as I looked at the folder. "He's connected with at least ten women."

There were tears in my eyes when I looked up at her.

"Don't worry," she said with a forlorn look. "This is going to work in your favor. I'll have the divorce documents ready for you next week."

It was hard, but I continued to play my part. Right after finding out how many women my husband had been with, I had to go home and get back on the website. By the third day, Wade's conversation turned sexual. He talked about his secret fantasies and the things he wanted to do with me. It was all filthy, grimy, and turned me off. But, I didn't let him know. In fact, I turned it up, told him I couldn't wait to meet him and suggested our first meeting.

"Why don't we get together on Monday?" I asked.

"Monday? That's three days from now. I don't know if I can wait that long."

I convinced him that he could and told him where I wanted to meet for dinner.

"Just look for the lady in all black," I said, thinking that it would be perfect to mourn the loss of my marriage.

Then, I suffered through the weekend, listening to him calling me Beautiful, staying in the living room late into the night, not even wanting to get into the bed with him.

The only time I felt good during this time was when I stepped away from the computer and I began to dream. I began to think about all the years that had gone by and I wondered how I could make the future great for me.

By Monday morning, I had a mixture of excitement and anxiety, especially when Wade told me over breakfast that he was going out of town for the night.

"It's a business meeting that came up suddenly."

"Really... suddenly," I said, sipping my coffee. It was surprising. He was sure about me, or rather Angela. And he planned on spending the whole night out?

I didn't ask him questions the way I normally would and now, of course, I wondered how many of his business trips in the past had been rendezvous with women?

He kissed my cheek, and the moment his car rolled out of the garage, I called the locksmith and alarm company; things were changing right now.

It was hard to concentrate on everything I had to do and by noon, I wished that I had set up a lunch with Wade, rather than dinner. But I was able to go through the paperwork for my new business, then take my time getting ready for my date.

Though absolutely nothing was going to happen with me and Wade, I wanted him to see the best of what he was giving up. So, I wore a black form-fitting dress with five-inch heels. I curled my hair and let it hang loosely, before I applied some makeup and my favorite red lipstick.

Then, with the four portfolios in my hand, I got into my car. So many thoughts were going through my mind as I drove. This restaurant meant so much to me. It was truly the place of my new beginning.

I arrived a few minutes late -- on purpose -- I wanted Wade to be sitting down when I walked in. I had called ahead, giving the staff instructions on where I wanted Wade to be sitting, far enough away so that he would think I was Angela, at first.

My legs were shaking as I walked inside, greeting everyone. I was at the maitre-d's stand when Wade spotted me. I gave him a little wave. He stood, he smiled and I walked toward him. With each step that I took, his smile faded more and his head tilted as if he were trying to figure something out.

I was doing the total opposite, my smile got wider the closer I got to him. By the time I got to his table, his smile was frozen.

"Hi, honey, or should I call you Shon?"

"What are you doing here?" His voice shook.

My voice was surprisingly steady. "Sit down!"

He did as he was told, but started stumbling as soon as his butt hit the seat. "I...I can explain," he stuttered.

I held up my hand. "No need for you to explain, but let me introduce myself. My name is Angela for the night."

I could actually see his hands trembling. "Relax dear; I just have some things to give you," I said.

I handed him the first portfolio. Slowly, he opened it and took in the copies of our financials, his business financials, and our wills. Then, I gave him the others, and his eyes widened when he saw the transcripts from his sweetsensation account. The third portfolio contained a copy of the restraining order I filed. There was only one I held onto.

When I slipped the last folder to him, he hesitated and I wondered if he knew what was coming. But the way his eyes widened even more when he read the first page of the divorce petition let me know that I'd totally shocked him.

For a long time he sat there looking from the portfolios to me. Not one word escaped his lips. So since he had nothing to say it was time to end this.

But before I could say anything, the waitress brought the bottle of wine that he ordered.

"Oh," I said, holding up the bottle of 1999 Domaine de la Romanee Conti La Tache . "Expensive." Then to the waitress I said, "He'll be paying for it."

He waited until the waitress walked away before he sneered, "I'm not doing this with you. I'm not leaving my house; you're not getting a dime."

I raised my eyebrows, surprised at his reaction and mine. Did he really think he could fight me on this with the evidence I had? But what was better than that was that I was pleased with how calm I felt.

"Honey, you are already out my house, and as for that dime you were just talking about, I'm going to get a whole lot more. Something like half," I said. "Oh yeah, all your assets are frozen as of this afternoon and I informed your partners about your escapades with women."

His eyes got so wide I almost laughed.

"Why would you do that? What does the firm have to do with this?"

I shrugged. "I don't know. Maybe it's the company's money that you used." I paused as his eyes watered.

"How could you!" he yelled. Then, he looked around and lowered his voice. "I can't believe you."

I didn't care about the tears in his eyes. "You can't believe me?" I shook my head. "Get out of my restaurant right now before I have you thrown out."

"Excuse me?" His face was etched with confusion.

"Pay your wine bill and then get out of the restaurant I purchased last week with my non-career-driven behind." I waited just a moment before I stood and then walked out of the door.

And I have to say, I had never felt so good.

Venita Alderman Sadler is originally from New Jersey but currently lives in North Carolina with her family. Venita hold degrees in Education, Business Management and currently pursuing a Masters in Accounting. Venita is currently working on a trilogy titled A Family of Secrets. Venita is a member of Victorious Ladies Reading Book Club. To find out more about Venita and her upcoming projects, you can visit her website at www.venitaaldermansadler.com.

Her Sister's Boyfriend

By Tamika Tolbert Lucas

It was the perfect October night. The air was crisp and invigorating. A cool breeze brushed against Kendall's cheek. She was on top of the world, literally. Her boyfriend, Trent, had reserved the entire rooftop at Sky Lounge for a private candlelight dinner to celebrate her 25th birthday. Every day with Trent was like a fairytale. From the diamonds, cars, designer clothes, and exotic trips around the world, Kendall never knew what to expect.

Kendall reached for her strawberry mojito. She smiled as her eyes met Trent's. After two years, she was still amazed at how fine he was. His muscular build, dimpled chin, and green eyes made him popular among the ladies. Whenever he walked into the room it felt like Christmas.

"Happy Birthday," Trent said, placing a square shaped gift box in Kendall's hand.

This! Is! It! Trent is finally going to propose! Kendall's face lit up. She could hardly contain her excitement. Trent was one of the most eligible bachelors in Atlanta. He was a philanthropist and the son of technology entrepreneur and inventor, William Herring of Herring Electronics.

As Trent got down on both knees, Kendall's heartbeat accelerated. She tore into the box, but then as she opened it, her eyes narrowed to a squint. *Is this some sort of joke?* Kendall held up a tiny opal gold- plated ring that looked like it came out a Cracker Jack box.

Trent wrapped his arms around Kendall's knees and began to sob. "Baby, I'm broke."

Kendall batted her eyes, hoping to awaken from a dream. "What did you just say?"

"I'm broke. Herring Electronics filed bankruptcy yesterday. All of my family's assets have been seized," Trent said, weeping.

Kendall liked her men tall, rich, and handsome. And rich was non-negotiable. She watched emotionless as the man she once respected, roll into a ball like a wounded animal in an Armani suit. Instead of coming to Trent's aid, Kendall stood and made a beeline for the door.

"Kendall! Kendall! Wait!" Trent hurried behind her. Frustrated, Kendall came to a halt. "What is it, Trent?"

Trent sighed. "I need the keys to the Bentley."

Kendall wasn't sure she heard correctly. "You need the keys to my Bentley, the one you bought me for Christmas?"

"Well, I didn't exactly buy it. It was a lease."

For a few seconds, Kendall couldn't move. Her legs were stiff. She could not believe Trent wanted to return her white 2015 Bentley Continental GT. This was her dream car. *Was he crazy?* "No!" Kendall shrieked.

"But Kendall, I have to. You and I both could face criminal charges."

"Okay, fine." Kendall handed Trent the keys to her car. Kendall started removing her watch and earrings. "Do you want my Cartier watch and diamond earrings, too? These are real diamonds, right?"

"Of course they are. Kendall, why are you acting like this?" Trent said, baffled.

Kendall folded her arms. "You gave me a cheap ring and took away my dream car. How do you expect me to act?"

Trent turned to Kendall with tears in his eyes. "I just lost everything. I expect you to understand."

"I understand that you can no longer provide the kind of lifestyle I am accustomed to. Trent, I'm sorry. This isn't going to work. It's over."

"Are you serious? Are you really going to break up with me on the worst day of my life?"

"I'm sorry," Kendall said, turning her back on Trent and walking toward the door.

"But baby, wait a minute!" Trent shouted as Kendall continued to walk away. "How are you going to get home?"

"I'll take a cab."

***

Krista ogled her sister as if she were insane. "What did you just say?"

"I have a date with Young Boss," Kendall repeated.

"The rapper?" Krista said, cocking her head to the side.

"Yes. He's an actor, too. I met him a few days ago. He's taking me to his movie premiere at the Rialto," Kendall said, beaming.

Krista thought her sister was smoking something stronger than Newports to break up with Trent for the likes of that clown.

Young Boss, whose real name was Dexter Lewis, stood about 5'4. He was loud, obnoxious and disrespectful to women. He was in the news for assaulting his ex-girlfriend last year.

Besides having the same mile-high cheekbones and smooth chocolate skin, twin sisters Krista and Kendall were complete opposites.

Kendall never left the house without makeup and five-inch stilettos. From her Malaysian weave to her designer clothes, she always looked like she stepped off a runway, even if she was going to the grocery store. Kendall dabbled in modeling and acting, but ran away from gigs that required a real commitment. Besides making guest appearances on a few sitcoms, Kendall made her living dating rich men.

On the contrary, Krista's style was simple yet chic. She preferred natural hair styles as opposed to weaves. She seldom wore makeup and would probably break her neck in a pair of stilettos. Passionate about helping people, she was the director of Community Outreach at

Victory Tabernacle Church in Atlanta, Georgia. Krista was also studying pre-med at Emory University. Becoming a doctor was Krista's way of saving the world.

"I still can't believe you left Trent. You were so happy with him. What happened?"

"He's broke. I am Kendall James. I don't date broke men."

Krista shook her head. She couldn't believe what she was hearing. "But it's been three weeks. Don't you miss him at all?"

"Of course I do. I miss the weekends in Venice, the shopping sprees on Fifth Avenue and my Bentley, yes, most of all I miss my Bentley," Kendall dabbed the tears forming in the corners of her eyes.

"I think you should call him. He's going through a lot. I'm sure he could use a friend."

"Then you call him. I'm leaving." Kendall sashayed across the room in a black strapless Chanel dress. "How do I look?" It was as if thoughts of her date immediately dried her disappointment over the Bentley.

"Stunning as always," Krista replied.

Kendall smiled. "Thanks sis. Wish me luck."

***

Trent tossed Herring Electronics' Mid-Year Audit in the trash. He had been working nonstop to find ways to increase sales and reduce costs at his family's company. So far he had nothing.

Trent figured his father's attorneys found a way to keep the bankruptcy filing confidential because the company's stock price remained steady. But that wouldn't last much longer. Trent knew as soon as the shareholders found out, it would plummet.

Trent never cared about his family's business. He just showed up for the photo ops and cashed his checks. But now that his family's legacy was at stake, he had to do something.

Trent let out a hoarse cough. Not only was he fighting sleep deprivation and thoughts of Kendall, he had to contend with a bad cold. The timing couldn't be worse.

He got up to get a cup of water when he heard the doorbell ring. It was after 10 p.m. Trent had no idea who could be visiting him at this hour. Deep down, he hoped Kendall was coming over to apologize. He missed her something serious. He gulped the ice cold water down between coughs and headed to the door.

"Krista? What are you doing here?" Trent had just spoken to Krista a few hours ago. She called to see how he was doing. The two had become good friends throughout the years. Krista's church was a major benefactor of the Impact Center, Trent's nonprofit organization.

"You sounded really bad on the phone. I made you some chicken soup."

The aroma of the fresh herbs and spices hit Trent's nostrils. His stomach reminded him he hadn't eaten all day. "Thanks. Come in."

Trent poured himself a bowl of soup. He paused as the broth quieted his throat and cleared his nostrils.

"I don't mean to intrude. I just want to make sure you are taking care of yourself. How are you, really?" Krista asked, her eyes peering over her square framed glasses.

Trent summoned for Krista to sit next to him at the kitchen table. "You're not intruding at all. I appreciate your concern. I am stressed out. I haven't slept in weeks."

"I'm sorry," Krista said, her face etched with concern. "But corporate bankruptcy really isn't a big deal. Companies do it all of the time."

"I know. But I just don't understand. Herring Electronics was doing so well. Then all of a sudden we're in trouble. I just don't get it."

"There are a lot of things I don't understand. That's why I pray. That's exactly what you need to do."

Trent nodded. "I did."

"Then wait. That's what we call faith."

Trent's mouth formed a slow smile. In a manner of minutes, Krista had managed to calm him down and give him a sense of peace about his situation. "I guess you're right. I need to stop worrying so much and have faith."

Krista grinned. "I know I'm right."

"Would you like something to drink? I have tea." Trent pointed to the K cups next to the Keurig machine on the counter.

"No thanks."

Trent slurped the last spoonful of soup. "This soup is delicious. I'm already starting to feel better. You know you didn't have to do this."

"I know. I wanted to. I feel really bad for the way Kendall treated you. You are a good man, Trent Herring. You deserve better."

"Thanks, Krista. I appreciate you saying that. How are things with you?"

"Good. I've started planning the annual coat drive for the orphans at the Impact Center."

"That's awesome. I appreciate your dedication to the cause."

"No problem. I can't bear the thought of kids being cold in the winter."

Are you still dating Jeffrey?"

Krista's eyebrows knitted together. "Are you talking about my friend who usually comes with me to the Impact Center?"

"Yes. That's the one."

Krista snickered. "Jeffrey is my friend and he's gay. I haven't had a boyfriend in over three years."

Trent felt like a fool. He wanted to ask Krista out long before he met Kendall.

Krista was smart, authentic and had a heart of gold. Unlike the other women he had been with, Krista didn't have to be painted with makeup to be noticed. She was naturally beautiful. He always assumed the husky gentleman who accompanied her to the Impact Center was her beau. That's what he got for assuming.

Trent surveyed Krista's body while she wasn't looking. He was impressed. Krista was a perfect ten. She had curves for days, but she never flaunted them. Trent became even more intrigued. Now that he and Kendall were over, there was nothing keeping him from asking her on a date. Because of Krista's loyalty to her sister, Trent figured she would say no. So he had to be subtle.

Trent cleared his throat. "Krista, no one has ever done anything like this for me. When I get better, you have to let me cook dinner for you. I make a mean oven roasted chicken."

Krista raised her eyebrows. "You? Cooking? Oh, this I have to see."

***

Krista grabbed her M.A.C. makeup kit from inside her bathroom vanity. She buffed the foundation across her face and rolled her cardinal satin-colored lipstick over her lips. Krista only wore makeup for special occasions. Tonight was special.

Krista had butterflies in her stomach. Last night when Trent called and invited her to dinner, it sort of sounded like a date. She had no business being nervous. It was just dinner with a friend, nothing more. She would be lying if she didn't admit she wanted more.

Krista hadn't stopped thinking about Trent since she visited him last week. If she didn't know better she would have sworn they made a connection. But she was fooling herself.

What would a man like Trent Herring want with me?

Every woman she had ever seen him with looked like they just stepped off the cover of *Vogue* Magazine. Not to mention he had just broken up with her twin sister a month ago.

"Wow! You look great!" Kendall said in amazement, walking into the bathroom. "It's been a long time since I've seen you wear makeup. What's his name?"

"You don't know him," Krista said, clenching her jaw. Although Kendall never had true feelings for Trent, Krista wasn't sure how she would feel about them having dinner.

"He must be some special guy to get you to wear makeup."

Krista ignored Kendall's pestering and continued to primp. She pinned her two strand twists into a sexy updo. Krista smiled at the image she saw in the mirror. The navy halter dress and navy mid heel pumps complemented her shapely figure and long legs. Kendall was right. A "wow" was definitely in order. Krista hoped Trent would agree.

***

Kendall inched away from Young Boss's sleeping body. She hoped to catch a few minutes of sleep before he woke up. Young Boss had given her a closet full of the latest designer fashions, but she paid for them ten times over. Her vagina was sore and she was absolutely exhausted. At least four times a day, Young Boss had her body twisted like a pretzel for his sexual pleasure. On a few occasions, he invited his friends to participate.

Young Boss was abusive and Kendall couldn't even understand what he was saying most of the time. But that was the price she was willing to pay for a life of riches.

Young Boss rose out of the bed. He yawned, stretched, then said, "Bitch, get up and fix me some breakfast."

Kendall pulled the Versace sheets off her body and did what she was told. She'd found out the hard way that he did not play about his food.

It was times like these when Kendall thought about Trent. He was so good to her. He never barked orders or treated her like a sex slave. He was one of the good ones. Too bad he lost all of his money. If Kendall was one of those women who ate off the dollar menu, things may have worked out for them.

Kendall grabbed the bacon out of the refrigerator and turned on the television. When the bacon began to sizzle, Kendall grabbed the carton of eggs.

She saw a picture of Trent on the television so she turned up the volume.

"In Financial News, William Herring of Herring Electronics is retiring. His son, Trent Herring has been named his successor. Herring Electronics had a substantial gain of twenty percent this quarter since the emergence of their wristband computer."

Kendall dropped the carton of eggs on the floor. She turned off the stove and tiptoed to the bedroom to retrieve her overnight bag. Young Boss was in the shower; so she threw on a wrinkled t-shirt, a pair of spandex pants and headed out the back door.

If the news report was true, Trent wasn't broke after all. Kendall had to congratulate him and apologize for breaking up with him. She knew he still wanted her. The day after they split, he left at least five messages practically begging her to take him back.

***

Kendall waited anxiously outside her ex's front door. For a minute, she didn't think he would answer. When the door swung open, she was all set to get her flirt on, but the sight of her twin caused her mouth to fall open.

"Aww, hell naw! What are you doing here?" Kendall asked.

Krista was the last person she expected to see at Trent's condo at 8:45 a.m. She had on the same clothes she wore the night before, so Kendall knew that she had spent the night. "Answer me," Kendall shouted, when her sister just stood there looking stupid. "What are you doing here?"

Trent appeared in the doorway with a smirk on his face, wearing only a pair of Nike jogging pants.

"I invited her," he said. "What are you doing here?"

Kendall decided she would deal with her sister later. There had to be some explanation to this anyway. She stepped inside and wrapped her arms around Trent's neck.

"Hey, baby. I wanted to tell you how sorry I am for overreacting on the rooftop. I never should have left you." Kendall rubbed her hands all over Trent's chest. She could see out the corner her eye, the act made Krista cringe.

Trent grabbed Kendall's hand and gently pushed her away. "That was a month ago," he said. "You didn't return any of my calls, yet somehow you show up at my doorstep on a Saturday morning. You saw the news, didn't you?"

Kendall's fidgeting gave her away. She finally broke her silence. "You said you were broke."

Trent released an exasperated laugh. "My parents made the whole thing up. They knew you were with me for my money. They saw that we were getting too close, so my mom froze all of my assets and made up the bankruptcy story so I could see who you really were. It worked, too. I was furious with them. I couldn't believe the lengths my family went through to get you out of my life. But I should thank you. Because of you, I stepped up to the plate at my family's company and I found a remarkable woman in the process."

Trent wrapped his arms around Krista's waist. Kendall pushed between them, breaking their embrace.

"Krista, are you two sleeping together?"

"Kendall, it's not like that."

"I've only been gone a month. How can you do this to me? Trent and I are soul mates."

Krista heaved a sigh. "You said you never had feelings for Trent. But I do. You just want him because he's still rich. I'm sorry, but you're going to have to accept that Trent and I are together now. And no, we haven't slept together. We stayed up all night talking."

Kendall gasped in disbelief. But while she wanted to be furious with her sister, she loved her too much. And if she was being honest, everything Krista said was the truth. She never loved Trent. She only loved the things he gave her. If Krista truly cared for Trent, she wasn't going to stand in the way of her happiness. Kendall walked away, conceding defeat. Deep down, Kendall wanted to find love. More than that, she wanted to find love with a rich man. But while she waited for love, she would settle for a rich man.

Kendall glanced at her watch. "Shoot," she mumbled. She had to hurry back over to Young Boss's house. Maybe she still had time to make him breakfast.

Tamika Tolbert Lucas is a writer with a passion for contemporary fiction and poetry. She is currently working on her debut novel, A Change of Plans. She lives in the greater Atlanta area with her husband, Michael and their two girls.

Only BeWeave

By J. P. Miller

I was in my own world minding my own business when I first spotted him tucked away in a thicket of Georgia Live Oaks. I don't know what it was that alerted me to his presence, but with my peripheral vision, I caught a glimpse of his slanted eyes glaring at me. His head began to rise and my heart stopped! I knew immediately someone was about to be struck by his venomous tongue. From experience, I'd learned that this type of wrath was reserved for either the one at the beginning of the pack or for the one at the end of the pack. So I darted into the middle, cutting off the little old lady next to me to get out of striking range. *Don't judge me!*

I looked over my right shoulder just in time to see his massive shiny black body slither from his hiding place and onto the path I had just traveled. He quickly caught up to the pack. Every time I changed directions he would aggressively follow. Finally, he got behind me and threw on his blues. *The 'ol sneaky snake got me!*

I pulled to the side of the road and tried to mask my annoyance with one of my Sunday morning "turn to your neighbor" smiles, so when the *nice* officer approached my car I wouldn't draw any more attention to myself than necessary. But all I could think of was how quickly life could change. Last month this time, I would have been pissed at Officer Unfriendly for wasting my time.

My girls would have already arrived at Only BeWeave Hair Salon & Spa. Not only would I have missed out on some of the latest gossip, but it would have no doubt put me behind a couple of shampoos, a relaxer, and possibly a flat iron or two.

Officer Unfriendly tapped on my window with the butt of his

flashlight, shocking me back to my current situation. I ran my fingers over the door panel controls and pushed the button for my driver's side window. The smoke tinted window dropped slowly exposing my identity.

"Ma'am, I clocked you with my radar going 85 mph in a 55 mph zone. Is there a reason you're driving so fast this evening?"

I wanted to tell him that one month ago today I betrayed my friends. I wanted to tell him that I filled up the tank to my Porsche Panamera Turbo S with the intention of driving until I reached the edge of the earth. But I looked into his expressionless face and simply replied, "No."

"Then I'll need to see your driver's license and registration, Ma'am!"

I reached for the console to retrieve my registration when it dawned on me that 'Sampson,' my Glock 22 was laying there in wait. With images of Sandra Bland in my head from the recent coverage of her arrest and death all over CNN and FOX News, I knew that things could get ugly real fast if I did not address this. A sistah could never be too cautious with the police, even when driving a $200,000 luxury car and wearing a $400 Stephen Burrows original. *After all, this is north Georgia!*

"Officer, I need to inform you that I have a Concealed Carry Permit and my weapon is in the console along with my car registration. May I?" I asked.

I could see fear shroud his face. He immediately positioned his right hand on his service revolver and tightened his fingers around the handle. He was very deliberate with his next command.

"Ma'am! I'm gonna need you to place your left hand on the door where I can see it and move slowly with your right to retrieve your registration! No quick moves!"

I complied without hesitation.

Officer Unfriendly walked backward to his squad car to run my information. I couldn't help but wonder if he had friends. Did he ever laugh so hard with his friends that he forgot all of his cares?

The Ex Chronicles

My nerves were on edge, but all I could think about was my beauty shop girls and how much I already missed them. That was the joint on Friday nights. I didn't have that much fun when I was a student at Texas Southern University.

I had not heard of *Only BeWeave Salon & Spa* before I moved to Flowery Branch, Georgia and you can best believe I'll never forget it. I remembered my first visit to the salon just like it was yesterday. During my initial consultation, Perri Buckner, owner and CEO of *Only BeWeave,* explained to me that she had the best weave this side of the Mississippi.

"I don't use that synthetic hair!" she boasted while contorting her face like a skunk had just walked past us. "I only use the best! Human hair straight from Venezuela! My clients all know that they can have 'good hair' if they only be-weave! ALL things are possible if you only be-weave!"

AAAhhhh, hence the name of the salon! I didn't know what was funnier, the joke itself or seeing how Perri's play on words tickled her so.

The chime on the door indicating that someone entered the salon had caught my attention. I turned in time to see a lady who looked to be in her mid-fifties enter the building. When I tell you that she owned that moment, I mean she OWNED! THAT! MOMENT! All eyes were front and center as she made one of those Fashion Week runway turns on the balls of her feet allowing her gorgeous African Dashiki dress and hair to catch air. They both fell into place when she stopped and began to sashay down the catwalk of her mind toward the receptionist's desk.

"Hel-looooo everybody! Ce—leste is in the houuusssse!" she hissed not missing a beat on her stroll.

Celeste's grand entrance did not seem to faze Perri or the other clients in the shop. I, on the other hand, was still staring in amazement at her hair. Her asymmetric cut cupped her face and lined her neck perfectly.

Perri must have heard my thoughts. "That's the type of work that I do here at *Only BeWeave.* But that type of hair doesn't come cheap! A Venezuelan Weave can run anywhere between $500 to $2500

168

depending on the length you want."

My jaw dropped to my knees. It was now Perri's turn to laugh at me. She laughed so hard she could barely speak. But as quickly as the second hand moved from one point to the next, her laughter abruptly stopped.

"If you need something cheaper, you can go to Blunt Cutz in Gainesville off of E. E. Butler." With all the laughter cleared from the air, it was confirmation to me that Perri was all about that cash money!

Now it was my turn to flex. "Did you see what I drove up in?" I said taking a sting out of Perri's attempted insult. "Do I look like a Blunt Cutz type of gurl to you? Put me on your books for Friday night! Yvette at 6:30!" I said matter of fact like, turned and walked out of the salon knowing that all eyes were on me and feeling that I had one upped Perri. *After all, it's not costing me a penny! My job is paying for this weave!*

I arrived for my first appointment around 6:15 p.m. When I walked in, Perri was putting the finishing touches on a weave set and there were two ladies under the dryer. One of the shampoo girls summonsed me to come to the back. There she began to cut out my old weave.

There were two ladies under the dryer. One was fast asleep. Most of her updo was bobbing out from under the dryer. Her mouth was wide open. At times her chin touched her chest, steadying her head momentarily. Someone had written a note and placed it on her rising chest that read:

Order what you want! Dinner is on me tonight! ~Stacie~

From that day forward I called her Sleepy Stacie!

I looked at the lady seated next to Sleepy Stacie and saw a reflection of myself. The shock of seeing my likeness sent a jolt through me and I quickly looked away. I glanced out of the corner of my eyes to get a better view.

Her face was so familiar to me. Her skin color matched mine. Her slanted eyes match my slanted eyes. It was as if I were looking at myself in the mirror. She removed a flask from her taupe Christopher Augmon handbag, twisted off the top and took a sip, all the while looking at me.

"Hi, I'm Bobette," she said from across the room.

"Hi, I'm Yvette."

"Yvette, do you have relatives that live in Newtown?"

"No, I'm not from here."

Bobette turned to Perri. "Don't she look like my daddy's people over in Newtown to you, Perri?" By that time everyone in the salon was checking me out. One by one, they commented on how much Bobette and I resembled each other.

"Y'all just might have the same daddy!" I heard someone say from the back. We both chuckled at that.

"See, you two even laugh alike!"

To tell the truth, I did feel a kindred spirit to Bobette. From that day forward I called her Sistah.

Without warning, the draft from a passing tractor trailer truck sucked my car in and released it so abruptly it startled me. I reached for Sampson, ready to stand my ground on any would be intruder, until I looked in my rear view mirror and saw Officer Unfriendly sitting in his squad car. I had lost track of time in my thoughts.

How long does it take to write a speeding ticket? I could feel the perspiration forming on my nose. Suddenly, I regretted ever coming back to Flowery Branch.

In the background, I heard Lil Wayne and Bobby V on V-103 making a siren sound singing *"Mrs. Officer"* and it took me back to my Academy days. I spent twenty-weeks of intense training and several undercover assignments too numerous to count to get to where I am today. Nothing I experienced at Hogan's Alley could have prepared me for this. Hogan's Alley was the mock town at the Academy where different scenarios were played out so trainees would know how to react to real world situations.

It was early spring 2010 when the Bureau got a tip from an anonymous caller alerting us to an operation in Flowery Branch, Georgia that we dubbed the Venezuelan Hacking Crime.

It was reported that the shop's owner was involved in a black market scheme to get human hair to the States to sell in her salon *Only BeWeave*. It was alleged that the suspect, Perri Buckner had connections to the Spanish speaking city of Maracaibo, Venezuela where thugs would walk up to unsuspecting victims and hack off their hair. They would sell the human hair to Perri and she in turn used it to quench the thirst of her aristocratic clientele of Flowery Branch. From the Falcon football wife who wanted to look like Beyonce to the new executive diversity hires at Wrigley's who wanted Yolanda Adams hair, Perri gave them all what they desired. The price or how she acquired the human hair was of no importance.

I started the assignment like any other mission. I learned my pseudo job as Senior Vice President, Fan Experience for the Altanta Falcons. I studied maps and became familiar with the lay of the land. I knew the demographics of the area well before stepping foot on north Georgia soil.

By the time I made initial contact with Perri Buckner, I had already visited Flowery Branch twice and lived there for two weeks. I liked the feel of the area. It welcomed me to a life of small town living and stability that I inwardly longed for. Perhaps that was my first breach.

Despite policy, the beauty shop girls became my best friends. They were the sisters I never had, the mother I lost at age eight, and the grandmother who poured her everything into me. The Sunday we all attended Friends and Family Day at Mount Calvary was an epiphany moment for me. I even warmed up to Ivy that day. *What black mother would name their child Ivy?*

Ivy had a standing appointment at *Only BeWeave* for every Friday at 8:30pm. By day she was the Chancellor of Brenau University, but on Friday nights, she would leave her sophistication at the door and immediately begin cleaning and sweeping. Doing anything to tidy up the place before the distributers delivered product. To me it was a nervous energy. *But why?*

On Friends and Family Sunday, I saw a different side of Ivy. It was a comical yet sensuous side I had never seen before. She leaped from the pew and began to clap and sway with the 40+ member adult all male choir at the first note from the organ. Her worry free curls trickled down her back like waterfalls and her sleeveless Athena Bride dress swayed rhythmically with her movement. She turned to me and gave me a 'gurl you better get up and work this room look.' I stood and began to clap, sway and lip-sync all the while laughing inside at my friend's attempt to market herself in church. *Of all places!* This would be the beginning of my bond with Ivy.

It took a year for me to collect the information that ultimately led to the breakthrough in the Venezuelan Hacking Crime. During that time there came a point when I was so torn that I could not sleep. I reeked of betrayal.

It was easy for me to disconnect when I went undercover as a poacher baiting Elk in Wyoming. Or the time I was a male transitioning to a female to bring down a doctor performing surgeries without a license. I never expected this assignment to be any different.

I went in. Did my job. *A damn good job I might add!* Delivered the bad guy to the Bureau and kept it moving.

Only BeWeave was different. I saw myself in the ladies at every stage of life. The college students with their low maintenance weaves filled with hope and dreams reminded me of my youth. The young mothers with their let-me-get-out-the-house-quick braided weaves made me question my own maternal skills. The been-there-and-now-doing-me baby boomers dared anyone to question their sassy style or their weave. I so admired them that at times, I craved for a peep into my own future.

I had stayed to myself growing up in Brownsville, Texas with my grandmother. The beauty shop girls became the girlfriends I never had. Over the course of the year we were there for each other through life celebrations, sickness and death, and looked forward to our Friday night social. We did other things like dinner and a movie, ballroom dancing, horseback riding, Falcon games, and of course, church.

"Special Agent Suzanne Godlock?"

I heard my government name for the first time in a year. The bright flashing lights and loud sirens surrounding me confirmed what I already knew. Tears began to well in my eyes and roll over my cheeks. I could see Officer Unfriendly standing outside my car with his weapon drawn.

"Yes," I surrendered.

"I have been ordered to escort you to the Atlanta Office of the FBI."

I complied. *What else could I do? I had run long enough!*

Running was never the plan. Being AWOL was very uncharacteristic of me and the level of professionalism I brought to the agency. In my mind, all I needed was one day to see them, talk with them, explain myself and that would make things right again. The thought of losing the beauty shop girls shook me to my core. Guess you could say I snapped.

Officer Unfriendly called down the other officers surrounding my car. Maybe it was my imagination, but I thought that I saw a hint of empathy in his once emotionless face.

"Do you know why I have to take you in?" he asked as he helped me out of the car.

"Yes, I violated Bureau policy by getting too involved with my case. I did not report for my debrief last month. I am within fifty miles of my last undercover assignment." Even I hadn't realized how deep I was in this until I verbalized it.

I saw Officer Not So Unfriendly's Adam's apple scale up and then back down his neck slowly as he swallowed hard and inhaled before placing me in his unit.

Our drive through Flowery Branch was surreal. Each crossroad we passed reminded me of the beauty shop girls in some way. A restaurant we ordered food from on a Friday night at the salon. The corner where Sistah and I tried to help Sleepy Stacie change a flat tire. The upscale boutique Celeste turned me on to. Even the sweet smell of gum when we passed Wrigley's on I-985 heading south had evoked a memory of its own. I sat staring out the window watching all of my memories pass me by. I was sharing the same Flowery Branch sky with my friends for the last time! *All but Perri at least.*

The last time I saw the beauty shop girls was at Only BeWeave the Friday before the bust. Finally after filling her voicemail up every day with messages, I heard from Sistah. She was the one who told me that the judge handed down a ten-year prison sentence to Perri and seven years each to her two accomplices "Slim" and his sidekick

"Hombrecito." For her involvement, Ivy ended up testifying against them all and was able to walk away without any charges.

Silence between me and Sistah was unheard of. So when the first lull occurred during our call, I knew things between us had changed. It was my guess Sistah concluded I was a "snitch" and no longer worthy to be called friend.

"We've been through so much. Do you think that the beauty shop girls can bounce back from this?" I had asked Sistah.

Silence.

"Do you at least think everyone can forgive me?"

More silence.

Just as I was about to end the call, I heard Sistah's faint voice singing as the beauty shop girls had done so many times before.

"Onn-llly be-weeavvee! Onn-llyy be-weeaavvee! All things are pos-si-ble if you only be-weave!"

The call disconnected and my heart sank. I'd lost my sister girls, my friends, and my job. Never before had I felt so scared and alone.

J.P. Miller is the author and creator of the Sally B. Lipscomb Archangel Series for youth. Each novel in the series has the potential to tear down cultural barriers and encourage acceptance through diversity by sharing a message of spirituality, family, and African American History. Check J.P. out on her website at http://www.lipscombarchangelseries.com/index.html.

I Will Love You So For Always

By Dwon D. Moss

Today was pure foolery at work. I worked as a supervisor at a large insurance company and I swear I worked with pettiness every day.

"Miss Turner, can you do this, can you do that…" That was a staple in my daily conversations. I was forever putting out fires among grown folk, but right now, I was sitting in my comfortable recliner, right leg hanging over the right arm of the chair and my left leg hanging over the left side of the chair, greased up with some SassiSoul Lavender Body slush, trying to soothe this fire in between my legs.

I was what some people call full figured fine, but these thighs felt far from fine. I called myself hitting the pavement for a little running, make that jogging, in an effort to relieve my stress from today's shenanigans. I don't know what was worse - the feeling of not being able to catch my breath from exercising or the chaffing from jogging in these thin leggings. I deserved a break, so I planned to just sit here for a while, nibble on a few Oreo Thins and a Diet Dr. Pepper and visualize the reunion of me and my first love, Khalid Davis, tomorrow night at our high school alumni ball.

***

"You're the perfect one, for you and me forever will be, and I will love you so, for always…"

That Atlantic Starr song boomed in the background as I daydreamed about the past. Me and my girl, Kelly, decided to throw a Blue Lights in the basement party at her house since her parents were out of town. It was our last year in high school and we wanted this to be a party to remember. Blue, yellow and red lights took turns lighting up the room. Every ten minutes, the fog machine would spray vanilla scented mist out into the crowd.

And of course, our deejay did not disappoint. We danced like Kid and Play to "Ain't Gonna Hurt Nobody," jammed to "Teddy's Jam," and shook our butts to "Doing Da' Butt." Then, the deejay slowed it down. Atlantic Starr started singing about love and Khalid, Kelly's twin brother, came up behind me, turned me to face him, pulled me close, placed both hands in the back pockets of my Jordache jeans and we slow dragged in slow motion. I held my arms around his neck tightly to let him know I would never let him go.

***

That was ninth grade. Khalid and I were inseparable after that. He was my best friend; we did everything and nothing together. My favorite moments with him were in the recliner I'm in now. He would sit behind me and we would take turns reading poems we had written for each other. It was an innocent love, pure love, and my parents loved and trusted him.

The closer graduation came, the more concerned I got about how the separation between Khalid and I would affect our relationship. He would be leaving for the Marine Corps in four weeks and I would be leaving for college in two weeks. I still remember the advice my Mom gave.

"Tangie, you two have been together your entire high school years. Right now, your lives are about to take off in different directions. Take this time to grow up, live life. Allow him to do the same and if this love is meant to be, it will be. Souls always find the way back to their mates."

I heard her, but I wasn't trying to listen.

***

The deejay played the song I had requested by New Edition.
"I'm lost in love, I can't live without you. I'm lost in love, all my dreams around you.
And I'm lost in love, and it's true. I can't live without you. Oh no…"

That song was my cue to take Khalid to his bedroom and prove to him that I was forever his lady. Besides, I had heard all about boyfriends leaving for the military, traveling the world, falling in love, and leaving their first love behind. I was about to make sure that would never happen.

Inside his bedroom, I closed the door behind us, reached on my tippy toes to give my man a long and slow kiss; he tasted like Grape Now and Laters. I removed my clothes, slid under the bedding and invited him under the covers and into my soul. No one told me it would hurt and they certainly didn't tell me that it would be over so quickly. It didn't matter, though. In fact, the only thing that mattered was that we had exchanged something special, something that could never be returned. Our virginity.

***

Graduation was bittersweet. It was time to say goodbye to old friends and start living like grownups in a grown up world with grown up temptations. Leaving Khalid behind was difficult. I thought my heart would literally break. I remember holding him so tight before getting into my parents' loaded down car. I gave him a kiss and whispered, "I will love you so, for always."

Weeks and months passed by. I settled in at Florida A and M University, in Tallahassee, Florida. Khalid went off to boot camp at MCRD Parris Island, SC before going to MOS school at Camp LeJeune in Jacksonville, NC and adjusting to his first duty station at Camp Kinser, in Okinawa, Japan. I could count on nightly calls from Khalid. Our conversations were long and filled with excitement as we talked about our days and the things we were experiencing. We planned our future together. We ended each call with plans to see each other soon. We both held the phones long after saying goodbye. I could still hear him breathing and I'm sure he heard me breathing until we fell asleep.

We kept in touch regularly for a year and a half. College was harder than high school and I was trying to get acclimated to the college life while missing Khalid and my family. Because we were several thousand miles away, we only saw each other twice a year and our conversations were not constant because he was being deployed quite often. We did our best by writing letters to each other weekly. I cried every time I opened his letters. He'd always write the most heartfelt poetry to me. His letters were truly love on paper. And the dog tags he sent me burned love in my skin and I swore, I would never take them off.

But then it happened…life. I was loving the college life. I mastered the art of getting my school work done as soon as I could so that I could catch every party thrown by a fraternity and sorority. I was partying with the upper classmen, became an expert on drinking but never got use to the hangovers. The college boys were fine. They had the body of Greek gods and had silver tongues. I eventually knew what the hype about sex was.

The more I enjoyed college life, the more I forgot about my old life, including Khalid. He still sent letters every week and I never had time to read them. The dog tags that I swore I would wear forever were replaced by a silver thin necklace, with a heart, with my new boyfriend's name in it.

I graduated from college a few years later and thankfully graduated from my college boyfriend. I was really ready to spread my wings and fly and I felt as though moving back to Atlanta wouldn't be the best thing for me. Besides, Khalid wasn't there and if he was, I'm sure he would never forgive me for the way I abandoned him and his heart.

***

"We're gonna have a good day, and ain't nobody gotta cry today, Cause ain't nobody gonna die today, save that drama for another day heeeey…" by Nappy

Roots and Greg Street blared from my alarm clock and jolted me from my deep sleep. I got out of bed, said my prayer of thanksgiving, and slowly climbed into my tub of hot water, scented with Lavender Essential Oil. I needed everything I could get to calm my nerves. I was excited about seeing Khalid, but worried about his reaction to seeing me after twenty-seven years. It seemed as though I had waited forever to tell Khalid I was sorry and ask for his forgiveness. I would explain to him that it was a huge mistake and I never married because no one loved me like he did and I could never love anyone the way that I loved him.

***

"Hello, it's me. I was wondering if after all these years you'd like to meet. To go over everything. They say that time's supposed to heal ya, but I ain't done much healing..."

Adele's song played in my head as I walked toward the hotel, feeling confident about the way I looked. I may have been full figured but my stomach was snatched to the gods, I had a butt like Serena and Tina Turner legs. Baaaby, I was looking fierce. But my nerves were shot. Thank God for those two Ativans I took a few minutes ago.

As soon as I stepped into the ballroom, a flood of emotions took over. I felt like I was that twelfth grader at the prom about to slow drag with the love of my life. I mixed and mingled, but my mind was far from the conversations and my eyes were scanning the room for Khalid. That's when I heard our song, *"Girl, you are to me, all that a woman should be and I dedicate my life to you always."* My heart fluttered fast because it was at that moment, I knew I would see Khalid. He had to be the one to request the song.

I turned around and that's when I saw him. But I frowned at the faces around him. Why is he in the middle of THEM? He didn't belong with that crowd. I walked slowly toward him. I heard people calling my name, felt them pulling at my arms, but I kept walking. I only had eyes for my forever love.

I stood before him; tears falling on my cheeks. I took my fingers and traced his thick eyebrows. I touched the tip of his nose, smiled at his contagious smile, and leaned over for a kiss, wondering if he still tasted like Grape Now and Laters. As my lips touched him, reality slapped me like a jilted lover. The cold panel of glass that held his photo wouldn't allow us to reconnect.

This can't be.

I was shaking as I picked up the orange and black frame, then slowly placed his picture back on the table among the rest of the classmates who had passed on to eternity. I realized I was dizzy from holding my breath. My body involuntarily trembled. I was numb but somehow felt the tears slowly streaming from my eyes. My knees buckled under the pressure of my heavy heart. I slowly exhaled. I felt a hand on my shoulder and heard a familiar voice.

"Hey Tee."

I turned around and fell into the comforting embrace of my high school best friend, Kelly. The look of anguish on her face matched mine.

"He. . .He's gone?" was all I managed to say.

"I tried to call you several times to let you know Khalid was killed last month. I know we fell out of touch after high school but I thought that you may have wanted to attend his funeral. You never returned my calls."

I dropped my head. "I know. I got your messages. I was too embarrassed to call back because of the way I treated your brother and for not keeping in contact with you after we graduated. My intentions were to come here and apologize to you both. Now I'll never have the chance to tell him goodbye and that I loved him," I said between sobs.

"Let's take a walk outside and find the bench where we used to sit and gossip back in the day." She grabbed my hand and we walked outside.

It was a good thing that she was holding my hand, because if not, I wouldn't have made it. The thoughts in my head were paralyzing as she explained what happened.

"We got the call late at night. We knew something was wrong when we saw his commanding officer on the doorstep. Mama didn't even want to open the door. The officer said Khalid was walking back from chow when he stepped on a land mine that blew up. The only grace that I could see in this was that the officer told us Khalid was never aware of what happened. One instant – he was here, the next, he was gone," she said.

I was blinded by my gushing tears. My tears had not stopped, not even once we reached the bench, but Kelly sat down and I followed. "I have something for you." She paused for a moment as if she was giving me a moment to gather myself.

I tried, but it wasn't working. She continued, "Khalid lived life to the fullest. You know that he traveled to every place imaginable, buying souvenirs for you from everywhere he lived. He always said that he had to save a little piece of his travels for you so that you'd feel like you'd spent all these years experiencing life with him." She blinked as if now, she were fighting her own tears. Still, she spoke, "When I was finally able to go through his personal property, I found a box addressed to you." She reached into her purse. "I was hoping to see you here to give it to you."

I slowly took the box, opened it, stared at the contents and then, blacked out.

***

The radio softly played Cyndi Lauper. "If you're lost you can look and you will find me. Time after time. If you fall, I will catch you, I'll be waiting. Time after time."

It had been four days and I finally had the strength to get out of bed. I opened the curtains to let some sunshine in, then walked slowly to my living room. I climbed into my recliner, our recliner, and picked up the box that I had set last night on the side table.

My finger slowly traced the beautiful pattern on the cover before I removed the top. Once again, I stared at the most beautiful ring I'd ever laid eyes on.

For the first time, I lifted it from the box and slid the tear-drop shaped diamond onto my finger. Just like I knew it would, it fit perfectly.

My glance returned to the box and my eyes stayed there, staring at the paper that had been folded several times. I inhaled, then released a long breath, sure that I had enough emotional courage now. I unfolded the letter until the eight-by-ten piece of paper was laying flat in my lap. And then, I read.

Dear Tangie,

I'm praying all is well with you. It's strange not having you in my life experiencing the world with me. But then again, you were and will always be my world.

I know it's strange that I'm writing you again, after all of these years. I'd stopped all those years ago when you stopped returning my letters, but I never stopped loving you. No matter how many years have passed, no matter how many women I've met, you have been in my heart. It may sound strange, but every day I breathe you, smell you, touch you, taste you and hear your voice.

I'll be retiring soon and that's why I'm reaching out now. As Marvin and Tammy sang, "Ain't no mountain high, ain't no valley low, ain't no river wide enough to keep me from getting to you, babe."

I'm ending this letter, praying that you will receive it and hoping that we'll be able to see each other when I get home. There is something that I want to give you and a question that I want to ask you.

Until then, just know that I will love you so, for ALWAYS,
Khalid

Huge teardrops smeared the letters on my love note. I closed my eyes and felt him with my heart. I placed the letter in the box, looked at the ring on my finger and whispered, "I will love you so, for always."

Dwon D. Moss is an upcoming Author, Entrepreneur, Marine Corps Veteran and Motivational Speaker. She launched her Soy Bath and Beauty line, SassiSoul Soy, in the mid 2000's. In addition to SassiSoul Soy, she has her own Greeting card line, SassiSentiments. She writes personalized cards that caters to the recipients and his/her unique situation.

Tangled Webs

By Elle Jaye

Aaron stretched his legs out and leaned back on the sofa. He was tired of having this same argument and the only way to permanently end it was to tell Laila the truth, a truth he had not spoken to anyone other than Michol.

"Hellooooooooo, are you even listening to me? Before I started dating you I always did things with my family. You act like you can't co-exist with them. Tell me what's really going on. Do you know how frustrating it is to have to keep my worlds separate? I mean, I love you and everything, but I feel like you're trying to isolate me." Before she could finish her statement, Laila realized that she had said too much.

As she pondered her next move, Aaron sat up straight and met her eyes with a gaze so sad, so intense that she just knew he was about to reject her and her feelings.

He sighed heavily before he spoke. "Laila..."

"Aaron, you don't have to respond to that. I really don't know where it came from. I'm sorry, I... I didn't mean to put you in an awkward position."

"Let me speak, Laila. We will address your..." he stumbled over the words he should use, "we're going to talk about your statement, but not right now." He noticed her eyes looking everywhere but at him. He wanted to ease her pain and comfort her, but first he had to tell her the truth.

"Look at me." She continued to look everywhere else. He got up and walked over to her, cupped her face in his hands, and gently turned her head so that she had no choice but to look at him. "Laila, look at me when I'm talking to you."

"What is there to say?" she asked. "I love you. You don't love me. I get it now. This is why you don't want to be around my family. You don't want anything serious with me. I get it." she said to him with as much strength as she could muster.

"Don't speak for me. You don't know how I feel unless I tell you." He let go of her face and grabbed her hand, gently lifting her from her seat. "Come here," he demanded as he pulled her toward the couch where he previously sat.

He sat down and urged her to do the same. "I will address your statement, but there is something else more pressing that we need to discuss right now. I don't have a problem with your family, well not all of your family."

Laila frowned. "What has anyone in my family ever done to you? Who do you have a problem with?"

He laid his head back and answered, "Michol. my problem is with Michol."

At the mention of her cousin's name, Laila made a move to stand, but she was pulled back down by Aaron. She then positioned her body on the couch so that her back was against the arm and she could look directly in Aaron's face. "What the hell happened between the two of you? She's not exactly fond of you either."

Not wanting to give Laila the opportunity to get off the couch, Aaron draped his hand over her and gently cuffed her thigh "It's complicated, we..." he paused trying to lessen the shock with carefully chosen words, "we..."

"Yooouuuuuu what?" Laila asked, growing frustrated and fearing the worst at the same time. "What did you do? Oh my God! Are you...did something intimate happen between you and my cousin?"

"What do you mean 'intimate'?"

Pulling away from Aaron, Laila asked, "I mean, are you screwing my cousin?" Aaron's evasive answer had propelled Laila's suspicions into overdrive and as her apprehensions increased, her patience lessened.

"Am I currently? No. Have I ever? Yes."

"What kind of answer is that?" she asked as she jumped up from the couch. "You slept with my cousin? When? Where? How long?"

Aaron dragged both hands down his face. "Sit down and let me explain." The bass in his voice caught Laila's attention, but it did nothing to assuage her anger.

"I'd rather stand because I'm about five minutes away from walking out the door. What can you possibly say to justify keeping me in the dark for the past three months? "

"Laila, I know you're frustrated and I'm gonna let you have that, but in order for us to get anything resolved you're going to have to let me explain. I promise you this not as bad you're making it out to be. Let me make things clear for you so that we can go back to the statement you made earlier. Can you do that for me, Lai? Will you let me explain?"

Laila just stared at Aaron. She was going to let him speak but if she didn't like what she heard, she couldn't guarantee that things were going to play out the way Aaron hoped they would. "I'm waiting."

"Could you at least sit down? This is difficult enough."

Laila sat down only because she wanted to hear what he had to say. "Look I'm not interested in the play-by-play details. When did this happen?"

Aaron ignored Laila in order to regain control of the conversation. He began, "Michol and I dated at one time."

"When? I never heard of you until Bryce introduced us to each other. Does he know about you and Michol? Is sharing women something you two do?"

"Laila. Let. Me. Speak. For the last time, let me speak," he shouted.

Aaron's tone got Laila's attention. It was not threatening, but she thought it was in her best interest to be quiet for the moment. He started speaking again, this time in a more agreeable tone.

"Michol and I kicked it before Bryce, before you. It was a long time ago. When I met her and Bryce for dinner it was the first time I'd seen her in years. Bryce doesn't know any of this because Michol asked me to let it go. She said that it was so long ago that it didn't matter."

She tried to hold it in, but she failed. "I've known every guy Michol has dated since she was sixteen. You've never been mentioned."

"That's because I knew Michol before she was sixteen."

"Well, when the hell did you meet her because I know for a fact she dated Aiden's father for two years before she moved here, so if the two of you dated it had to be when she was really young and if that's the case, I'm really pissed that you interrupted my day with some puppy love B.S."

"Laila," he barked, "shut up and let me speak. I started dating Michol when she was fourteen. We were together for two years and I'm pretty sure that Aiden is my son."

Laila was about to go off on Aaron for raising his voice at her, but his last words stopped her. Instead of speaking, her mouth just hung open. There was an awkward silence that felt like it lasted for hours, but in reality it didn't last a full minute.

"Now, Laila, now is not the time to get quiet. What are you thinking?"

"I'm thinking that I'm sleeping with my cousin's baby daddy. Ain't this about a...I can't...this is too much."

"Look, in your defense, you didn't know. Don't be so hard on yourself."

Laila laughed. It wasn't a laugh that indicated she was amused; it was laugh that dripped with incredulity. "Let's be clear, I don't need you to defend me. You're absolutely right. I..." she said while pointing to herself, "didn't know anything. You, on the other hand, knew everything. So worry about defending yourself. I'm good."

"So you don't want to talk about this?"

"Talking isn't going to make you any less trifling, so with that being said, I'm out." She raised herself up from the couch, grabbed her purse and attempted to walk out the door.

Aaron grabbed her arm and pulled her back. "I wasn't done talking."

"Too bad because I was done listening." She tried to jerk her arm away, but he pulled her back.

"I know you're hurt and you need time to process this. I told you because I didn't want to keep anything from you."

"You're about three months too late, buddy." She succeeded in getting away from him and made her way to the door. She opened it, but quickly closed it again when she realized she had more to say. "Yes, Aaron, I'm hurt, but not for the reasons you think. There is nothing I can do about your past with my cousin, but I could have decided not to get involved. You took that choice away from me. Yes, the act happened before me, but the deception is new and that's what hurts. You and my cousin allowed me to get close to you knowing full well that once the truth came out, I would look dumb as hell. But that thought never occurred to either of you, so no, I don't have anything else to say to you. I'm done."

Aaron tried to maintain eye contact with Laila because he knew that as a man that was the least he could do, but he felt like less of a man looking into her pain filled eyes. "Laila, I don't want to be done. I...we...what about what you said earlier."

"Forget what I said earlier." She walked out and left him alone with his thoughts.

***

Once she was securely in her car, Laila took several deep breaths. After each one she exhaled slowly in an attempt to expel the hurt feelings and the shock. When she felt a tear forming in the corner of her eye, she scrunched up her face in order to keep it from falling. She would not cry. Not this time.

As soon as she put the car in reverse, her cell phone rang. She prayed it wasn't Aaron. She wasn't sure if she could continue to reject him if he persisted. Unfortunately, it was Aaron's partner in crime, Michol.

"Yeah," Laila answered dryly.

"Hello to you, too. I guess judging by your dry attitude you will not be joining the rest of us for dinner. Aaron really has you on lock, huh? I mean, what is so great about him that you ditch your family every chance you get?"

"I don't know, Michol. You tell me."

"What?"

"You tell me what's so great about him. He was your man first, right?"

Laila heard a loud sigh before an overly dramatic Michol exclaimed, "I can't believe he told you. Why did he tell you? Do you see, Laila? Do you see what kind of man you're dealing with? He has only been in this city for four months and he's already causing problems for me."

"Seriously, Michol, you're the victim? Is that what you're saying to me?"

"That is exactly what I'm..."

Laila ended the call before Michol could finish her sentence. Aaron had invaded her world and became everything she never knew she needed and craved, but he was also her cousin's ex-boyfriend and the father of her teenage son. She now shared an ex-love with the person she shared so many other sacred things with. She wanted so badly to erase the events of that night, but it was pointless. Family didn't go behind family and family definitely didn't go against family, so the decision was made for her. She had to let Aaron go and that thought brought her to cry the tears that she swore would not fall. As she pulled out of Aaron's driveway, Laila reasoned that she should not be the only one crying tears that night. She drove until she found a place to stop and park. She picked up her cell phone that she had tossed onto the passenger's seat when she hung up on Michol, and for one fleeting moment, guilt permeated her thoughts. What she was about to do could cause major damage to her cousin's current relationship, but she swept that thought aside when she thought of the damage that had been done to her own. She scrolled through her contacts until she landed on Bryce's name. Without hesitation she pressed the call button.

***

Michol calmed down once she heard the sound of the garage opening. Bryce was home. Her peace was home. She knew she would eventually have to deal with the can of worms opened by her ex, but for the moment she just wanted to seek solace in the arms of the man she had loved for almost a decade.

She went to embrace him as soon as he walked through the door. Michol was so consumed with her own thoughts that she initially failed to notice the sadness in Bryce's eyes. His failure to respond to her embrace is what caused Michol to finally step back and study Bryce's face. The look in his eyes told Michol that he knew about Aaron, but she refused to be the first to speak on the subject.

Bryce watched Michol. He saw the uncertainty in her eyes, and he waited for her to say something. After a few minutes of silence, it was evident to Bryce that Michol wasn't going to confront the issue and he knew that if given the opportunity, she would ignore it all together. This revelation fueled his emotions and he began to speak. "I'm a simple man, Mich. I love you, I provide for you. I treat your son as if he's mine. I've done everything I could have possibly done to make you feel secure in this relationship. I only asked one thing of you. Do you remember what that was?"

He was only met with Michol's silence and her pensive gaze.

He nodded as if he was agreeing to something only he could hear. "Of course you don't remember. Because if you remembered you would have made sure that you carried out the one thing I ever asked you to do for me. I asked that you always be honest with me, but you have been lying to me since day one."

Michol shook her head while tears fell. "Bryce, I..."

"No, Michol. You don't get to speak. You had ten years to speak, Mich. Ten. You chose to say nothing, so I think you should do what you've been doing. Don't say anything."

"I haven't been lying to you the whole time. I didn't know that I would ever see him again. When he showed up here, I panicked."

"Why? Why panic about a relationship that happened sixteen years ago?" He prodded her with his eyes. "I'm waiting. Nobody cares what you did when you were sixteen, Mich. So why keep this a secret?"

"I..."

"Math was never my strong suit, but I can handle the simple stuff. You know, stuff like basic arithmetic. I know the answer to this next question, but I'm going to give you an opportunity to come clean. Is Aaron Aiden's father?"

"Aiden's father is the man that has been raising him for the last ten years. You are his father, Bryce."

"Wrong answer, Michol." For the first time since encountering Michol that evening, Bryce stopped talking. He looked at his love of ten years and dropped his head. "We have a lot of things to discuss Mich, but it's not going to happen tonight."

She breathed a sigh of relief believing that his willingness to discuss anything was a sign that their relationship would remain intact. "So we're gonna work through this, right?"

Bryce closed his eyes and rubbed his hand over his face as if he were trying to erase the thoughts going through his mind. "Michol, when I walked through the door, I thought that we could work this out. I thought that you would confront the issue and we would work through it. When I realized you weren't going to say anything, I realized I can't trust you. On our first date, you told me that Aiden's father was dead. From day one, you have been lying to me and you're still doing it. If I hadn't said anything, you would still be acting like everything is good with us. To answer your question, no we are not going to work this out. What we will do is sit down and untangle all these webs that we've created. We are tied together because of the house, the cars, the accounts, and most importantly, Aiden. These are the things we have to discuss. Our joke of a relationship is over." Bryce walked out of the house in a defeated manner, and Michol cringed with every step he took. She stood in her kitchen for a while allowing the events of the evening to register. Her sadness gave way to anger in a matter of minutes. She walked to her bedroom to retrieve her cell phone and once she crossed the threshold, Bryce's scent overwhelmed her. She never realized how strong his presence was until she was forced to deal with his absence. Shaking off the sadness once again, she grabbed her cell phone and called Aaron. Bryce had programmed the number into her phone shortly after Aaron moved to town.

"What?" He answered with an apparent attitude.

"Why couldn't you keep your mouth shut?"

"I warned you, Michol. When I realized Aiden was my son, I told you to fix this."

"You didn't give me time."

"You had weeks to do this. It's bad enough that I don't have a relationship with my son because of you, but now my relationship with Laila is over because of you."

"Your relationship with Laila should have never happened in the first place. I told you to stay away from my cousin. By the way, if your relationship is over it's because you caused it by being impatient. I told you I would handle it, but no, you had to tell Laila and Bryce."

"What are you talking about? I didn't say anything to Bryce."

"Cut the games, Aaron. If you didn't say anything, who did?" In her mind, Michol answered the question before she even got it out of her mouth. "I can't believe Laila would do this."

Aaron sighed. "I can believe it. She was pretty hurt when she left my house."

"She didn't have to be. If you had just…"

"If I had just what, Michol? Look, the damage has been done and the reality of the situation is that both of our relationships are in a dangerous place. The only thing that will help is time. Right now, I'm more concerned with getting to know my son, so you need to tell me how you're going to fix this."

"First of all, your little fling with my cousin does not compare to the years that I have put in with Bryce. Our situations are not the same. You waltzed into town and managed to hurt me, Bryce, and Laila. Do you really think I'm going to give you an opportunity to the same thing to Aiden?"

Aaron had had enough of Michol's theatrics. "You really are delusional Michol. This is all because of you and your lies and your secrets. I have run out of patience and I'm not about to play games with you. I want to build a relationship with my son. If you are determined to keep him away from me then I have to tell you that things are going to get a hell of a lot worse for you before they get better or did you forget about this law degree that I hold?"

"I don't care how many degrees you hold. You are still the same thug who left me alone and pregnant when I was 15…"

"I didn't leave you alone. I was arrested and you left. If you had stuck around long enough, you would've known that those charges were dropped. You left me, Michol. You are NOT the victim in any of this."

"Aaron, I can't do this with you right now. My world has been turned upside down over the last few months and I need to regroup. I will talk to you another day, and you can miss me with the threats. Your introduction to Aiden will be on my terms and you can bet your degree on that." She abruptly ended the call and laid on her bed. As much as she wanted to close her eyes, she knew that sleep would have to wait. She needed to get a handle on the events of the day. Laila was the least of her worries, not because she didn't love her cousin but because she knew that in time, they would get back to a good place. They always did. She wasn't even mad that Laila told Bryce. She wasn't sure how Aiden would react to the news of Aaron being his father, but she was confident that her bond with her son was strong enough to weather hurricane Aaron. Her final thoughts before she allowed sleep to overtake her were of Bryce. She had never seen him as hurt or angry as he had been that evening, but she had hope that ten years of love would be enough to repair their relationship. It was this hope that sustained her at that moment and allowed her to rest. She missed dinner with her family that night, but it was probably for the best because Laila, refusing to wallow in self-pity, made sure she was in attendance and she also made sure she gave her family an earful regarding Michol. Aaron had been right about one thing. Things for Michol would definitely get worse before they got any better.

Elle Jaye currently resides in Savannah, Georgia with her two children. She is currently working on both her first full length novel and her Master's thesis which she hopes to finish by year's end. Follow her @ElleDJaye on Twitter.

Memory Full

By Princis Lewis

It rained throughout the day and into the late evening hours, but Erika didn't mind. . . especially after the crazy disastrous blind date she'd had last night.

The date started off great, and they'd actually had a good time dancing and drinking at Le Bain, one of New York City's most popular night clubs.

But the minute they left the club, they bumped right into a guy in skinny jeans, a skin-tight tank top, and hair that was laid better than her Keratin-treated shoulder length mane. Erika could tell by the way he was glaring at her date, things were about to get ugly.

"So you ignore all my calls to hang out with this yellow bitch?" the man yelled, his neck wiggling as he jabbed a finger in her direction.

"I-I. . . I don't even know this chick," her date had stammered.

Erika was about to give him the serious side eye, but the skinny jeans guy hauled off and slapped her date in the face and that was Erika's cue. She made her way through the gathering crowd – many of whom already had their cell phones out to capture the fight - hailed a cab, and headed home.

Whatever happened to good ol' fashion honesty? Erika thought as she leaned back in the cab. All she wanted was a man of her own. A feat, that at thirty-four, she'd yet to accomplish.

Erika made her way back to the high-rise she shared with her best friend, Paige. As a real estate broker, Erika was always coming across good real estate deals. When she'd found this place, she just had to have it. The only problem was she couldn't afford it alone. That's why she'd been ecstatic when Paige had stepped in.

Paige and Erika met three years earlier at a social gathering with mutual friends. They immediately connected and their friendship grew from casual to hanging out at the clubs, to traveling and having fun. Paige had become the sister she never had.

While Erika was still loving for love, Paige had found it. Her fiancé, Evan Pryce, had it all – a successful career as an attorney, an esteemed family (his father was a superior court judge) and looks that would put Idris Elba to shame.

With just a touch of envy, Erika found herself gravitating toward Paige's never-ending love story... how Evan first met Paige at a business meeting and how he couldn't take his eyes off her. How he later asked her out for drinks, and then again the following week for dinner. He made her feel special. After they started dating, they occasionally traveled to exotic islands for the weekends. They'd visited Jamaica and Aruba. Evan flew her to Toronto for lunch at Kayoto's and Chicago for soul food at Pearl's. Paige once shared with Erika that she loved Evan more than she ever thought she could love "another" man.

Through the years, Paige had introduced Erika to nine different men who were either too short, too chubby, no money, too many kids, didn't want kids, too serious, not serious enough, and so on. The closest Erika came to finding a man she enjoyed was the young trumpet player she met at the jazz club. He soon became her "boy toy" and the one she called when she desired the company of a man. He could've been around longer if she hadn't found out about his wife. But letting him go hadn't been hard. She just refused his calls and moved on.

So, until her Prince Charming came along, Erika buried herself in her work and tried desperately not to make loneliness her new friend.

The real estate business was booming around New York City and

Erika was in the midst of it. She enjoyed her job, and when one of her regular clients called her to check out commercial property in Twin Hooks, New York, she reluctantly agreed to meet him. Even though Twin Hooks wasn't in the nicest area, she couldn't turn down a possible deal.

As Erika was hailing a cab, her phone rang.

"Hey girl!" she said, answering when she saw Paige's name. "How's the beaches in Florida? Ooops! I meant to say, how's the conference going?"

Evan had whisked Paige away to some legal conference in Florida, but Erika knew her friend was spending all her time at the beach.

Paige laughed. "Gurrrrrl, it's so damn hot down here, I'm ready for some New York weather like yesterday! What are you doing?"

"About to go meet a client in Twin Hooks," Erika said, climbing into the cab and giving the driver the address.

"You'd better be careful in the Hook, and don't hang around too long," Paige warned.

"Believe me! I won't! In and out, that's my plan!" she responded. "Besides, I have a date tonight with a cup of hot chocolate, some fuzzy bedroom slippers, and the Sparkle movie with Whitney Houston, and you know I can't be late!" They both laughed, and then Paige continued.

"Oh! But if you happen to pass Chip's Diner on the corner of 21st and Pine, stop in to get a cheesesteak with chili! You won't be sorry! Okay, girl, we'll talk soon, Evan and I are on our way back to the beach. Ooops! I meant to say, we're on our way back to the conference!" They laughed again and hung up.

Erika grinned at the thought of Paige's suggestion, because she most likely wouldn't be stopping at any diners in Twin Hooks.

After the meeting, her client was so impressed with the property, he told her to expect his bid in the morning. To celebrate, Erika told the cab driver to drop her off at the corner of 21st and Pine so she could treat herself to a delicious cheesesteak smothered with chili since she was starving after all.

It only took one bite for Erika to know that Paige was right. The cheesesteak was delicious. Erika sat alone, devouring her meal. She was so focused on her sandwich that she almost didn't notice the tall, handsome man in the business suit standing at the counter admiring her.

Embarrassed at how she must've looked, she quickly dabbed her mouth with a napkin, pretended to check a text on her phone, and prayed he hadn't seen her gorging... but he did. As if she wasn't totally embarrassed by her eating display, she felt mortified when he started walking toward her.

"Your man won't be mad if I sit with you, will he?" he asked in the sexiest, smoothest voice she'd ever heard.

Dabbing her mouth once more, she struggled to find her words. "He won't. . . I mean, no man. I'm here by myself," she said. "I usually don't eat alone. . . so. . . and I usually don't eat this fast. . . because I usually don't eat alone. . . and I'm. . . .I'm babbling, aren't I?"

"It's the cutest babbling I've ever seen." The handsome man smiled and extended his hand. "Hi, I'm Christopher. And can I say that you are much too beautiful to be dining alone."

Erika blushed. She was flattered that he would even refer to the way she was just eating as 'dining.'

"You mind?" he asked, pointing to the seat across from her.

"No, please," she said, dabbing at her mouth again just to make sure she didn't look like some kind of pig.

He slid into the seat and she had to catch herself from slipping into a trance from the scent of his mesmerizing cologne. His light brown eyes were just one of his many gorgeous features. He had almond colored skin and short wavy light brown hair.

"Pretty good, huh?" she asked after he took a bite of his cheesesteak.

He closed his eyes, savoring the sandwich as he nodded.

"So, you live around here?" Erika asked.

He finished chewing, licked the sauce from his lips then said, "I'm in town on business from California. I used to come here as a kid, and whenever I'm here, I try to stop by for a cheesesteak. What about you?"

Surprised at how comfortable she felt with a stranger, Erika began to tell Christopher all about herself.

She'd learned from their conversation that he was thirty-three, single, and made a decent living in Los Angeles as a popular nightclub owner.

Erika and Christopher didn't realize how long they'd been talking until the waitress mean mugged them.

"Ummm, I think she's mad that we're taking up booth space for so long," Erika said.

Christopher smiled, then much to the relief of the waitress pulled out a twenty dollar bill for the tip.

"Let's get out of here."

Erika didn't want the evening to end. "Oh, okay," she said, slowly gathering her things.

Just as they reached the door, he said, "Do you want to catch a cab to the city?"

"I'd love that," she replied.

From the bright flickering city lights, the soft jazz sounds oozing from the cab's radio, and the arousing fragrance of a sexy man, Erika found herself traveling down that 'what if' road. *You just met this man,* she reminded herself.

It didn't feel that way, though.

In the city, they'd walked around with her arm snuggled comfortably inside his, before stopping at a hookah lounge for drinks. They talked for a few more hours and then ended the night in his hotel room. Everything in Erika's mind said no, but her body didn't bother listening.

That night, Christopher did things to her that she only read about in romance novels or watched online! And by the time they were done, her body and her mind knew that this man was the one.

The next morning, Christopher flew back to California. He and Erika kept in touch regularly. Mostly, Erika would fly out to California to see him. They texted all day, every day and soon found themselves in a committed relationship. For seven months, they dated. At her age, Erika was ready to settle down and have the family she always wanted.

***

This was going to be the perfect Valentine's Day, Paige thought to herself. She was finally going to meet Erika's new man. They were doing a double date for dinner and Paige couldn't wait to meet the man who had brought such joy to her best friend.

The evening started like any other. Paige and Evan arrived at the restaurant early and were engaged in their own romantic conversation when Evan looked up to see Erika and Christopher walking toward their table.

"Well, you must be Christopher." Evan stood to greet Christopher with a handshake.

Paige turned to greet them as well, but when she laid eyes on them, her heart felt like it had stopped. She had trouble catching her breath as she forced herself to smile. When she looked into Christopher's eyes, the silent stare he gave her back told her immediately what he was thinking. But before he could say anything, Paige held out her hand toward him.

"Nice to finally meet you, Christopher," she said.

Obviously shocked at her greeting, he reluctantly went along. Throughout dinner, Paige did everything she could to avoid eye contact with Christopher. When she laughed, he laughed. When she spoke, he couldn't stop staring at her mouth. Paige tried her best to lessen the fixation he had on her every word and prayed no one else had noticed the odd behavior between them. They hadn't.

Somehow, she got through dinner, but when the four of them hugged before ending the evening, that all-to-familiar tingle returned with a vengeance and she remembered what she desperately pretended to forget.

Sitting in her office early the next morning, Paige was staring out the window, thinking about the previous night. She and Christopher had not seen or spoken to each other in over ten years.

Why had he stayed away so long? she wondered.

Her thoughts were interrupted when her secretary buzzed in.

"Hi, Paige. You have a call on line three. He says his name is Christopher."

Paige's heart raced. She almost said to take a message, but she couldn't do it. She couldn't turn her back on him when he was her lover, and she couldn't do it now.

"Hello Dre," she said.

"Hey baby girl... I missed you."

The sound of his voice brought nostalgic tears to her eyes. "I – I'm sorry I couldn't let them know we had history," she told him.

"It's okay, I understand. I didn't think I'd ever see you again... you are as beautiful as I remembered," he said.

"You still got your charm I see, still smooth with the tongue." Paige smiled, relaxing. As the Director of Marketing, she pretty much did as she pleased. She closed her office door, lounged back in her seat, and indulged in conversation and laughter for well over an hour.

For the next few weeks, they continued to secretly text and call each other when on one was around. By this time, Paige was in a whirlwind of confusion. The undying love she had for Christopher was reborn... the passion for him, rekindled.

"I want you back," he'd told her during an earlier conversation.

Those words had caused her to toss and turn all night. What happened to the woman who was so self-assured and confident about what she wanted? Evan meant the world to her and could give her the life she always dreamed of, but Christopher was the once love of her life, a love she thought was long gone. Yet, the thought of breaking Evan's heart was unbearable, because he loved her with the deepest kind of love. And of course, there was Erika.

That's why she made the decision to tell him their secret conversations had to stop.

When she finally got up the nerve, her heart sank as she found the words to end what never should have started.

"Fine," he said firmly. "If that's what you want, I'm out!"

His words hurt like open heart surgery with no painkillers. Yes, she was the one ending it, but how could he give up just like that?

Over the next few days, Paige buried herself in her work, trying to put Christopher out of her mind. It hadn't been working. She missed reading his naughty late night text messages and the calls that made her blush during the day and giggle late at night the few times she lay alone in bed.

"You will never believe what I'm about to tell you!" Erika screamed when Paige walked in the door the next evening after a long day at the office. "Christopher asked me to move to California with him and I said 'yes'! I'll be leaving in two weeks!"

Paige was having trouble finding the right words to say. She tried to appear excited for her friend, but inside her heart was shattered. The thought of him with Erika living happily ever after was torture.

Two agonizing weeks passed, and Erika was returning to New York to gather the last of her belongings before leaving for good. Paige had planned to take Erika out for drinks that evening as she'd summoned up all her strength and convinced herself that it was for the best.

"You have to let him go," she mumbled to herself right before opening the front door and stepping inside the apartment.

The door had barely closed when Erika came stomping toward her.

"When were you going to tell me?" she yelled. "When were you going to tell me that Christopher was your ex-husband and that he was still in love with you?"

"I-I. . ." Paige couldn't get her words to form.

"You should've been the one to tell me, not him," Erika cried. "Why would you do that to me?"

"I'm so sorry, Erika," Paige said. "I didn't know how to tell you."

"So you were just going to let me run off with a man who was in love with my so-called best friend?"

"I-I. . ."

"Do you love him?" Erika snapped.

"It's not like that," Paige stammered.

"Like what?" Erika snapped again.

In tears, Paige tried to explain her love for Christopher and why she had buried those painful memories.

"You can't have them both, Paige!" Erika yelled, then took a deep breath. "I've waited all my life for a man like Christopher and I'm not losing him now. I'd rather have a man who quietly longs for another woman, than to be alone one more day. He has assured me that he will never act on his feelings for you. Now I need to know... will you do the same?"

"Christopher is your ex-husband?"

Both Erika and Paige turned to see Evan standing in the doorway. The hurt look on his face was heartbreaking.

Erika didn't bother saying a word as she picked up her suitcase, brushed past Evan, and walked out the door.

"Is it true?" Evan asked, his eyes filled with tears. He continued when she didn't respond, "And he still loves you?"

Paige took his hands. "I wanted to tell you, but I didn't know how."

"Why did you lie?"

The pain in his voice told her she owed him an explanation. She took a deep breath.

"Back in the day, Christopher was known as Dre and we were very much in love. We grew up in the streets and used our hustling skills to make money. I was his ride-or-die and helped him with his drug business. At twenty-one, I got pregnant and we got married. Dre didn't want me to be alone. Just before our baby was born, we were both arrested on drug charges. Dre took the rap for me and was sentenced to two years. Some thugs broke into our place looking for money and drugs, but found me instead. I couldn't tell them what I didn't know, so they beat me and left me for dead.

When I lost my son, a part of me died, too. With no Dre, no baby, and nowhere to live, I left Twin Hooks vowing never to return. After the darkness was over, I promised myself never to talk about it or think about it ever again... until now."

She stopped there, telling him as much as he "needed" to know.

When Paige finished, Evan was still sitting there. Although the pain remained etched across his face.

"Please forgive me." When he didn't respond, she added. "Please don't leave me."

He released a heavy sigh, then didn't say a word as he took her into his arms.

***

Eight weeks later and the void in Paige's heart was nowhere near healing. But she knew she had to move on. She was moving in with Evan and she owed it to him to give him her all.

It was a perfect day for packing as the rain continued to fall. Paige had just taped up one of the last boxes for the movers when the doorbell rang. She swung the door open, thinking it was the movers. She was stunned to see Christopher.

"Can I come in?" he asked.

Paige reluctantly stepped aside and let him in.

"What are you doing here, Dre? You shouldn't be here."

Christopher closed the door behind him. "I had to come. I can't get you off my mind, I'm crazy without you baby girl. I left Erika at home in California and jumped on a plane. I came to get closure."

He placed his hands on both sides of her face and pulled her close to him and said, "I've loved you all my life and I never stopped loving you. I can go on without you, if that's what you really want, but I need to know, do you still love me?"

Paige tried to back away, but he wouldn't let her go.

"I need to know do you still love me?" he asked again.

"Why?" she replied. "All I have left from us are memories and my memory of you is full. I have no more room for new memories. What difference would it make if I still loved you?"

Christopher whispered in her ear, "It makes a difference to me. Do you still love me?" He lifted her chin and looked her directly in the eyes. "Do. You. Still. Love. Me?"

Paige could no longer hold back. "Yes! Yes Dre, I still love you!"

She burst into tears. He held her close, their bodies as one, hearts pounding, and burning with desire. They stood still, his cheek gently touching hers, and she felt the warmth of each breath he took. His lips were soft on her neck. His hands gently caressed the sides of her face, down her shoulders to her waist, and then her hips, and down to her thighs. He kissed her tenderly on her lips. He stopped, kissed her again.

Strong passion overtook everything they tried to resist. They could no longer control themselves or deny the burning they both hid deep inside for months. He lifted her up high against the wall and pressed his body hard against hers. They kissed passionately as he undressed her slowly. He removed each layer of clothing, piece by piece. He slipped away her bra straps, exposing her breasts. The rain fell hard and long and strong, and the thunder was like their personal love song, beating uninterrupted for the next hour and twenty-two minutes.

Afterward, Paige lay still not knowing how to feel. But despite her conflicted feelings, the two of them agreed to meet later that evening around 6:00, so they could figure out how they were going to be together again. They got dressed, embraced with a kiss, and Christopher left.

Paige cried as she continued to pack her things. While packing, she came across photos of her and Evan having lunch in Paris, skiing in Switzerland, and enjoying the beach in Hawaii for her thirtieth birthday. She stared at the smile on his face and the love in his eyes. Paige wiped away her tears and sent Evan a text.

Let's meet tonight for dinner, 7:00, Cafe Burgundy.

Just as she knew he would, he replied: *Anything you want.*

At six that evening, Paige sat patiently in the backseat of a cab in front of Christopher's hotel. As much as she loved him, she'd decided that he was her past. Evan was her future and she had to let him know. By 6:30, there was no sign of Christopher, nor had he called or answered her texts.

She began to wonder... *did he change his mind? Did she herself make the right decision? Or maybe he got what he came for and wasn't coming back.*

At 6:45, she checked her phone one last time in case she missed his text, but she hadn't. Paige released a sigh of relief. She turned off her phone, placed it in her purse, wiped away a final tear and told the driver, "Take me to Cafe Burgundy on Park Boulevard."

***

The rain came down in a steady fall. As soon as Paige's cab pulled off, Christopher exhaled. He'd been sitting in another cab across the street, watching her the entire time. He wanted so badly to get out and be with her, but he couldn't. After watching Paige leave, he turned to his driver and said, "Take me to LaGuardia Airport."

As they pulled off, he glanced at his phone and re-read a text he received earlier that evening from Erika.

I love you and I can't wait 'til you get home! We're having a baby!

"You can't leave her hanging like that," Christopher mumbled to himself as he sat waiting on his flight to California. He took a deep breath, picked up his phone and dialed Paige's number. He held the phone close to his ear, waiting for her to answer. It rang. . . and rang. . . and finally he heard the familiar voice of the automated answering machine saying, "The person you're trying to reach is unavailable... Memory Full!"

Princis Lewis is a writer of several intriguing fictional stories and a book of poems. As a wife, mother and grandmother, she is creative and enjoys writing, painting and making arts & crafts. Her personal journey can be found on youtube entitled: My Story - After The Fire. She earned her Master's degree in Education, is actively involved in Alpha Kappa Alpha Sorority, Inc., and along with her husband Kenneth "Tony" is co-owner of Art & Soul Paint Studio in New Jersey.

The Plot to Take Over Washington

By Michelle Mitchell

Tracee Hughes paced the length of the cherrywood floors in front of her friend, Charis Watts. She had all but chewed her nails down to the nub as she waited.

"*Ugh*. Okay, so what do you think?" Tracee asked.

"Don't rush me," Charis responded. "Go sit down. I can't read with you hovering."

"I can't sit still. Do you know how *major* this could be for me?"

Tracee was interviewing to be the Director of Residence Life at Georgia Southern University. She had been a Resident Director for four years, and she was eager to be the one to add some diversity to the predominantly male, campus leadership.

"Presentation looks great. I would put your talking points on another document and just use bullets to highlight your subjects."

"Thanks. Now, I need to make copies."

"About that—I forgot to buy ink."

"It was on the grocery list. How'd you miss that?"

Charis began fiddling with her hair. "I didn't make it to the store. I ran into *Wallace* and we went out for dinner."

"*Really*? So we don't have ink or food? Wait, Wallace Washington?"

"Yep," Charis answered. "He finally asked me out. He said he was waiting for an opportunity to see me alone—since I'm always with

---

you."

Tracee shook her head. She asked Charis not to date any of her coworkers. She did not want to wake up to anyone she worked with walking around the kitchen in their boxers. Plus, she couldn't stand Wallace. They were friends—until Tracee got the attention of the higher-ups. When word got out that Tracee was being considered for a promotion, Wallace's bigoted, alter-ego surfaced. Tracee overhead Wallace telling one of the men in the office that a woman should know her place, and that he would never work for a woman. She could not understand what Charis saw in him.

"Why him? You know how I feel about mixing my life and work."

"Uh—last time I checked this was my life. *Not yours*, so you'll just need to *get* into this because it's happening."

Tracee grabbed her purse from the kitchen table, shaking her head in disgust.

"I hope you know what you're doing. I'm going to Staples."

Tracee walked out the door and got into her car. She could not believe that Charis went against her wishes. Tracee put the car in reverse, turning up the radio to try to help relax her mood. She rolled her eyes when the beat kicked in for TLC's single, *What About Your Friends*.

"My thoughts exactly," Tracee mumbled.

####

Charis sat on the sofa still looking toward the door that Tracee exited. She did not understand why Tracee thought she could tell her who to date. She turned back toward the laptop and realized that Tracee left her flash drive.

Charis jumped up to try to catch Tracee, to no avail. She grabbed her cellphone to give Tracee a call.

"Hello," Tracee answered.

"You left your flash drive. How far are you?"

"Dang, far enough that I would hate to have to drive back. Listen, can you *please* load the file to Staples.com and request same day pick-up?"

"Yeah. I'll do it right now."

"Thanks…and sorry about earlier. It's your life."

"It *is* my life. Glad you came to your senses. Who would I get to be my maid-of-honor?"

"See. That's what I'm talking about."

Charis laughed. "Lighten up, Tee. It was a joke. Well anyway, loading the file now."

"Thanks and that wasn't funny."

###

Charis leaned over to tighten up the laces of her sneakers. She loved going for Saturday morning runs. She had been trying to get her roommate to join her, but Tracee was not into jogging.

Charis had lost ten pounds since joining Black Girls Run and was starting to slim down in all of her problem areas. She still had her full hips and that nice dip going toward her round behind, but her waistline was almost snatched how she'd always wanted. She would be too fine by the summer time.

Just as she was opening the door to leave, she ran into Wallace.

"Oh—ouch," she said, hitting her head on his raised arm.

"I'm the one in pain," he said, rubbing his elbow.

They shared a laugh.

"What are you doing here?" she asked.

"I thought I would come by and see if you wanted to grab breakfast." He paused. "I'm not even gonna lie and say I was in the neighborhood cause I wasn't."

Charis blushed. "Wow! I like it. A man who knows what he wants. Come on in." She stepped aside. "I was just about to go for a run."

She smiled hard as she watched him look her over.

"I can see that. I can wait while you change. That is…if you want to go?"

"Absolutely. Let me go freshen up. The remote is on the table."

Charis could not believe how great things were going. They went from occasional flirting to two dates in the same week. She was going to have to put on her I'm-the-only-woman-you-need dress for this date. Tracee was clueless; this man was not here to play games. She may be asking her friend to be a maid-of-honor after all.

As soon as Wallace heard the water running in the bathroom, he quickly stood and started looking around the room. While he thought Charis was nice, he was not into her. He knew Tracee and Charis were roommates and thought this was his chance to see what she had planned for her interview presentation.

While he knew he could do the work, he knew that Tracee was an overachiever and she would stretch herself to impress the committee.

He started in the kitchen and looked through some files on the table. No luck there.

Wallace combed through the letters and papers on the desk by the entryway, but that proved to be another waste of time.

Feeling defeated, he sat back down on the sofa, nearly knocking the laptop off the table with his knees.

"*No*," he said aloud. "It can't be that easy, can it?"

He reached for the laptop and hit the space key. To his surprise, it wasn't locked and on the screen was Tracee's presentation. He threw his head back and cheered silently.

"God is good," he murmured.

He opened the web browser, logged into his yahoo account, and emailed himself a copy of the presentation.

He heard some motion from the room where Charis was getting ready, and put everything back as it was, right as she came out of the room.

"Sorry I took so long. I'm ready," she said.

"Trust me, you were worth the wait. Besides, I managed to keep myself busy with thoughts of how good you were going to look."

"*Wallace*," she said swatting at his chest. "You are too much."

"Hopefully, I'm just enough for you. After you, my lady," he said, gesturing toward the door.

As she walked in front of him, Wallace glanced over at the laptop and smiled. *Nothing like a hard day's work.*

Today was the big day.

Tracee felt prepared and confident that she could win over the search committee. She walked over to the receptionist, Angela, to sign in for the interview.

"Good morning," Tracee greeted.

"G-good m-morning," she stammered.

"Are you okay?" Tracee inquired.

"Well," Angela lowered her voice to a whisper, "they moved your interview time back."

Okay, now she was nervous.

"I was scheduled for eight, what time do they have for me now?" Tracee asked. "And can you tell me what happened?"

"That snake, Wallace got here at seven o'clock this morning talking bout he had a family emergency and needed to interview earlier. I think he lied, but anyway, they moved you back by thirty minutes."

Tracee released a sigh of relief.

"Okay. That's cool. You had me a little scared."

"You might still need to be. That Wallace was looking sketchy like he was up to something. I don't trust that boy."

Tracee shrugged and kept her face neutral. Angela was cool, but she was also the campus gossip.

As Tracee sat down in the lobby, she sent up a silent prayer and positive thoughts. She had been researching other institutions for a while, so she knew what it took to get this job and she did not take this opportunity lightly. She knew this was the job for her, now she just had to convince them.

She sat up straight as she heard the door opening.

"Gentleman, it was a pleasure meeting with you. Thank you for the opportunity."

They caught eyes briefly before Wallace turned back to the group to throw what he thought would be a dig in her direction.

"Dean Witherspoon, don't forget, I reserved a tee time for us this week."

"I'll have Angie put it on the calendar, son. Great presentation."

As the committee closed the door to discuss Wallace's future, Tracee diverted her eyes to one of the collegiate magazines on the table. She reached over to grab one.

"Allow me to help you with that," Wallace said before placing a magazine in her lap.

He was so inappropriate, she thought. Angie caught the exchange and gave her a sympathetic look.

"Have a great afternoon, Wallace," Tracee said, dismissing him.

"My day has already started off great. I only anticipate it getting better. Can't say the same for you," he chided before walking away.

"What was that about?" Angela whispered.

Tracee didn't respond, she knew better.

Wallace thought women shouldn't be allowed to hold positions of authority; she was about to be the exception to his crooked rules.

"Mrs. Hughes? You can come on back," one of the interviewers announced.

"It's *Ms.* Hughes," Angie stated, giving Tracee a wink.

This caused him to frown slightly. *Noted,* Tracee thought. They think a married woman should get this role. She inhaled and smiled. *Got to remain positive.*

"Good morning, Dean. How's your wife, Kathy, doing? Recovering well?" she asked.

He smiled. "She's doing wonderful. Her surgery went great, thanks for asking."

"No problem. The students really enjoyed participating in the letter of encouragement project I implemented in the dorms. I hope she received them."

He looked stunned. "That was your brainchild? Here, we thought Mr. Washington was behind that. She did receive it and loved it. Thank you. Come on and have a sit."

Tracee stiffened when she heard Wallace tried to take credit. *No worries,* she thought. *He will not defeat me.*

She finished setting up her presentation to the SMART Board, and turned to the group preparing to blow them away.

"Gentleman, thank you this opportunity. I want to discuss how I plan to elevate residence life programs through what I like to call the three P's, Planning, Preparation, and…"

"Partnership? Is that the final P, *Ms.* Hughes?" Dean Witherspoon asked. She noticed his brows furrowing.

"Yes. Exactly, great minds think alike," she said, turning back to her presentation.

"Or slow minds steal the ideas of great minds," one of the committee members mumbled.

Tracee raised an eyebrow. The air in the room was getting thick with tension. She could feel herself beginning to sweat under her arms.

"Gentleman, if I may, I would like to present to you how I plan to use those three P's to accomplish my goals for residence life initiatives."

"Young lady, this is absolutely unacceptable. For you to come in here with your head all high and commit this unethical act is beyond me."

Tracee looked from one frowning face to another, she was confused.

"Sir…I'm not following. Did I do something to offend?" she asked, looking over her outfit and presentation materials.

Dean Witherspoon stood up and pointed at the screen. "Are you really going to sit here and act like you didn't steal this presentation from Mr. Washington?"

Steal from Mr. Washington?

"Excuse me? I've been researching this subject matter for almost a year and started the presentation months ago. I can show you my data."

"We'll be investigating this, but for now we will not be moving forward with you, unless you want to come clean and have your own work to share."

"I have my flash drive right here, and I can quickly have my personal laptop here. I have the proof."

"Very well. We will discuss this with human resources and get back to you soon."

"What about the interview?" she asked, desperately hoping to change their minds.

"That's the least of your worries, gal," one interviewer said.

"*Gal*. Oh, no he didn't," Angela said from behind the door, completely blowing her cover.

Everyone in the room looked toward the door.

"Fine. You contact HR, and I'll be contacting my lawyer and filing an EEOC claim as well. Excuse me," Tracee said as she collected her belongings before leaving the room.

So Wallace wants to play games? She knew how to play games, too. He should have never thrown the first blow because she did not plan to fight fair.

Tracee burst through her front door. She was livid. *How could this have happened?* The only people who had access to her presentation was Staples and Charis. *Charis?*

She paused. Instantly shaking off the thought. Charis would not betray her for a man, or at least she hoped not. Tracee walked over to her laptop and opened it up.

She went into her browser history, hoping for a clue. Just when she thought everything was normal, she looked and saw that a Yahoo page was open.

Tracee clicked on the page, and almost wanted to laugh when she saw that Wallace never signed out. Oh, this was going to be good.

As soon as Charis walked through the front door, Tracee pounced on her.

"Charis. Come sit down."

She casually strolled over to where Tracee sat.

"What is it? You know I worked third shift at the hospital and I'm too tired to surf the web with you."

"Sorry. Umm, was Wallace at the house this past weekend?"

She knew the answer, but she wanted to see how Charis would respond and gauge whether her friend was an accomplice.

"Oh yeah." A smile spread across her face. "He surprised me and took me to brunch on Saturday. I didn't mention it to you because you don't like him. Why?"

Charis looked confused as Tracee inhaled deeply and stared blankly at the computer screen.

"Okay, walk me through this. Did he come in or did he just walk up and you walked out?"

Charis sat down on the sofa, visibly annoyed.

"He came in. I got in the shower," she said, following Tracee's eyes to the computer. "I wasn't in too—oh…oh no," she said, understanding before Tracee said anything else. "I cannot believe this. I'm so sorry."

"It's not your fault. I should've told you to close my document and shut down my laptop after you sent the file."

"Wow. That's why he didn't mind waiting. He probably planned this."

"I'm going to print this email as evidence, but not before I make sure he knows not to mess with me. I'm thinking mental warfare."

Tracee got up and walked over to the desk to get the cartridges she had purchased. Usually she would not seek revenge on someone, but he had it coming for more reasons than one.

As Tracee went to the printer, Charis leaned in and looked through the rest of Wallace's emails. Just when she started to feel guilty for snooping, she saw the email exchange between Wallace and a woman named Danielle.

Danielle, I can't wait to see you. Thank you for being patient, baby. I just need to kiss up to Charis a little longer so it won't look like I used her to get close to Tracee. If I leave her alone now, she may not vouch for me if this whole thing blows up in my face. I hate to admit it, but Tracee's a smart woman and will eventually put the pieces together. I need to keep Charis' nose open, she's hooked and will defend me. I love you and can't wait to see you in that bikini in Mexico.
--Wallace

Tracee looked over her shoulder to see Charis reading Wallace's email.

"Tracee, what do you have planned for Wallace?"

"No offense, but I don't want to tell you anything. I know you're upset now, but I'm trying to maintain us while you figure whatever *that* is out."

"Bump that. According to this email, he was just using me. So whatever you need, I'm down."

Tracee leaned her body back and to the side in surprise at Charis' response. A smile emerged upon her face.

"*Well, all right then.* Let the plot to take over Washington began."

They high-fived.

"And I know just how we can set it out," Charis said bringing the laptop closer to the printer. "Safety off, let's do this."

####

It took almost a month and several conversations, but they were finally ready to put their plan into action. . With a majority of students going home for the summer, Charis and Tracee agreed it would be best for her to meet Wallace on campus. Charis asked him to meet her at the student union.

Charis was nervous, but she really wanted everything to go well. As she saw him approaching, she sat up straight and smiled.

"Hey baby!" *Gag.*

"Well don't you look gorgeous," he said, looking around.

Charis joined him in his search and said, "Looking for someone?"

"No. It's just been an odd day," he said.

"Oh, how so?" Charis quizzed.

"For starters, Tracee greeted me this morning, as if nothing happened."

"Did something happen between you two?"

"Oh, *nah*. I just don't think she likes me very much."

Charis nodded. A mischievous grin appeared on her face as their plan started to come together.

"Hey, Wallace," Danielle said smoothly, as she crept up from behind, taking Wallace off guard.

"Hey, *heeey*. How are you?" Wallace looked drained.

"Good. Aren't you going to give me a hug?"

Wallace shrugged in Charis' direction, but stood to oblige Danielle.

As he leaned in for a long embrace, Charis quickly called Tracee on her cell to set up the second part of their trap.

"Hi, I'm Charis."

"Charis? I've heard so much about you. It was really cool of you to help Wallace with his presentation for the interview. With your help, I'm sure he'll get that promotion."

"I didn't help him. Outside of showing him love and affection. Were you giving me credit for your work, honey?"

"*Honey?* You're confused. He only befriended you to get Tracee's presentation. Right, Wallace?"

"No, we've been dating. He's been lying to you about who I am."

"*I don't think so*," Danielle uttered.

"Whoa. Let's everyone calm down," Wallace stated. "Dani, why don't you go stand over there while I handle this."

Danielle did as she was told, but not far enough that she would miss the show.

"Charis, you're a great friend, but you're not my girl. You and Tracee don't know your place. What I look like having Tracee as a boss?"

Charis smiled and moved closer.

"I understand. A woman can't be a leader. You did what you had to do."

"Exactly. I guess you do understand."

"So, how'd you do it?"

"Do what?"

"How'd you get Tracee's presentation?"

"Oh that." He laughed. "A leader knows not to leave their laptop open for anyone to steal all of their hard work. That's just stupid."

"So do you consider us stupid as well, Mr. Washington?" Dean Witherspoon said while holding up Tracee's cellphone.

"Of course not, sir. I was merely telling Char—," he paused when realization suddenly hit him as he saw Tracee, the Director of Human Resources, and campus security behind the Dean.

"Stan, come on. You know I'm right. She left herself open," Wallace stated.

"It's Dean Witherspoon, Mr. Washington." He frowned, showing his disapproval. "Tracee was in her home, where she should've been safe to do that and not have to worry about schmucks like you. Ms. Hughes, you have our deepest apologies and we would love to hear that presentation on next Monday."

"Thank you, sir. I appreciate the opportunity."

Turning toward Wallace, Dean Witherspoon said, "Oh and Mr. Washington, you're fired."

"Actually, sir, he'd make a great assistant. What do you say, Wallace? Want to work for me?"

He gritted his teeth. "Let's go, Dani."

"Nah…your services aren't needed here either."

Tracee laughed in Wallace's face as the three woman walked away. She was about to get the job of her dreams, and though this position was in a man's world, she knew that she could play right along with the big boys. If they needed a reference, she would just have them call Wallace Washington.

Michelle Mitchell is a Georgia native and graduate of Georgia Southern University. She is the author of, Truth Is… released under the Jacquelin Thomas Presents imprint for Brown Girls Books. For more information about Michelle Mitchell, please visit www.authormichellemitchell.com.

Intuition

By Karen E. Williams

My mind was telling me something was wrong. Johnathan and I had our third fight. I couldn't understand why he didn't want me to go to the clinic with him. The surgical procedure on his foot had been scheduled for over a month, and my plan had been to take the day off. He told me not to come. Just go to work. He had it taken care of. My cell phone rang as I prepared for work.

"Diane, this is Aunt Mary."

I held the phone with one hand as I slid my keys into my uniform pocket. The office that I managed was five miles from the clinic and would give me time on my lunch break to go see Johnathan. My boss allowed me to make up the hours. Nights and weekends, I did medical billing work. "How you doing?"

"I'm fine. I was just wondering what time is the surgery?"

"Nine o'clock," I said and looked at the wall clock in the kitchen. My clock read 7:49 a.m. and my coffee was brewing on the counter. While I talked, I went to the cabinet to get sugar.

"Will you give me a call when you two get there and let me know what's happening?"

Outside, the sky darkened and threatened rain. "Well, Johnny already left."

"By himself?"

"He didn't want me to come." I tried to sound nonchalant. "He said it is a minor procedure and that I should go ahead to work."

"Baby, I don't feel right about this. You should be with your husband."

"Aunt Mary, I don't think he wants me there."

"Nonsense. He's just being a man. Trying to be strong and not worry you. You go on to that hospital and call me. Please?"

"Only for you, Aunt Mary." I tried to smile, hoping she could not sense my hurt through the phone. I pushed the END button, and then called in to work.

After having my coffee, I left for the hospital. Johnathan and I saw very little of each other, with me working all hours and he starting his business. He said the business was for us, so we could retire in style. All I saw was money leaving as fast as it came in. My biggest purchase was the new fully loaded Escalade for my husband. The vehicle cost almost as much as our house that we bought twenty years ago and I had only rode in it twice. He expressed his love for the car with weekly detailing. He said he needed it because clients judged the car you drove. My 2000 Honda Civic had seen better days and so had I.

Arriving at the front desk, I recognized the physician's assistant. "Could you tell me where Johnathan Greene is? He's having a procedure on his foot this morning? I'm his wife."

She looked at me as if my hair was on fire.

"Is something wrong?" I asked. My pulse quickened and I placed both of my hands on the counter to try and see Johnathan's name.

"He is," she said, staring at the chart, "being prepped." She returned my concern with a smile. "You can wait for the doctor in the waiting room."

"Thank you." I followed the yellow line that led to the blue line that would take me to the waiting room.

The room had rows of chairs that lined all but one wall. On the bare wall was a coffee station that housed paper cups, napkins, creamers, and sugar. A flat screen hovered above the station. The only other occupant when I arrived was an older man. I sat down across from the entrance and clasped my hands. I watched reruns of "Divorce Court" for a while and remembered that I needed to call Aunt Mary.

Although she was Johnathan's aunt, she welcomed me into the family and treated me just like a daughter. I pulled out my cell phone and dialed.

"Aunt Mary, they said he was in the prep room, so I couldn't see him. I'll call you when I know something."

"You want me to come wait with you?"

Adjusting myself in the chair, I moved my purse to the empty one next to me. "You don't have to do that."

"I got a meeting at the church, but I'll come after that."

I shook my head. "Okay, I'll keep an eye out for you."

Moments later, an attractive woman walked into the room. She looked toward me, then strutted toward the middle of the room.

Butterflies fluttered in my stomach and a chill ran through my body. Something wasn't right. She tossed her dark weave over her shoulder like models did on commercials, pulled a compact out of her purse to check her lipstick before she sat down in the corner out of my line of vision. I waited a few minutes before I got up. At the coffee station, I poured a cup and then sat on the opposite end of the room where I could watch her. I also didn't want Dr. Bradley to see me if he walked into the room.

An hour passed, while I tried to concentrate on the television screen. The woman I watched had dozed off. A nurse came into the room and called my husband's name. I didn't move. I wanted to see if my intuition was right. The woman didn't move either. The nurse called his name again. I took a deep breath and began to relax. I was acting silly.

The nurse spoke again, "Is there anyone here for Johnathan Greene?"

Before I could rise, the woman jumped up. "Did you say Johnathan Greene?"

"Yes, the doctor can give you an update now."

She followed the nurse out the door and I followed both of them. As we approached Dr. Bradley, he smiled my way. "Mrs. Greene."

"Yes," I said and watched the woman's eyes dance around, trying to avoid looking at me.

"And who is this?" Dr. Bradley glanced at the woman and returned his gaze to me.

"That's a good question. Who are you?"

"I--, I--, I'm just a friend, friend of the family."

"That's funny, seeing that I'm family and all, I don't remember meeting you."

"Well, I used to date Johnny's brother."

She called him Johnny. Such an amateur. Dismissing her would be easy. "Oh yeah, which one?"

"I haven't seen him in years."

"Well then, it must be Jason." I kept my expression blank, no reaction.

"Yeah, Jason. We were real close a while back."

That answer would have been okay except that Johnathan did not have a brother named Jason. I willed myself to remain calm. I did not want to cause a scene in the hospital. Have everybody thinking I didn't have any home training. My mother always told me that you never deal with the woman unless she's a relative. The relative should know better. But I thought *Johnny* would know better or at least know me. Obviously, I would have to remind him just who I was. My blood pressure was rising and the only way I knew to release it would be to act ignorant on his ass when we got home.

Dr. Bradley looked between my face and the woman's. "The procedure was successful. We removed the embedded toenail. There are no signs of infection. Mr. Greene is in recovery and he should be ready to leave in about thirty minutes. So *someone* needs to drive around to the Receiving door and pick him up." He turned and left.

"Did you drive my husband here?"

"He said that his wife had to work."

"You drove my car?"

"No, he left the Escalade at my house. I drove him here in my car."

"Well, you can go. I got things under control."

She backed away, turned and hurried down the hall. She looked afraid. I couldn't imagine what Jonathan must have said about me.

I took in big gulps of air and blew them out. I stared at the floor. I was not going cry, act a fool, or cause a need for security to escort me out of the building. I started following the blue line when I heard a voice. I looked up into the concerned eyes of Aunt Mary.

"Diane, baby, how's Johnny?"

"Everything's fine," I said. "I'm going around to get the car. Why don't you come with me?"

"Okay."

Aunt Mary asked about the surgical procedure, and was delighted that Johnathan would be able to go home. I managed head nods, and one-word responses as we drove around to the entrance where we were to pick him up. My skin felt tight and I sucked hard on my bottom lip to keep the emotions from bubbling out. The sky darkened with black-gray storm clouds to match my mood. How could he do something like that to me? I had been working two jobs. I was paying for a brand new Escalade and struggling to make the monthly house payment. His business brought in little to nothing. We left the Civic parked near the entrance and waited. Moving toward us, I saw the wheelchair with my husband. He didn't realize who we were until Aunt Mary called his name. I smiled.

His expression morphed into fear. "Oh no!" he said.

"What's wrong?" Aunt Mary looked at me, and then approached Johnathan.

"I can't go with her." He struggled to get out of the wheelchair and return to the safety of the hospital. "She'll kill me."

I remained smiling, but walked to the driver side of the car. My icy glare had him shook. I wasn't thinking about killing him, yet.

"Baby, what's the matter?" Aunt Mary's concerned eyes widened.

He had no right upsetting that sweet woman. *That's all right, Aunt Mary. I'm gonna get him good.*

"No, I won't go. You can't release me to her," Johnathan said to the nurse pushing his wheelchair.

The nurse gave him some papers and walked away. Another nurse and Aunt Mary tried to calm Johnny down.

"She gonna hurt me bad," he pleaded.

"Boy, you talking crazy. That's Diane, your wife. Diane would never hurt you."

I kept my face neutral. "I'm gonna take real good care of you when we get home."

"See Aunt Mary? I can hear it in her voice."

"Aunt Mary, I'm gonna go start the car. It must be the pain killers," I said, my tone calm.

Raindrops began to hit the windshield as I started the car and waited for my husband to get in. Aunt Mary followed behind with Johnathan in the wheelchair.

"I said, I'm not going. Call me a cab," he said.

Aunt Mary looked deep into his eyes, as if she were trying to read his thoughts. "Johnathan, stop all this foolishness. Diane is going to take you home so you can rest."

"Can't I go home with you?" Johnathan gave her a puppy-dog look.

"Don't you want to go home to your own bed?" Aunt Mary said. She looked confused and turned to me.

By that time, I was real tired of his shit. I began to pull away. Aunt Mary ran to the driver's window. "What's going on?"

I stopped and yelled out the window. "If he don't want to go home, I can't make him."

"Just wait a minute, please."

Aunt Mary went back to Johnny and talked with him for a few minutes. He must've acquiesced because he let her wheel him to the passenger side. He took his time easing into the seat, eyes trained on me. He sat as close to the passenger door as he could as if he needed to make a quick exit. We drove in silence until I felt my head was going to explode, or it could have been the rumble of the storm cloud above.

"How dare you?" I wouldn't let the first tear drop.

"She's just a friend."

"Liar. You had that woman up there in my place."

"I just needed someone there who wasn't going to nag the hell out of me."

"You disrespect me like that. What you think, I wasn't gonna find out?"

"If you were doing your job, maybe. . ."

No he didn't. No he didn't just tell me if I was doing my job. For the last three years, I had been doing my job *and* his. Taking care of his monkey ass. Paying the bills while he started his business. I tried to compose myself, but the well of emotion threatened to drown me. Anger, Fear, Depression, Love, Hate, then Anger again. The tears ran and blinded my vision.

"I'm sorry," he said and I could hear the hurt in his voice.

"Where is my car?"

"No, Diane. Let's just go home."

"Home? What makes you think you got a home to go to? I pay the mortgage there." Sixteen years of marriage was circling down the drain. "Where is my car?"

Johnathan exhaled. "It's our car and I am not taking you over there. Look, I'm tired. Why don't you drop me at–"

"I'm only gonna ask one more time. That's *my* car and I want to know where it is."

Resigned to my determined mood, he pointed to the left. "Go east on Michigan."

"How long this been going on?" I pushed down on the accelerator.

"I know you're angry."

He was actually trying to reason with me. "Angry? I'm way past angry."

"Listen, baby," he said and reached out to touch me.

I whipped my head in his direction and he huddled closer to the door frame. "Where am I going?"

"Turn right on Forest. Go to the middle of the block. The Escalade's in the driveway."

The house was a nice brick bungalow, with red awnings, reminding me of Aunt Mary's home. Usually the sight of that house would give me a warm feeling. I did feel warm, all right. "The car keys."

He looked confused. "Keys?"

"The car keys," I said, with a bit more force as I slowed the car to a stop and mashed hard on the break. He lurched forward. I narrowed my eyes and flexed my fingers. "Get out."

He looked at me with pleading eyes. "Diane."

"Keys," I said and watched him ease out of the car keeping his eyes on my hands. Before he closed the door, he rummaged in his pocket and tossed the keys on the seat. I picked up the keys and fingered them. He wouldn't need them anymore. I placed them in my pocket.

Outside, Johnathan limped toward the Escalade as if to protect it. The rain continued to fall.

My heart raced as rage threatened to overtake me. I couldn't see anything for a moment. But when my vision cleared, I lifted my foot off the brake and returned it to the gas. He saw me coming and hobbled over to the front porch. I drove up on the grass and stopped. I put the car in park and gunned the engine.

"What the hell is wrong with you?" Johnathan said.

I cut the engine and popped the trunk to get my tire iron. He saw the instrument in my hand and I could see the panic on his face.

"Stop playing, Diane."

"I got a game for you." I took a power swing and heard the sound of glass breaking.

"Oh shit," Johnathan said and stumbled up the porch.

Next, I turned my fury on the headlights. Batter up!

"You must be out of your damn mind. Don't let me have to come down. . ."

I turned to face him. "Come on." I smiled and began to approach.

"Go on now. You play too much."

Returning my focus to the car, I took the sharp edge of the tire iron and ran it lengthwise along the sides.

"I'm calling the police."

I moved toward him and he hopped closer to the door. Adrenalin ran through my body like an electrical current. "Call the police. Maybe I'll get a female cop who'll hold your ass while I beat it."

The door to the house swung open and a woman came out the door. She placed both hands on her hips. "Oh, no. You gonna have to take that shit someplace else."

I tried to focus on the woman. I could hear her voice, but I didn't comprehend her meaning.

Johnathan turned to the woman and held up his hands, motioning her back in the door. "I'll take care of this, baby."

No, he didn't just call this woman, baby. My eyes locked on her. I tightened my grip on the tire iron.

A steady drizzle wet the pavement.

"You can't be doing this in front of my house. I have neighbors."

"I told you I would take care of this," Johnathan repeated.

"I didn't sign up for this ghetto shit," she said, raising her voice an octave higher than before.

"Go inside and just let me talk to my wife."

"You can have him." My anger had bubbled over into words. "I can have all of his belongings, including his dirty drawers back here in fifteen minutes."

"He can't stay here," her words rang out.

The shock in his eyes was matched by the delight in mine.

"What?" Johnathan said.

"Listen, Johnny. We had some fun, but I'm not looking for all this drama. I don't need no broke down man. You need to go home with your wife."

He looked from her face to my smile. He knew he couldn't come home with me. That bridge had been blown up and now lay burning. Johnathan limped down the porch toward me. "Can we talk about this?"

In that moment, I realized I was done. I looked at my 2000 Civic, the smashed windows, the car's long scratches and dents. I felt bad, but not for long as I climbed in my Escalade. It still had that new car smell. There was no reason to destroy a new car I was paying for. I took out my key and started the engine. The car seemed to welcome me as I settled into the leather seat. I pressed a button and the seat adjusted forward. Another button began to warm my seat. I adjusted my mirrors and backed out of the drive. The woman's door closed, leaving Johnathan standing on the walkway.

"You gonna just leave me, Diane. How am I gonna get home?" I heard him scream.

I rolled down the window. "Call Tyrone," I sang out the chorus from a popular Erika Badu song.

Heading back toward Michigan Avenue, I pushed the radio button. As the lightning flashed, I heard a familiar oldies beat and I began to bounce along with it. Johnny Mathis was singing, "I can see clearly now the rain is gone." and I joined in for the chorus. Throwing my head back, I sang, *"It's gonna be a bright, bright, bright sunshiny day."*

Karen E. Williams is an author and avid reader. Her short stories have been twice selected by the Cranbrook Writers Guild. She is a graduate of the University of Michigan.

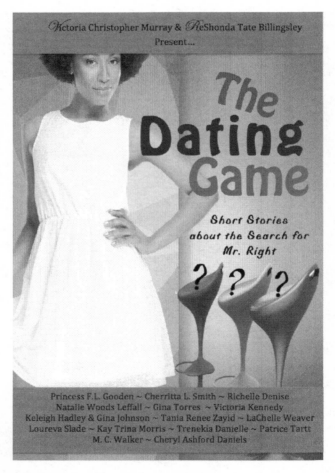